# FALLEN REBEL

## C.G. BLAINE

*To Emmily, for believing in angels.
And in me.*

# ONE

## *CASS*

In the beginning, there was only darkness. Then there was bullshit.

And just so we're clear, "darkness" was never really darkness. Most of the Bible and other religious texts are metaphors and symbolism or misinterpreted completely. The apple Eve eats? A metaphor for the burden of knowledge. Jonah being swallowed by a big-ass fish? A tale of second chances. Watcher Angels teaching humans about art and technology before God wanted them to know and being punished for it? Now we're getting to some facts. Although the story falls apart on the Nephilim topic.

Another one humans got right, to a degree, is the crystal ball. Those things are real. They only show you the present, need to be connected to a particular soul, and are inconvenient as fuck to use in public.

I lean against my motorcycle, parked against the curb, and light a cigarette. Hannah Kelley has another twenty minutes left in whatever bullshit class she takes on Thursdays at two-fifteen. As I gaze into the clear orb at her, she twirls a strand of auburn hair around her finger, diligently taking notes on the lecture. Back when she was a sophomore in high school, she'd pass notes back and forth, giggling with her friends. Teachers caught her more than once and sent her to detention. She'd sneak out early and smoke behind the school or end up in a senior guy's car, fogging up the windows.

But that's not her anymore. Now she hangs on every damn word the sixty-year-old professor says. She'll wander to the front after class, making sure she wrote something down correctly. His eyes will drop to her chest, the smile and nod he delivers not at all in response to her question. She'll accept it as one, though, and scurry away.

A gorgeous five-foot-nothing blonde struts by my bike for the third time in the last half hour. I tuck the crystal ball in my jacket and follow her down the sidewalk toward the building Hannah's walking out of. The blonde's flattered I'm paying attention, but it's short-lived.

It always starts in my chest. A warmth that almost makes me feel whole again. I look at my hand, palm up, fingers stretched out. The heat shoots down my arm, and the tips of my fingers emit a white glow. Divine light. I only enjoy the sensation for a second before I scan around. A city bus is closing its doors at a stop a block away. Given Hannah's trajectory, she'll walk right in front of it when she crosses the street because she's watching her fucking shoes instead of where she's going.

The blonde tries to say something as I jog past, but I wave her off. Women tend to take a backseat when your eternity is on the line. My jog turns into a fast stride by the time Hannah reaches the corner, and we collide. Our impact knocks her back from the curb, and the bus passes. The power fades from my body within seconds of her being safe, the loss as painful as ever.

I glance at her over my shoulder, her surprised eyes meeting my glare. "Watch where you're going."

"Sorry," she says.

She should be fucking sorry. After thousands of years, she's the last thing standing between me and home, and she almost ruined it by stepping in front of a bus.

And this is why I hate Hannah Kelley. My forever is tethered to her life.

# Two

## *HANNAH*

Some days I want to fast-forward through. Or some weeks, months, years. This is one of those days. Or weeks, months, years.

As soon as the apology leaves my mouth, I want to add, *you're an asshole.* But the guy's already crossing the intersection. I watch him gliding away as if he hadn't almost knocked me to the ground and then looked at me like I'd insulted him by existing. His dark hair and even darker eyes were familiar in the way a moment reminds you of a dream. An incredibly angry and intimidating dream.

I let it go, checking for traffic before I step into the street. Since I wasted time asking my professor a question he answered by staring at my chest, I'm late to drive Terra to work. Music floods the hallway when I rush into our dorm room. The naked guy in her bed scrambles for his jeans, and I shield my eyes with a hand, walking to my side.

"Sorry," I say. My mantra for the day. But my apology goes out to Terra for being late, not the guy with a heart tattooed on his ass. I drop my bag, and once he makes his exit, I spin around.

Terra's pulling on a white top that does little to conceal the red bra underneath. "Are you sure you don't want to come out with everyone later tonight? It's just a movie, not a rager or anything."

"I've already fulfilled my required two social events for the month. Try again in October."

She wiggles her jeans up over her hips. "We should have renegotiated at the beginning of the school year. I'm shooting for four outings a month senior year."

"Good luck on even reaching three." I toss her a sweatshirt off the floor and follow her out.

She and I have come a long way since we were assigned as roommates freshman year. Her sole purpose was to party; mine was just to get through the next four years. Nothing has changed in that aspect, but we stopped hating each other after the first semester. By the end of the second, we were spending time together outside of the room. Enough to upgrade us to the Friends category at least. Last year, we requested to room with each other, and now, I can't imagine my life without her.

She chatters the entire drive across town to the clothing store, which leaves the silence on my solo return trip all the louder. Any other day, I would turn on the radio. But not today. Today, I tune out the world the best I can. No music, no TV, no movies or books. Nothing that can remind me of *them*.

The only exception I make is to study, and when I get back to the dorms, I curl up with a textbook.

Linguistics. Some people collect stamps. I collect languages. I've always picked them up quickly. The patterns and similarities stick out in my mind and piece together with roots from others. I speak French, Spanish, German, and Italian. I know enough Latin to be dangerous, and last year, I took a class in Sanskrit.

The words blur after an hour or so, my eyes dry from a lack of sleep. I close them, letting them rest before I switch to accounting.

I jolt awake when the book slides off the bed and crashes to the floor. My eyes search around, and as they reorient to the dark room, they land on Terra's alarm clock.

*Shit.* The campus cafeteria closes in twenty minutes.

I grab my phone and pull on a sweater before I rush out the door.

# Fallen Rebel

The crisp air helps clear my head from the grogginess of an accidental four-hour nap. Just as I start feeling like myself again, I step into the dining hall, and everything inside me dies. Music plays over the speakers in the ceiling, echoing through the empty hall and bouncing off every smooth surface. It's one of the many songs they claimed as theirs. One he would dance her around to in the kitchen, singing every word just for her. She'd laugh and throw her head back and then rest it on his chest. All I hear is the music. All I feel is the loss. And all I want to do is run.

So, I do.

I run out of the building and down the sidewalk until it turns into a stone path. I keep going after the trail ends, across a field and through the trees. I'm running away from the way she always smelled like vanilla and how he could make me feel so loved with just a smile. Away from the social worker and police taking me out of class and how my life imploded, and all they could say was, *"I'm so sorry for your loss."* Away from everything and toward nothing. I run until I can't breathe, tears streaking across my face, and then I drop to my knees on the cold, hard ground.

That's where I stay until I forget what it's like to lose everything all at once. Until I forget how to feel and remember how to survive without them.


By the time I calm down enough to function again, it's late. I step into the trees that block the lights from campus. The stars and moon disappear too, hidden by the canopy. I'm not far in when the first shiver shoots down my spine. I stop.

My breathing picks up as the feeling of someone watching settles over me. I think of the stormy eyes of the stranger cutting through me earlier. I force my feet forward, convincing myself it's just this day. This terrible day that needs to end.

# THREE

## CASS

As I follow Hannah out of the woods, a stick snaps under my foot. Her adrenaline spikes again, and she picks up her pace without looking back. The imagined danger sends a surge of energy through me that wanes once the branches overhead open to the expansive night sky. She tips her head back, admiring the handiwork that took eons to perfect, and continues across the field.

I stay hidden behind the trees, watching her until she finds the path that leads to her dorm building and disappears inside. She finally settles down enough to fall asleep around three in the morning, and I can relax.

*One day closer to going home.*

When you spend your existence shadowing someone else, you don't require much in the way of an apartment. Mine is fully furnished, though, to keep nosy neighbors and maintenance from asking questions. I drop my keys and crystal ball on the counter and swipe the open whiskey bottle.

A knock on the door turns me around as I walk into the living room. Being the middle of the night, I ignore it and settle in on the couch. The bottle's barely touched my lips when my phone vibrates. The unknown number continues to ring after I decline the call. If I had a damn pager, that would go off next. Maybe a fax machine or carrier pigeon.

*"Tamiel."*

I light a cigarette, disregarding the disembodied voice filling my apartment. I've been Kasdaye since before Lydia came into existence, Cass since the nineteenth century, but she uses my old name—the first one given to me—to assert her authority. The *Tamiel*s continue, each more bitter than the last, until she appears between me and the TV.

"Why do you have to be such a dick?" She tosses straight blonde hair over her shoulder, glancing around the apartment, annoyed.

"Sorry, sweetheart, but unless they changed how long a century is, you're about seventy years early for my check-in."

Lydia's usual unimpressed expression is in place. She gives off a powerful vibe for such a small package, shoulders back and straight, chin up to offer an illusion of height, staring me down in her business suit. "I'm not here for *your* report, asshole. I can't find Samyaza for his."

I shrug, downplaying my interest. "Samy's not here."

"When's the last time you talked to him?"

"Four, maybe five decades?"

A lie she doesn't buy.

She crosses her arms and juts out a hip, like the cool mom trying to get the kids to rat on each other. "Look, I get it. You've been brothers since your beginning, and you cover for each other. But—"

"But in this situation," I interrupt, "I really have no idea where he is, Lydia. The last I knew, he was bouncing between three states to keep up with his charges. If you want me to, I'll ask the others."

I won't tell her anything even if they do know something, but my offer eases her tension. Over the centuries, the four of us remaining on Earth have learned how to keep her from hovering.

She eyes my crystal ball in the other room. "Since I'm here, I might as well ask about your charges."

"Charge," I correct.

"The last time, you reported three," she says, interest piqued.

"Anthony Kelley passed away thirteen years ago in his sleep at the age of eighty-six." I tick them off on my fingers. "His sister,

Cynthia 'Kelley' King, three years later from cancer. And five years ago yesterday, Brice Kelley and his wife were killed in a plane crash."

She cocks her head to the side. "Why did the plane go down?"

I hold up my hands, already knowing where she's going. "Lightning strike. A true act of God. Which leaves me with their daughter, Hannah Kelley."

"The final Nephilim in their lineage. Wow, Cass." She shakes her head, finding it hard to believe another one of us might make it home. "Well, good luck. Don't let her die."

"Or get knocked up," I add.

Her eyes roll, and then she's gone.

I polish off the bottle of whiskey and trade it out for a full one. Walking back to the couch, I roll the crystal ball off the counter, bringing it with me. I fall onto the cushions and scroll through my phone to a number Samy texted me from a few years ago. He drops off the grid from time to time. As our leader, the guilt of us being punished still weighs on him even though none of us blame him for what happened. We all knew what we were doing when we decided to help the humans.

The twenty Watchers were sent to Earth to ensure man didn't fuck up God's plan. But that meant watching them suffer through disease, famine, and at times, utter stupidity. Samy couldn't handle it anymore. His compassion wouldn't let him sit idly by while they died off. So, we taught them astronomy, meteorology, how to forge weaponry, and other sweet skills. Some dumbasses veered from the syllabus, though, and spent the better part of a millennium screwing their way around the world, creating the Nephilim. Legends say the hybrids were giants, but the only thing abnormal in size was their egos. Because they were half-angel, they thought themselves all-powerful, and clans started warring with one another. God's solution was to flood the Earth—an actual flood, essentially hitting the reset button on creation. God then passed down punishments for us. The playboys were sentenced to live out human lives, and their souls were condemned to sit outside the gates of Heaven for eternity. As for the seven rebels who gave away knowledge, we were "cast into darkness and chains." A metaphor for no longer being welcome in the light of Heaven, and now bound to the humans we'd wanted to spare. God saved seven Nephilim, commanding we keep watch over them and their descendants until the lines die off naturally— disease, self-sacrifice, an act of God. Only then will we find redemption and reenter Heaven as angels.

The number Samy sent me rings through to voicemail.

"Hey," I say. "Lydia let herself into my apartment tonight, looking for you. Where the fuck are you? I think I bought you some time, but let me know if you need me to send her off in the wrong direction. Check in soon, man."

A tingle trips down my spine, and my hand runs over the orb. Hannah's restless. Nightmare. They bother her more this time of year, sending out a lot of false warnings of her in distress. My powers react to both actual danger she has yet to perceive and her adrenaline responses, which means, right now, both of us are exhausted. Not that I need much sleep, but she's pushing my limits.

Once she settles down, I stretch out and balance the ball on my chest. And then we sleep.

Over the next few weeks, our pattern returns to normal. Hannah lets me sleep more than an hour or so a night, and I keep enough distance that she doesn't begin to recognize my face.

The world around us transitions into fall the first week of October. The leaves change color at such random intervals and different paces that no one would believe it was all by design, each leaf falling off the trees in an ordered sequence.

I try Samy a few more times with no answer, but even so, I hold off on calling Chaz and Rosdan. They'd lie their asses off for either one of us without hesitation, but until Lydia pops back up, the fewer in the know about Samy's disappearing act, the better.

One morning, while Hannah's in class, I spread out on a bench outside the building. Despite my claim of being better rested, I doze off, waking to her voice. I peek an eye open, and she's standing right in front of the bench, facing away from me. Moving would only draw her attention, so I do as any good stalker would and stay perfectly still. She fake laughs, not something she does often. It almost sounds like she doesn't want to embarrass herself if her snort makes an appearance. Then I hear a guy chuckling along with her, and my eyes fly open.

*Who the fuck is this jabroni?*

A few inches taller than her, so at least six less than me, sandy-blond hair, too wide of a smile. But forget the fact that he looks like he goes skiing in Vail on the weekends with his fellow future MBAs. He's leaning into her, his hand rubbing her arm.

I risk it, pulling out the crystal ball, and concentrate on her face until it appears in the globe. She looks nervous, chin tilted slightly down, eyes cast up at him, a hint of color in her cheeks. And when she smiles, I feel it ripple inside me, barely there … but there. She likes him. The ball goes back in my jacket pocket, so I'm not the weird guy on the bench, and I listen.

"So, I'll call you," he says. "But not too soon, so you think I'm cool."

"And I'll let it go to voicemail, so you think I'm unavailable." She shifts her weight to one leg, fidgeting.

"Perfect." He walks backward, off the sidewalk and into the grass. "I'll *not* talk to you soon, Hannah."

"I'll be ignoring you, Gabe."

*Gabe.* I bet it's short for Gabriel, and he's going to prove to be just as annoying as the original.

Hannah's suitors' goals and mine directly oppose one another. They want to fuck her, and I don't want anyone fucking her. She's not a virgin. She gave that up to a guy named Ricky in the back of a van by a lake in high school. Even though it was tempting to "suggest" all my charges remain virginally pure to speed up my sentence, I'm an asshole, not a sadist. But Hannah's freshman year, a condom broke, triggering the most nerve-racking two weeks of my entire existence. I don't intend to ever repeat it, especially now when I'm so close. Which means it's time for some sabotage.

# FOUR

## *HANNAH*

"Not a chance I'm letting you out in public like that." Terra's head jerks back and forth, further emphasizing.

"Why?" I turn around, checking the mirror, not seeing her issue with my costume.

"You look like a fucking nun."

I hold out the rosary and gesture to the habit. "I am a nun."

She rolls her eyes on the way to the closet. "We can do better. And by better, I mean sluttier because that's the entire point of Halloween."

"Agree to disagree." I sigh, pulling off the headpiece of my now-vetoed costume.

Our choice of Halloween activities differs as much as our Halloween attire, but I owe her a social event, so the Omega Haunted House Party is on the agenda.

She reaches up on a shelf and retrieves a pair of over-the-knee black stiletto boots and lays them on the bed along with a black dress. Then she digs through my underwear drawer until she finds black lace panties.

"I detect a theme here," I say, picking up the dress. The very short dress with a nonexistent back. "Sexy goth girl?"

She smiles and fishes a shopping bag out from behind her bed.

I narrow my eyes at her as she reaches in. "You just happened to have this lying around in case you hated my costume?"

"No. I saw the ugly sack you planned to wear and picked you up something this morning." She pulls out a pair of black wings and a flower crown made of black roses.

"A dark angel." I smile, running my finger along the soft feathers.

"What's sexier than that?" she asks.

The answer: Terra's interpretation of a demon.

While I change, she zips into a red latex catsuit with strategically placed cutouts covered in mesh. A long leather whip with a point at the end acts as a tail, and she slips a horned headband in the wavy black hair cascading down her back. Since her crimson heels spike even higher than my boots, she still stands a few inches taller as she adjusts my "halo."

She pulls out her phone and snaps a picture of us in the mirror. Neither of us looks enthused—my disinterest genuine, hers for aesthetic.

My phone vibrates with a message from Gabe a few minutes before we leave.

> *Sorry, held up at work. Rain check on our rain-checked rain check?*

Even though he said he wouldn't, he texted me the same day we met. But we haven't seen each other again because every time we make plans, something happens. He has to stay at work late; I lose my keys, phone, and ID all at once; three of his tires go flat.

I send, *Next week?*

> *It's a date. One with both of us in the same place at the same time.*

I smile on my way out, and Terra whips me with her tail.

The only way to enter the party is by going through a haunted house set up by the fraternity. Once we get our wristbands, Terra drags me up the steps without any hesitation. A few couples are ahead of us as we walk inside, but they disappear when the door slams behind us, leaving us in the dark. I jump, and Terra squeals, clasping on to my arm.

We rely on each other for protection and maneuver our way through a room full of dolls. Cracked porcelain faces stare at us from every side, some with missing eyes, as a little girl's voice keeps asking if we'll play with her.

A pile of broken doll bodies in the corner starts moving, and a person rises out of it. "Stay with me," she says, stumbling toward us. "Stay forever."

"Fuck that." Terra dashes through a doorway, and I laugh, more creeped out than anything.

We follow glowing tape on the floor to move us in the right direction down an unlit hallway. Every now and then, someone screams from somewhere. Then I'm the one screaming at the hands grabbing at my legs.

The next room is set up as an insane asylum with patients drifting around. One of the actors, a guy dressed in gray sweats and a dirty T-shirt, pulls at the back of his hair. He wanders toward us, mumbling. The closer he gets, the louder he chants, and the others are surrounding us and shouting nonsense. As they close in, my heart hammers in my chest, my breath coming faster. All at once, they jump at us as the lights cut out. Terra's hand slips out of mine.

"Hannah!" she shrieks.

A strobe light blinks from a ceiling corner. They're pulling her away, but whenever I try getting to her, someone bumps me in the opposite direction. The mumbling guy in sweats stalks toward me, his movements choppy in the flashes of light. None of it's real, but the yelling and strobe disorient me, and I panic.

"Back the fuck off, man." A guy steps between us and reaches back, moving me behind him.

Once the actor changes direction, my new hero turns around. Blunt metal spikes decorate the front of his jacket. His dark hair points every which way.

I'm still catching my breath when he takes my hand. The punk rocker keeps me close behind him and leads me around the perimeter. He pushes through plastic slats hung in the doorway and holds them back for me. I look for Terra, but knowing her, she's hooking up with someone in zombie makeup, so I follow him.

In the next room, a white-and-black-checkerboard pattern covers the floor, walls, and ceiling. There's no door other than the one we came through, and a single lightbulb hangs down in the center. As he steps closer to the light, I struggle to figure out how I know him. The heavy eyeliner and hair throw me off, but I've seen the chiseled features and scruffy jawline.

He taps the bulb, sending it swinging, and our shadows bounce around the room. The light glints off a doorknob straight ahead, the door painted to match everything else. We head toward it, and a person perfectly camouflaged against the backdrop lunges at me. I let out a yelp and latch on to the rocker again. He stops and looks down at our hands, his dark eyebrows drawn together.

*Oh God, Hannah.*

"Sorry," I say, heat flooding my cheeks.

I start to pull my hand away, but warm fingers curl around mine and lead me forward.

"Welcome!" A bubbly voice meets us from behind a surgical mask in the next room. A stainless steel table on one side holds a body with trays of surgical tools scattered around. The girl in a sexy nurse costume struts over. "I'm Nurse Joy."

She tugs the rocker over to the table by the zipper on his jacket, and I come along, welcome or not. Her skit includes giving an autopsy to a still-alive man, while giggling the entire time. We're almost out of the room when she taps me on the shoulder. I turn around and scream. Her mask is off, and it looks like her skin's been torn away, muscle and teeth exposed. I cling to the guy's arm as he hauls me out of the room and into a dark hallway. The walls move, knocking into us. I bounce back and forth until he tucks me under his arm.

He keeps me there for the next two rooms—a demon baby's nursery and a meat locker with bodies hanging from the hooks. We step into one more hallway. I relax, seeing the exit sign, but then a chainsaw growls to life. Since I've already proven myself unable to handle anything remotely scary, I unapologetically wrap my arms around the guy's torso, burying my face in the leather. Once the sound cuts off, his grip on me loosens. Cold air hits my skin, and I peek up, realizing we're outside.

I let go of him and straighten. "People actually enjoy those things?"

"You'd be surprised." One side of his mouth turns up, and a dimple appears.

*Fuck me, he's gorgeous.* I stare up at him in a stupid schoolgirl daze, and the feeling of knowing him creeps back in. "Have we met before? In class or maybe—"

Terra shouts my name from ahead. I turn to wave at her, and by the time I look back, he's walking away.

"I'm Hannah, by the way."

I expect him to stop or at least tell me his name in return, but he keeps going.

Terra calls for me again, the guys with her ready to go in. With my mystery man not interested, I click my way up the sidewalk to them.

We wait at the door while a frat brother checks that everyone has wristbands from the haunted house. I flash mine and look back on our way inside.

He's standing in a group of people, but our eyes meet, his full attention on me. Goose bumps rush over my skin, and as if he knows, he smiles.

He has two dimples.

# FIVE

## *CASS*

Hannah in a haunted house is a fucking drug. I want it. I need it. I'll do whatever it takes to get more. Enough adrenaline flooded her system that I'm still running warm with light when her gaze finds mine in the crowd. I want to tear across the lawn and carry her back in, caveman-style. Like she knows I need another fix, she gives me one before disappearing inside.

I hang around the rowdy group on the lawn. The ones too drunk to realize they don't know me. They keep calling me bro and elbowing me to laugh at their crude jokes.

Once they start to disperse, I make my way in to where her roommate is entertaining a group. Hannah lingers around the edge, so I take the winding staircase to a balcony overhead to do what I do—watch. She avoids engaging as much as possible, staring at the beer in her clear plastic cup.

A sexy unicorn sidles up next to me. She's wearing a white corset, a rainbow-colored tutu, and a pink wig with a horn on top. After being plugged directly into a power source, it only takes her finger brushing over my abs for me to lose interest in Hannah's inability to enjoy a party. We exchange a few sentences, and then her teeth are tugging at my ear, and my hand's up the tutu.

She's sitting on the banister, legs wrapped around me. My eyes flutter open to scan the people below for the face they always seek out. But it's not there.

"Fuck." I set the unicorn back on the floor, still searching the crowd for, of all things, an angel.

She touches my chest. "What is it, baby?"

I forget she exists and tear down the stairs. Terra's giggling by the keg, guys drooling on both sides of her, but no Hannah. The line for the bathroom is long, but she's not there either. And here's where the crystal ball becomes as much a blessing as a curse. It's the fastest way to find her, but I can't exactly whip it out in front of everyone. I make it outside and find a secluded area, my thoughts on Hannah's face before the globe's out of my jacket. Her image is dark, so it's hard to make out her surroundings as she walks alone.

*Where the fuck are you?*

And that's when it hits, dead center in my chest.

Someone wearing a mascot bunny head zips past her on a bike, then another on the other side. A third flies by, snatching the phone from her hand. They circle her, a fourth one laughing.

*Fuck. Fuck. Fuck.*

The glow almost breaks through the tips of my fingers as I duck behind a line of hedges. I shut my eyes, focusing on Hannah touching me, the feel of her skin on mine, the spark of light she supplies. The world drops out from under me, and when my feet land on solid ground, she's fifty feet ahead of me.

The jokers have climbed off their bikes, bunny heads still on. Hannah tries to run, but one grabs the wings of her costume and tosses her back toward the group. She loses her balance, falling down, and I almost lose my fucking shit.

"Hey!" I shout.

They're too busy with their new toy to pay attention to the only warning they'll get. I don't bother using my powers, ripping off the first bunny head I come across.

The guy's face gives under my fist, and I catch another by the shirt, jerking him back. His costume head lands next to the other. Since he's the one who took her phone, he earns a few extra kicks to the ribs.

Hannah crawls off the ground, distracting me enough that one of the remaining two lands a few punches. He sprints off when the other jumps on my back. I throw him off, onto the sidewalk, and am on top of him, pulling off his bunny head before he knows what happened. I leave him in the fetal position, face bloody, and I glance around for the lucky one with my blood on his knuckles. He's riding away on his bike with the other two.

As the last one hauls himself up, I take hold of his shirt. At first, he winces when I touch his busted-to-shit cheek, but then his expression relaxes, his eyes glazing over.

"The one who got away," I say in a calm tone. "Tell me his name and how to find him."

He answers without thought, "Barrett Lane. He works at the costume shop."

"You won't remember talking to me."

My hands fall away, and he stumbles backward a few steps, shaking his head. He reorients quickly and takes off on his bike, leaving his bunny head behind.

I barely keep my temper as I stalk toward Hannah, my patience worn thin. We've been through this a few times over the years, where something happens and I become too easily remembered. My power's fading with the danger gone, but she's still shaken enough to give me the boost I need to make her forget. But as I close in on her, I stop. Removing me from her memories also removes the faces of the guys who just tried to assault her. Not to mention the healthy fear she'll now have of walking alone at night.

"Shit," I shout, scooping up the bunny head.

Hannah jumps but not even the surge she supplies settles me down. I grab her phone, followed by her arm, and pull her down the sidewalk.

"Hey!" She tries to jerk away, so I tighten my grip, stopping to glare down at her. She swallows hard but lifts her chin and narrows her eyes right back at me. "I know how I know you."

"I have no idea what you're talking about," I lie.

"You're the jerk who plowed into me outside of Mercy Building last month."

"You're confusing me with someone else."

She shakes her head. "No. It was you. I know it was."

I can't catch a break tonight. The mascot head falls to the concrete, and I cup her face in my hands. Drawing on what energy remains, I wait until the moss-green eyes staring up at me soften and lose focus. "That wasn't me," I tell her. "The first time we met was in the haunted house."

She rests her hands on my wrists while her mind molds around my words. "And then you saved me from the evil bunnies?"

My lips twitch, and I blink a few times, caught off guard by her description of the event. "Yes, the men who were going to hurt you because you tried to walk home alone like a fucking idiot. Now, I'm walking you back to the dorms so that no more bunnies come for you and that dress."

I let her go, picking up the head off the ground, and she follows behind me without further argument.

At her building, I wait on the sidewalk until she's at the door. She pauses and looks back. Neither of us says anything, though, and after a second, she goes inside. In twenty-one years, it's the longest we've been together and the most we've spoken without the moment being erased. I no longer blend in with hundreds of other indistinguishable faces. She'll recognize me, be able to pick me out of a crowd.

God help me if this girl fucks everything up.

# SIX

## *HANNAH*

After the Halloween party, my eyes constantly search faces. Sometimes I look for the ones who attacked me but mostly the one who saved me. None of them appear, though, and slowly, I stop trying to find them.

My date with Gabe moves three more times. If I were the type of person to believe in signs, I would think the universe was telling me something.

By the second week in November, he promises nothing will stop him from seeing me. Even so, I expect him to call right before, apologizing and asking to reschedule yet again. About an hour before he's supposed to pick me up, someone knocks. I answer in yoga pants and a sweatshirt.

Gabe looks me over, raising an eyebrow. "If you look this good caught off guard, I have no idea what you're doing with me."

I roll my eyes. "You're early."

"I know, but I was worried that if I waited until eight, something would happen." He pulls a bouquet of white flowers from behind his back. "I've actually been outside for half an hour already."

He hands me the flowers, and I smile.

"Let me get changed?"

"Or you can wear that."

He leans to the side, so he can watch me until the door shuts. The flowers land on my bed as I rush to the closet. I change fast since Terra and I already argued over what I'd wear. For once, I won with skinny jeans and a V-neck sweater. Much more sensible than her miniskirt and halter top she claims are first-date musts.

I slip on a pair of sneakers. When I open the door again, the nerves kick in. My pulse quickens when Gabe smiles and extends his hand. I decide this time will be different. This guy won't be like the others who stop calling and drop off the face of the earth after a few dates.

Then again, I always tell myself that, and they always do.


Gabe's the kind of guy you expect to bring flowers. He opens doors and holds my hand while he drives and checks if I'm cold. Since our reservation isn't for an hour, we stop at an art gallery he says he's always wanted to visit.

We're in a small room, just the two of us, and he slips an arm around my waist. But it falls away after a vase crashes off a pedestal behind us and startles me. A few minutes later, someone tells us they're closing early, and we need to leave.

Since we still have time to kill, he takes the long way to the restaurant, and we walk in, right on time. Only the hostess stares at him, confused, when he gives his name.

"But you canceled your reservation. I just talked to you half an hour ago."

He shakes his head. "I never called."

She frantically checks the crowded dining room and stutters out an apology.

"We can eat somewhere else," I say.

And so we stop at the first fast-food place we find and cram into a booth together. He steals most of my fries, and every time I laugh, he smiles. It's sweet and uncomplicated. He really might be different.

I choose the movie, a cheesy romantic comedy I think he'll hate, but he dutifully buys the tickets and popcorn and those chewy cinnamon candies without complaint.

We're alone in the theater until the lights dim, and someone sits all the way down in front. During the previews, Gabe puts his arm around me, pulling me closer and trailing his fingers over my arm. The only other soul gets up and walks out. I look over, and Gabe's gaze lowers to my lips. His mouth inches toward mine until a loud buzz makes me jump. Lights high on the wall flash red as the sound continues.

"Fire alarm," Gabe says in my ear. "I think I'm bad luck or something."

Or I should start believing in signs.

We evacuate with the rest of the building, no one in much of a hurry. An usher walking out with us comments about it being a false alarm. Rather than stand around, waiting for them to sort everything out, Gabe and I head to his car.

"You want to go somewhere without people and alarms and reservation disasters?" he asks, opening my door.

I smile and nod.

He stops at a park I've been to a few times with a lake in the center. We walk down a lit path that curves around trees. By the time we reach the water, I'm cold, but we sit on a bench anyway.

"I came here a lot with my parents when I was a kid," he says. "Did you grow up in Boston?"

"Colorado."

"Do your parents still live there?"

I force a small smile and shake my head, hoping he won't ask anything more.

"You're lucky then. Mine have lived in the same house my entire life. I think they still eat the same breakfast as they did my entire life too. What about yours? Stuck in the same old habits?"

One of the first things I did after the funeral was sell their house. I was only sixteen, and in order to stay out of foster care, I went through the courts to become an emancipated minor. After that, I could sign all the documents without needing a guardian or permission. I told the realtor to price it below market value. She thought I was crazy, but it sold in three days, and I took my first real breath since they'd died.

My eyebrows pull together, and I look around for nothing. "It's freezing."

On cue, I shiver. He runs his hands up and down my arms. "Let's get you warm then."

His arm stays around me on our way back, but it drops away as we reach the parking lot. He rushes over to his car. "You've got to be fucking kidding me." He kicks at the flat front tire.

"Is that one you just replaced?"

"No, it's the only one that I didn't. I haven't replaced my spare yet, so I'll have to call someone."

Gabe pulls out his phone. As he wanders away, a motorcycle pulls into the parking lot. It stops near the car, and the driver leaves the headlight on. It blinds me until someone walks in front of it. The body takes shape with a bright white glow around it.

Before my eyes fully adjust, the figure stops in front of me and says, "Hannah."

His hair looks messy without gel, no eyeliner, and this black leather jacket is clear of spikes, but it only takes me a few seconds to recognize him. My mystery man from the Halloween party glares at me—tall, dark, and annoyed.

"What are you doing here?" I ask.

"It's a public park, Hannah. What are you doing in one after dark?" He glances at Gabe coming back in our direction and shakes his head. "Great."

"Someone will be out in thirty to forty-five minutes." Gabe nods at the guy who appeared while he was away. "A friend of yours?"

"We go way back," Mystery Man says, an edge in his tone. He points at the phone still in Gabe's hand. "Those places always take longer than they promise. How about I give Hannah a ride back to the dorms? Unless you want her stuck in a park with a history of stabbings."

Gabe wants to argue, I can tell. But being the kind of guy you expect to bring flowers, he looks down at me. "What do you want to do?"

"She wants to not freeze to death, for starters." Mystery Man shrugs out of his jacket, leaving him in a white T-shirt. He holds it out for me.

I slide my arms in. Sandalwood mixes with the leather, and I pull it tight around me, instantly warmer from his body heat. "Thank you."

He's rubbing the back of his neck, already walking away. "Let's go."

It's not a suggestion anymore, so I shrug at Gabe. "I'll call you when I get home?"

"We're doing this again." He pulls my hair out of the collar and brushes a finger across my cheek. "Soon."

He watches me back away. Mystery Man watches, too, waiting on his bike when I turn around. He holds out the only helmet, but I shake my head.

"I'm not going anywhere until you tell me your name."

His jaw works under the skin as he swings his leg over, off the bike. For a second, I think he might throw me on the back, but he sets the helmet on my head. "John," he says. "John Smith."

I huff and start pulling it back off.

"For fuck's sake." He shoves the helmet back down. "Cass, okay? My name's Cass."

His fingers yank the coat's zipper up, and he climbs back on the bike. I check over my shoulder at Gabe, still looking in our direction.

*Last chance, Hannah.*

The motorcycle roars to life, and before I change my mind, Cass jerks me forward by the sleeve. I grip his shoulder and climb on behind him.

As soon as my feet touch the pegs, he guns the throttle. I throw my arms around his middle, and he tears out of the gravel parking lot. He pushes every yellow light, takes each turn too fast. My damn life flashes before my eyes, even after I've squeezed them shut.

Eventually, I get brave and peek. We're farther from campus than at the start of this little joyride.

"Where are we going?" I ask at a red light.

Cass never answers, accelerating fast enough that the front end pops up. I cling to him tighter, and I swear he laughs, his abs contracting under my grip. For someone worried I might get stabbed with Gabe, he seems less than concerned about my safety now that I'm with him.

He slows down then, and we wind our way through the streets. We finally come to a stop in front of my building. I straighten up, cold when I let go of him. Even in short sleeves, he somehow remained warm the entire time.

"Do me a favor," he says as I climb off. "Stop taking douchebags to the lake at night."

I drag off the helmet and shake my hair out. "Should I bring jerks instead?"

An eyebrow lifts, and he snatches the helmet from my hand. Wild motorcycle rides apparently make me mouthy. He motions for his jacket. The wind cuts through my sweater when I take it off. I wrap my arms around myself, fighting off the need to shiver.

"Go inside," he commands.

The engine revs.

I step onto the curb, but after a few steps, I turn. "Goodnight, Cass."

When I say his name, he lowers his head, and his back rises with a deep breath. "Go inside, Hannah."

He still hasn't moved when I reach the door and look back. I hurry in and upstairs to my room. Terra sits up on the bed, but I go straight to the window and check through the slats of the blinds. Cass stares up, his gaze hard on me through the glass. I can't say why, but I feel like whatever just happened between us shouldn't have happened. This guy I want is someone I shouldn't want.

My phone vibrates with another call from Gabe. I tap the screen to ignore it and look out the window again, but Cass is gone.

# SEVEN

## *CASS*

It's not against any rules for a Watcher to engage with their charge. Chaz has one he skydives with on a regular basis, reveling in the power during the free fall. But I don't want to know Hannah. I don't want her touching me or saying my name. I want her to live out her life and die in her sleep, old and gray, and free me from the metaphorical chains.

So, I keep as much distance as possible the first week after her failed date with Gabe. A date that only happened because I paid a little visit to my friend Barrett Lane at the costume shop. His face when I walked in, swinging the bunny head around, was priceless. I bashed him with it until I felt a twinge. It was Hannah opening the door to fucking Gabe. Who shows up an hour early for a date?

A few days before Thanksgiving, she forces me downtown while she goes shopping. I duck into the doorway of an insurance building as she gawks at a mannequin in a storefront. The clouds hang low in the sky. Most people carry umbrellas, all bundled up and ready for a cold rain to fall. Not Hannah, though. She wears a fucking sweater and leggings, and if she steps on a patch of ice, her boots will land her on her ass. After much deliberation, she heads into the store.

While she's inside, the sky finally opens up, letting down sheet after sheet of sleet. I pull up the collar of my jacket, shoving my hands in my pockets. Without any light inside, my body responds to the cold like a human's.

By the time she reemerges with another shopping bag, slush covers the abandoned sidewalks. We're blocks away from her car as she contemplates her next move. *Go back inside and buy a fucking coat.*

Instead, she turns back the way she just came from. I follow at a safe distance, and after about a block, she dips into an alley that cuts across to the parking lot where she left her car.

The second she's out of sight, I'm too warm—no, I'm fucking hot. Energy burns through me, demanding and urgent as it propels me across the street. A car honks, narrowly missing me when I sprint in front of it. Reaching the opening between the tall brick buildings, I search for the threat. Only nothing looks out of place. A garbage dumpster, a few cardboard boxes stacked next to a wall by a handcart. I'm almost at full strength with no apparent reason.

"Hannah," I shout, slowing to a brisk walk so I don't scare her.

She's halfway down the alley and stops, turning at her name. Confusion washes over her face, and her mouth opens. Before anything comes out, a ripple appears in the air next to her. It only takes milliseconds for a being to materialize once the portal opens. Shadows swirl around the human form, my light instantly recognizing the dark.

*A fucking demon?*

I act without thinking, and an arc of light illuminates the alleyway, shooting from my hand and knocking him away from her. He bounces off the metal dumpster but teleports before hitting the ground. Hannah can't even blink in the time it takes him to reappear behind her and grab her shoulders. Demons always revert to self-preservation if threatened, and she's his best shield against further attack. While he keeps her between us, his eyes dart from me to the portal. The drop comes without effort, and my feet land on the concrete in front of it, blocking his escape route. Hannah's terrified gaze meets mine for a split second before he launches a fireball from his palm. As I dodge, he throws her aside, and I take the opening. A bolt of energy strikes him in the chest, blowing him back. Midair, he vanishes, and my power goes along with him.

I drop to a knee, the sudden void inside me overwhelming. I shouldn't feel like this, not a complete absence of light. Not until Hannah calms down. But I don't sense any divinity. Nothing. Then I see her lying by the wall, unmoving.

*No. No. NO!* My head starts shaking as I scramble over to her, colder than I've ever been. It can't end like this.

I press my fingers to her neck. Relief doesn't have meaning until I feel her pulse beneath my fingertips, steady. I drape my coat over her, and as I pick up her limp body, I notice her boot print in a pile of slush where she slid. Demon or not, I blame the fucking boots.

A flicker of warmth spreads through me when we reach the end of the alley, and her eyes flutter open. She lifts her head, panicked. "Cass?"

"You slipped and hit your head," I tell her.

Her eyebrows pull together, and she winces, touching the back of her probably cracked skull. "Let me down."

"Not a chance." I readjust my grip as she wiggles in my arms. "We're going to the emergency room."

She struggles for a few more steps and then huffs out a sigh, forfeiting the fight she wouldn't have won anyway. I want her checked over, inside and out.

Stopping by the passenger side of her car, I hold my hand out. "Keys."

Her eyes roll, and she digs through the purse hanging across her body. "This is ridiculous. I'm perfectly fine."

"Or you have a concussion, go to sleep, and die." I rip the keys out of her hand and set her down.

While I open the door, she pulls on my coat. I'm in for another week of it smelling like flowers. I help her in and rush around to the other side. Before I even try to fit behind the wheel, I move the seat back, and as soon as I turn the key, I shut off the crap she calls music.

As I pull out of the parking lot, she turns in her seat to face me but doesn't say anything. I glance over a few times, trying to gauge whether she remembers anything about the attack. If she does have a concussion, I'll need to wait until she recovers to wipe her memories. Unless I want to chance screwing up her brain permanently and condemning myself to a forever of misery.

"What?" I finally ask.

She squints, studying me. "How did you know this was my car?"

"I saw you park earlier."

"And why were you in the alley?"

"Why were you?" The irritation cuts through my tone. "Hoping to get mugged?"

She crosses her arms and sits back in the seat, pouting for the rest of the drive.


They won't let me back with Hannah for her scans, so I hover outside the door, not wanting her far away.

At one time, a demon attack meant very little. They scoured around like sewer rats, irritating but a part of the day-to-day you ignored. But over the past several centuries, they've tightened ranks. The last time I even remember seeing one surface was in the eighteen-hundreds. And I've definitely never had one come after any of my charges.

My phone vibrates for at least the seventh time, Chazaqiel unable to take a hint. I step around the corner and into a darkened room with the light boards for reading X-rays.

"What?" I answer.

"Fuck you too, dude," Chaz says. "From your mood, I take it that you also dealt with a little visitor today?"

I stop pacing, giving him my full attention. "Demon?"

"Low-level bitch who ran as soon as I showed up. He tried a snatch-and-grab on one of my charges."

"So, we think they're targeting Nephilim?"

"Not sure, but it sounds like more than a coincidence. We'd better give the other two a heads-up, just in case."

I rub the back of my neck, the tension building. "I'll call Ros, but Samy's MIA."

"Again?" Chaz sounds about as unconcerned as I'd expect. "How long this time?"

"No idea. He missed his hundred-year check-in with Lydia. She popped in a while back, looking for him. I haven't seen or heard from either of them since."

"Well, he always shows back up. Even if it takes two or three decades."

"True," I say. "I'll let you know when he does. Keep in touch."

"Yeah, I'll send a fucking Christmas card." He snorts as he hangs up.

I poke my head out into the hall. Since the crystal ball is still in my jacket, which lies on a chair inside the room with the rest of her clothes, I rely on good old-fashioned spying and peek through the small window of the door. All I see are Hannah's feet sticking out of a machine, explaining the sensation settling inside me. She's not a fan of tight spaces.

I return to the dark room and call Rosdan.

He answers on the first ring with an exhausted, "Demon attack on your Nephilim?"

I drop into a chair, his question confirming what I feared. "One of Chaz's too."

"Perfect."

A deep sigh comes through the speaker. I can't help but feel bad for the guy. Armaros—Rosdan for the past few centuries—never deserved any punishment. He merely suffered from the worst case of wrong place at the wrong time in the history of everything by being on Earth when the hammer came down on all of us. We call him the Cursed One, and he's earned the nickname over and over again. Every time he comes close to reaching the end of his line, someone has twins. Or triplets, as was the case last year.

"What's the plan?" he asks.

My turn to sigh because I have no idea. The role of leader belongs to Samy—always has and always will. Chaz fills the place of bro, Rosdan acts as our resident therapist, and I'm the asshole who mostly broods.

The lights flip on, and a nurse walks in. She gives me the evil eye for being on my phone despite the numerous signs telling me to shut it off. I'm the rebel too. I resume my post, waiting for Hannah, and switch to the Angelic language to avoid blabbing about demons in front of people. They throw out seventy-two-hour holds far too easily these days.

"There's a blood moon next week," I tell him. "If it's ritual-related, the threat will pass."

"So, keep our charges close?"

"I think it's our best option for now. Your five are all in one house. Chaz's two live in the same city. And last I knew, Samy was racing me to the finish line with one. He's missing, by the way."

"I figured." He pauses as a cry comes through the speaker. "Triplets are waking up from their nap."

"What are you, the nanny?" I chuckle at my joke, but when he doesn't, I stop. "Oh Jesus, Ros, you're the nanny?"

"Screw you, Kasdaye. Not everyone gets to follow a hot chick around, pretending she's such a fucking burden."

"She is," I say. "I saved her from the demon, so she could slip in a puddle and knock herself out. She's getting checked over right now, so I'll know how long I need to worry about her remembering that I lit up like a Christmas tree."

He laughs. "You do look pretty when you glow."

The cry becomes a chorus, so we agree he'll clue Chaz in on the plan, and then he goes to change a diaper or something.

It takes another twenty minutes for the door next to me to open. The same woman who took Hannah in for her scan walks across the hall. Once she disappears, I slip into the room.

I round the corner to find Hannah changing in front of a locker, facing the other way. She doesn't notice me, so I wait until she hooks her bra and step behind her.

"Do you have a concussion?"

She gasps and covers her tits with her shirt as she spins around. "What the hell, Cass?"

I smile and walk away, having scored my fix. Really, it's the least she can do, considering my trouble.

She huffs and turns back around to finish getting dressed. "You couldn't wait outside?"

Ignoring her, I flip through her chart that the lab tech carelessly left lying about. She has a mild concussion with no evidence of bleeding or swelling. Which means I should wait at least a week before messing with her mind. More to be safe. According to what Hannah told them, she doesn't remember anything leading up to her fall or immediately following. So as long as those memories stay dormant, she and I shouldn't have any problems.

*Hannah.*

She bends over to put on her boots. I toss the clipboard down and rush over. I catch her arm as she brings a hand to her forehead, and a second later, I catch the rest of her. I haul her back to her feet and guide her to the bench.

"Sorry," she says, her eyes staying closed a few more seconds. "Dizzy."

"Comes with a brain injury." I kneel in front of her, sliding her other boot on. After I zip them, I hand her my leather jacket from the chair.

"Let me guess. You're driving me back to the dorms whether I like it or not?"

I shrug. "Unless you prefer they call your emergency contact."

She looks away, not wanting to admit she left the spot blank on her forms. I consider the issue settled and help her to her feet. The crystal ball clinks against my lighter in the inside pocket when she pulls on my jacket, but she doesn't seem to notice.

By the time we walk through the large glass sliding doors, it's dark and cold. I check on her a few times during the drive, making sure she doesn't go to sleep. The exact opposite of what I usually want.

At the dorms, she doesn't wait for me to climb out of the car—her stubbornness on full display. I follow her inside and upstairs to her dorm room. When she stops at the door and turns around, I realize this is as far as I'm expected to go.

"Thank you for your help today." She pushes it open to a dark and empty room.

"No roommate?" I ask, already knowing Terra's in Rhode Island.

She shakes her head and looks at the floor. "Everyone already left for Thanksgiving break."

I snatch her discharge instructions out of her hand and read, *"During the first night, ask a friend or family member to wake you every two to three hours."*

She rips the paper back from me. "I'll set an alarm."

"What good does that do if you're unresponsive?" I pull my phone out of my pocket. "Give me your number."

Women rarely have a problem with giving me their number, but she hesitates before rattling it off. Since I already have it stored, I pretend to enter it. "I'll kick this door in if you don't answer."

She hands me back my jacket, and without another word, I leave her in the hallway. I'm in for a long night, camped outside her building on my bike. Maybe I shouldn't have given Rosdan such shit for being a nanny. Because that's essentially what I've become.

# EIGHT

## *HANNAH*

The first time the shrill ringtone goes off, it confuses me. Mostly because I haven't taken my phone off vibrate since high school. I check the blinding screen, not recognizing the number. It takes me a few seconds to remember why my head throbs. Everything that happened since the alley is a fog mixed with a dream. Pieces slowly come back, and I answer.

"What day is it?" Cass asks.

I let out a sigh and rub the sore spot on the back of my skull. At this point, he probably thinks I'm completely helpless. A damsel constantly in need of saving. And at this point, maybe I am.

"Hannah," he says, irritated I haven't answered.

"If it's after midnight, then it's Wednesday. The day before Thanksgiving."

"I'll call back in a few hours."

That's how it goes all night without fail, only with different quizzes each time. When I wake a few minutes to eight, I switch my ringer off and wait for him. But at eight sharp, rather than my phone vibrating, someone knocks.

Cass shoulders past me and sets a bag of groceries down on Terra's bed, pulling out a container of yogurt. "You didn't eat yesterday."

The gesture catches me off guard, and I almost ask if he bumped *his* head. I shut the door and sit on the bed, taking my yogurt with me. Before I can ask how I'm supposed to eat it, he brings over a plastic spoon. His fingers brush mine as he hands it to me, and unlike the other times, he's cold. Freezing, actually.

"Why are you so cold?"

"Because it's cold outside." He returns to the bag and shows me what else he brought. Magazines, snacks, food for my mini fridge. "This should last you at least a few days, so you can rest while everyone's gone."

"Why would you think I don't have plans for Thanksgiving?"

He stops sorting through the bag. "Do you?"

It sounds more like a challenge than a question.

He looks over for my answer. The way his intense gaze locks on mine feels oddly familiar. But the memory stays cloudy around the edges, not giving me anything other than his face and a shiver down my spine.

"No," I finally say. "I don't."

His attention drops to the container on my lap. "Eat."

I roll my eyes, but when he steps toward me, I pop the spoon in my mouth before he tries to force-feed me.

He almost cracks a smile. "Good girl."

We don't talk anymore while I eat my breakfast, and he finishes putting things away. He watches with a cautious eye as I throw the container away across the room. On my way back, I dig cash out of my purse.

"Here." I stop in front of him, holding it out.

He stares down at my hand, eyebrows drawn together. "What's that for?"

"For the supplies. It's the least I can do, considering all you've done for me, Cass."

We stand there for what feels like forever until he looks at me, his expression unreadable. It looks like he might say something, but then he shakes his head and walks out. I sigh as the door slams. I wonder if everyone's knight in leather jacket is as temperamental as mine.

# FALLEN REBEL

It's not until I stick the cash back in my purse that I remember my shopping bags from yesterday. My stomach sinks as I think about someone selling everything inside them for a quick buck. I peek out the window and wait for Cass's motorcycle to pull away from the curb. Once the roar fades away, I pull a sweatshirt from the closet and grab my purse, needing to know for sure if they're gone.


My parents' life insurance policies both paid out double for accidental deaths. One of the lawyers told me how lucky I was, and if I invested a little, I could live a cushy life well into my forties. I guess he and I have different ways of looking at the world because any time I spend money on something unnecessary, I don't feel lucky. I feel guilty.

So, when I park in the same lot as yesterday, I take a deep breath and ask the universe to give me this one. Let the bags with my entire next year's wardrobe in them be untouched and waiting for me, no matter how unlikely the possibility.

Someone must be listening for once because, about halfway down the alley, I spot them by a brick wall among a number of empty cardboard boxes. I laugh in disbelief and drop my head back. My eyes close, and I breathe with the sun shining down on my face, and life feels livable.

"Hannah," someone shouts.

I lift my head to see Cass stalking toward me, and it's like someone rips back a curtain in my mind. Everything rushes back. Feelings first, confusion and terror mostly, followed by images. Cass and a bright light and a man grabbing me from behind, and then Cass vanished into thin air. My gaze shoots to where he instantly reappeared. I shake my head, bringing a hand to my mouth. It's not possible, but it all seemed so real. Sleet hitting my face, hands crushing my shoulders, the smell of sulfur, and Cass's eyes meeting mine.

He stops moving when I look at him again, my heart pounding out of my chest and throbbing in my face.

"Calm down," he says.

"How did you know I was here?" My voice wavers, asking what seems like the least crazy of all the questions I could ask.

He holds his hands up and eases a few steps closer. "Let's go somewhere and talk."

I back away, keeping the distance between us. "Not until you tell me why you're here."

He licks his lips and shrugs. "Because you're here."

"What does that mean?" I ask.

The bags catch his attention, and he bends over, gathering them up. It takes everything in me to stand there while he comes toward me, his stare as harsh as ever. But even scared, I can't bring myself to believe he'd hurt me. Not after all the times he's come to my rescue since we met in the haunted house. Then again, that trusting nature probably makes me the perfect victim for a serial killer.

"Let's go," he commands, walking past. I stay unmoved, my mind still struggling to process, until his footsteps stop behind me. "Now, Hannah."

My hands tremble while my feet follow, but my mind stays at half-speed.

Cass loads my bags in the backseat of my car and waits by the passenger side for me to hand him the keys. I shiver after we crawl in. I don't think it has anything to do with the temperature, but he cranks the heater anyway.

As he pulls out of the parking lot, he turns on the radio, clearly not wanting to talk. I stare out the window, searching for a logical explanation for what happened yesterday. The most likely being that I never woke up when he called last night. He kicked in my door and found me unresponsive, and now I'm in a coma at the hospital. Or he's an alien. Or a science experiment gone wrong. Or maybe I lost it after my parents died, and he's part of a hallucination.

I don't notice we've stopped until he opens my door. We're back at the dorms. He gestures for me to lead the way, and I reluctantly climb out. We walk all the way in without a word, his eyes on me every time I peek back.

At my room, he stops next to me and dangles my keys off his finger. I take them, but as I turn to unlock the door, he tugs me toward him by the sleeve. His hands cup my face, tilting my chin so I look at him. I struggle to keep my breathing even, and I swear his skin grows warmer against mine. He searches my eyes, his softer than usual.

"How's your head?" he asks, low and quiet, the edge gone from his tone.

"My headache's coming back."

A torn expression appears, and he lowers his head, his forehead almost touching mine. "Promise to rest at least for today, Hannah. Give your body time to recover." He takes a deep breath and brings his gaze back up. "Do that for me, and tomorrow … I'll explain everything."

I want to argue, but my head starts to spin, so I nod. "Tomorrow."

Cass stares at me a few seconds longer before his hands fall away. My cheeks instantly grow cold where he was just touching them. He pushes the door open for me and walks away, but I stay there, watching him until he disappears around the corner. Despite our agreement, for the first time since meeting him, I think I might never see him again.

# NINE

## CASS

Even though we cleaned up the chaos, the cosmos never stopped being volatile. It just became more complex and organized in its hostile nature. Stars die, planets collide, galaxies merge and rip apart. All part of something so vast and flawlessly designed that it will carry on endlessly, never repeating. With or without us.

This is where Samy would usually jump in and tell me to take a shot before I go all existential. But since he's not here, I sit up and voluntarily take a swig of whiskey. Then I take a few more just to be safe. The bottle comes with me when I sprawl back out on the grass and resume staring at the sky. At one point in my existence, I could rattle off the exact number of stars in the universe at any given moment. By the time I finished, the number would have already changed, but it was a fun party trick. I think that's what I miss the most—knowing.

I crane my neck, so I can see the building behind me and up to Hannah's window. Her light's still on well into the middle of the night. The bottle balances against my rib cage as I pull out the crystal ball and swipe my hand over it. She's in a pair of shorts and a baggy sweatshirt, relaxed back on her bed with her computer. Homework is not what I consider resting.

I slap around on the ground beside me until I find my phone.

*Sleep,* I text her. *Or tomorrow's off.*

She hesitates to look away from the screen, but after she glances at her phone, the chill leaves my muscles. I wonder if it's excitement or fear. The mind of man has a difficult time with the two both causing the same biological response. It's why people die chasing the thrill. Fear is intoxicating.

Her teeth dig into her lip as she taps away on her phone, mine vibrating soon after.

> *I thought maybe you would change your mind and disappear forever.*

I laugh once, probably loud enough that she can hear me through the closed window.

> *Maybe I will if you don't go to sleep.*

Honestly, the idea crossed my mind, and if I thought I could get away with it, I would. But if another demon attacks, it would all be over for both of us. So, the way I see it, two options give me a chance in hell of ever going home again. I risk wiping her memories before she heals or tell her the truth. I'll try the truth first and keep the other as a backup if she freaks out. Or I'll kidnap her, and we'll live out the rest of her life in a remote corner of the world.

Make that three options.

The light in her room shuts off, and I lay the orb on my chest, watching her. The blue glow on her skin dims after the laptop closes. Lit only by her phone, she crawls under the blankets and sends back a message.

> *See you tomorrow, Cass.*

> *Goodnight, Hannah.*

She smiles, her eyes reflecting the screen. I feel her, my temperature rising. My eyes fall closed, and I ride out the wave.

I lied before; this is what I miss the most—being in the light.

# FALLEN REBEL

I'm still on the grass in front of Hannah's building when the sun rises, empty whiskey bottle cradled in the crook of my arm. My eyes open long enough to realize that the blinding sun and I will not be friends for the next few hours. At least not until Hannah is up and scares herself with her own shadow or something and my powers heal me.

My hands are cold and stiff as I roll over and force myself off the ground. Before I shove the ball in my jacket, I check to make sure Sleeping Beauty is in fact sleeping. Dark auburn hair fans out over the pillow, and an arm covers her face. I push my bike far enough up the street so she won't hear me leaving. The longer she sleeps, the longer I can pretend today won't potentially end with me as a human.

She starts texting around noon, wondering where I am and when I'll be there. Her nerves kick in when I don't answer. I let her fret until my hangover's gone.

I shower and throw on a hoodie under my leather jacket. On my way down to the parking lot, I finally text her back.

*Be ready to leave in an hour.*

*Where are we going?* she asks.

*Just dress warm.*

Another message buzzes through as I climb onto my bike, but I ignore her, pulling away from the curb.

It takes more than my allotted hour to run errands and drive over to the dorms, but she'll survive. I climb the steps to her floor, plastic bag in hand, then I shrug off my coat and knock on her door. My limbs tingle after the first thud, and for once, I have trouble distinguishing between her nerves and my own.

She answers, and I roll my eyes. As expected, her idea of dressing warm includes skinny jeans and a low-cut sweater. I hand over my jacket and let her pull it on before I give her the goodie bag. She pulls out the earplugs and gloves and tilts her head to the side, confused.

"In case you're sensitive to sound from your concussion," I say.

She looks up at me. "Why? Where are you taking me?"

"For a ride."

What should be a cold day at the end of November turns out to be one of the nicer days of the past few months. We start off slow, Hannah agreeing to let me know if it gets to be too much for her. Nephilim are known for healing faster than full humans, but not that fast.

Her hold on me tightens as I pull out onto the highway. The needle on the speedometer creeps higher and higher. I wait for her to tug on my shirt like she promised she would, but it never comes. So, I keep going, not paying attention to where anymore, and soon enough, we're all alone. Everyone is sitting around a table with their families while we speed down the road, not bothered by a soul.

Once we hit one hundred, I drop my hand to her wrist and push up the sleeve until I find bare skin. Her pulse drums against my fingertips, still picking up speed. I can't help but push it further. Enough light flows through me that the wind doesn't even touch my skin anymore. I feel everything I lost and everything I stand to lose again. But this time, forever.

Once Hannah's adrenaline peaks, I let off the throttle, letting us coast around a curve. We slow, Hannah's pulse steadies, and I sober the fuck up. I have no idea where we are when I turn off onto an unpaved road, but I follow it until we reach a field of tall grass, brown and blowing in the breeze. It seems as good a place as any to try and tell someone you're a Fallen Angel charged with protecting them until they die.

I help her climb off and lean the bike on its kickstand. She pulls off the helmet, and as she takes out the earplugs, I walk away. I keep walking into the field, having no idea what to say. I've never known any of us to even attempt this, and I'm not exactly the best choice to act as the guinea pig.

At the end of the field, a cliff overlooks the scenic view below. I force myself in the other direction before I reach it. The last thing I need is Hannah being anywhere near it with her track record.

She's about twenty feet behind me, arms wrapped around herself. A section of hair covers her face from the breeze. She has to unbury her hand from the leather sleeve to push it back behind her ear. She swims in the jacket, making her look small and fragile, and for the first time in her life, I see her as something other than an obstacle in my way.

*Hell of a time to lose your edge, Cass.*

I take a deep breath and ask, "Do you want all my cards on the table at once, or should we ease into this?"

The question gets me a hint of light. Not enough to do anything with, but it's there like a security blanket.

She nervously shifts her weight from one leg to the other. "How do you always know where I am?"

She tenses as I step toward her and grab the front of my jacket.

"Calm down," I say. "I'm just getting something from the inside pocket."

I fish out a cigarette and my lighter first, then hand her the crystal ball. She stares at it while I light my cigarette. Before she asks what it is, I wave my hand over it and walk away. I expect a thud as it hits the ground or a spark to shoot down my spine as she witnesses the globe in action. But neither happens, so I turn back around.

She's still looking at it, eerily calm. "I don't get it."

"What the fuck do you mean, you don't get it?" I stalk toward her, and she shrugs.

"How does this have anything to do with you finding me in the park or the alley?"

I rip it out of her hands and check. It shows me her face, and I realize, to her, it just looks like her reflection. So much for that idea. I drop it and regroup, switching to a more direct approach.

"Do you believe in God?" I ask, agitation apparent in my voice. "Angels and Heaven and all that?"

"About as much as unicorns and fairies." Her eyebrows pull together. "Why? Are you going to try and tell me you're an angel?"

The second she says it out loud, my throat seizes up. We're at the point of no return. My hand actually shakes while I take a drag off my cigarette, and all I can do is nod.

Hannah catches me off guard with an amused smile. "You want me to believe you're an angel?" Then she laughs and rolls her eyes. "Okay, John Smith."

I stare at the sky, placing my hands on the back of my head. She's starting to irritate me, and I want this done and over with now.

"You want me to prove it?"

She laughs again and nods.

"Fine." I storm off toward the cliff, my head shaking the entire way.

"Cass…" she says, panic in her tone as I reach the edge. "What are you doing?"

"I'm fucking proving it."

I jump off the cliff, Hannah's screams following me down.

# TEN

## *HANNAH*

I drop to my knees, my entire body trembling as the cool breeze blows at my back. Shock takes over, my mind refusing to accept what my eyes just witnessed. But it happened. Cass went over the edge.

My vision blurs, tears streaming down my cheeks, and short bursts of air suck into my lungs, releasing just as fast.

"Calm down," he says from behind me.

I stop breathing altogether and whirl around. He's standing there, cigarette still balanced between his lips. I'm not even thinking about the impossibility of it, stumbling off the ground and running to him. He lets out a grunt when I hit his chest, and my arms lock around his neck. An arm reluctantly holds on to me as my feet dangle in the air.

"I thought you were dead." I bury my face in his neck, his skin so warm that it almost burns. "You should be dead."

Everything clicks then, my brain finally catching up.

*He's a fucking angel.*

I push away from him hard enough that I almost fall backward. I catch my balance and keep backing away, wanting as much distance between us as possible.

"Hannah," he says, his strides matching my own, "calm down."

"Stop saying that."

I'm still backpedaling when he disappears from in front of me. I back straight into him and spin around. Only him and a few feet separate me from the cliffside. He reaches out, keeping his arm between me and the edge as I look over at the jagged rocks waiting at the bottom of a hundred-foot drop.

Logic says I continue panicking, but my thoughts become sluggish. Everything slows down. I bring a hand to my forehead. Cass's voice warbles in and out, and I feel the warmth of his hands on me. When I look up, his concerned face fades out of focus. Darkness bleeds in from the edges. As it takes over, I only make out one word: "Fuck."

Not much registers at first but the chill of the hard ground beneath me. My eyes blink open. I'm still in the field with the dry grass surrounding me.

"Welcome back," Cass says from above me.

I sit up too fast, the world spinning in response. With my head no longer in his lap, he readjusts, leaning on an elbow and facing me. I look around, like my surroundings will help make sense of everything, but my eyes return to him without any new answers.

"Should we try this again?" he asks.

Maybe it's because I'm tired and still partially convinced I'm in a coma that I nod. "You're an angel." I sound braver than I feel, and he studies me like he knows it.

"I am."

"And you use that ball to find me?"

After a few seconds, he drops onto his back and hands me the glass ball again. My pulse jumps when my fingers brush his, taking it. Like the first time, I examine it, seeing nothing but my face reflected. Without looking, he reaches over and places a hand on the sphere behind mine. The image changes, widening to show both of us, him lying on the ground next to me as I stare at the ball in my hands.

"Holy shit." I let go, and he catches it with a smirk, a dimple appearing.

"Worked that time," he mutters and sets it on his other side. "I was one of the original Watchers."

I start to ask a question, but he cuts me off, "If you call me a Guardian Angel, I'll throw your ass over the cliff."

My mouth clamps shut, and his eyes roll before he continues, "We were only supposed to watch, not get involved. Short version is, we all broke the rules in one way or another. Some knocked up a bunch of women and created a super-breed of angel-human hybrids called the Nephilim. The rest revealed information man wasn't supposed to learn yet."

"Which were you?" I ask, still not sure how much I believe.

He stares at me, eyebrow raised. "Astronomy. If I were in the other group, I wouldn't be here. As part of their punishment, they were all made human and died thousands of years ago."

"Wait, how old are you?"

"Angels aren't born, so we don't age. We simply exist."

Disregarding how crazy that sounds, I rephrase, "How long have you existed then?"

He half-smiles and says, "Since the beginning."

"Oh." I nod like I understand but can't even begin to process what he means. "The beginning of what?"

His expression returns to annoyed. "You're distracting me from my point, and it's going to be dark soon."

I glance at the horizon where the sun's lowering behind the clouds.

He sits up, lighting another cigarette, and exhales smoke through his nose. "The angelic properties in Nephilim blood never dilute. First or twelfth generation, they remain half-angel and, back then, they maintained certain powers. After a while, the Nephilim considered themselves gods and began feuding over who was more powerful. They recruited humans to go to war for them. And thanks to our interference, man had advanced faster than we could have anticipated, developing weapons and strategies for fighting. The entire world ended up a giant, bloody battlefield, and getting them under control required drastic measures."

I pull my hands back into the sleeves of the jacket, the temperature dropping as fast as the sun. "There's something in the Bible about the Nephilim, right?" My comment earns a dubious look. "I never said I didn't listen at church. I just said I believe in it as much as magical creatures."

He nods and ashes next to his foot. "You're right. It's in Genesis before the flood. God destroyed the Earth to kill them and everything else to start over. The thirteen angels who couldn't keep it in their pants were used to re-kick-start humanity since they had already proven themselves fertile—along with a few thousand new humans."

"What about you and the others?"

Cass rubs the back of his neck, taking another drag. "God spared seven of the Nephilim and released them back into the world after suppressing their abilities. For our punishment, God tied each of our powers to one, only giving us access when something threatened them. In order to reenter Heaven, we had to keep our Nephilim from dying anything other than a natural death. And then we were charged with doing the same for all of their Nephilim descendants." He pauses, his eyes meeting mine. "Every. Single. One."

He says the words with a staccato, and with each, I become more aware of what he means. If he's only here to watch over Nephilim, then…

"I'm a Nephilim," I whisper.

Not needing confirmation, I push off the ground and run toward the road we came in on. Twilight has set in, but I don't care. It's all too much. I can't be here anymore. Not in this field or with him.

"Hannah," he shouts, catching up with me. He jerks me toward him by the arm, my chest hitting his. I try to pull away, but his hands cup my face. "Stop," he demands.

I blink away the burning in my eyes, not looking at him. "Which one?"

"What?" He ignores the tears rolling over his thumbs.

My gaze finally lifts to his, and for once, I'm the one glaring. "Which one of my parents were you supposed to protect?"

"Hannah—"

"Which one?"

His jaw tenses as he swallows. "Brice."

The air leaves my body, and I squeeze shut my eyes.

"I couldn't save him, Hannah. It wasn't my choice."

I try to pull his wrists away, but he doesn't move.

"It was an act of God," he says. "They were meant to die on the plane."

I shake my head, desperate for him to stop talking. If what he says is true, not only is God real, but I hate him. I hate him for taking them away and leaving me alone. Because that's what I've been since the moment they were gone.

This time, Cass lets me break away. I walk back toward the cliff, not having anywhere else to go. I'm all the way to the edge when I feel his hold on my arm. Not tight, but protective as I lower down on the ledge. He sits next to me, our legs hanging over the side. Neither of us talks for a long time. The sky darkens around us, and the stars appear.

"How does it work?" I ask, finally breaking the silence. "How do you know when I need you?"

He rubs his hands together. "Do you trust me?"

Before I can answer, he shoves me over the edge.

I gasp, clutching on to him. "Cass!"

"You feel the rush?" he asks. "The adrenaline?"

"I feel like I'm going to fall, you asshole."

He pulls me back to a safe distance and holds his hand out, palm up. The light on his fingertips looks dim enough to be the moon reflecting, but the intensity grows, spreading down his fingers until his entire palm glows with a bright white light. I touch the center, feeling the heat of his skin and a pulse of static across my own.

"It's divine light," he says. "Energy created by heavenly beings."

The light lessens as my heart rate returns to normal, and his skin cools.

Once it disappears, he pulls his hand away and clenches his fist. "The only time I feel it is if you're in danger or your adrenaline spikes. Other times, I might as well be a fucking human." His mood changes fast, sullen again. He stands and hauls me to my feet. "Let's go."

We return to not talking as he impatiently waits for me to climb on the back of his bike. It's late, and the roads are as abandoned as they were earlier in the day. The air's colder though. I lost the gloves he gave me in the field, so when we stop at a gas station, my fingers are pink from the wind. Cass pumps gas, watching me hide them in the sleeves of his jacket.

"Where do you get your money?" I ask.

"Artifacts mostly." He hangs the nozzle and screws on the gas cap. "People pay a lot of money to own random shit from three or four hundred years ago."

He straddles the seat, and I crawl back on behind him. Before starting the bike, he shoves my hands in the front pocket of his hoodie. The back tire screeches and fishtails as he pulls back onto the highway. His driving stays erratic, and the faster my heart beats, the warmer he becomes, my body directly affecting his. We fly through the dark scenery, road signs flashing past in the headlight. It's easy to forget about the world. But then we reach city limits. He slows down, and it all comes crashing back in.

With everyone still gone for Thanksgiving, the dorms are dark, except for the main entrance. Cass hovers in my doorway after I switch on the light.

"When does Terra get back?" he asks.

I smile, hearing him say her name.

"What?" He crosses his arms and leans a shoulder against the frame.

"You know all these things about me, and I don't even know your last name."

"Daye," he says. He cracks a smile, and my belly flips at the dimples. They fade away, and he's serious again. "You need to eat."

"Want to order something?" I think about everything he's told me and add, "Wait, do you eat?"

He nods and pulls out his phone. "Just not that Indian crap you like."

His name is Cass Daye, and he's an angel who hates Indian food. Now I know three things about him.

By the time he finishes ordering pizza, I'm halfway through a bag of gummy bears from the stash he left yesterday. I lean back on the dresser and study him while he stands by the door across the room.

"What happens now?" I ask.

He shrugs, pocketing his phone. "They bake the pizza and drive it over here."

I guess grating sarcasm beats him not answering. "I mean, with you and me. Do you go back to following me around and not talking to me?"

He tilts his head toward his shoulder as he shrugs again.

That's exactly what he plans on doing. It bothers me more than it should. It's our natural state, him in the background without me aware of it, but I thought it would be different.

"You'll be around for the rest of my life, right?"

"That's the deal," he says.

"And if I have any kids, you'll watch over them too?"

Cass shakes his head, looking at the floor. "You're not having children."

He says it like it's a fact already decided.

"I'm not?" I challenge. Although I doubt I'll ever want any, I won't let him dictate the choice for me.

"No." His steely gaze rises to mine. "You're the last Nephilim in my line. After you, I go home."

"That's not really up to you, though, is it, Cass?"

He steps farther into the room toward me, a nerve struck. "Are you sure about that?"

I stand my ground when he reaches me and tilt my chin up, our eyes staying locked. He towers over me while I force slow, even breaths, not willing to back down.

"The tough act won't work on me, Hannah." His palm presses against my chest where my heart pounds. A warm spark skitters across my skin. I slap his hand away, glaring at him.

Cass smirks, holding up his glowing palms as he backs off. "Calm down, sweetheart. You can't have babies if you never have sex." He grabs his leather jacket off the bed. "Enjoy the pizza." Halfway across the room, he spins and keeps backing out. "And tell Gabe I say hi ... if you ever see him again."

"What's that supposed to mean?" I ask.

He grins, both dimples proudly displayed. "You'll figure it out."

My mouth falls open as he slams the door. The universe isn't guilty of fucking up my dating life. It's my fucking Guardian Angel.

# ELEVEN

## CASS

I'll be the first to admit, I underestimated Hannah. Not once, but three times. She proved herself perfectly capable of handling the truth about me. She accepted the fact that she's Nephilim. And now she's bound and determined to screw Gabe just to show me she can. Unfortunately for her, she's also underestimated me and my well-crafted skills in sabotage.

Saturday night, she struts out of her building, wearing a light-gray sweater dress that barely reaches mid-thigh, black boots that hit above her knee, and nothing but skin in between. Rosdan would be drooling as much as one of his charges.

I've seen the outfit, and I know exactly what she plans to do with it. Well, what she *planned* to do anyway.

She should be leaving for a date, dinner at Gabe's—he cooks. Instead, she comes to a stop in front of me. My gaze catches on her legs before making it all the way up to her face.

She sets her jaw and crosses her arms over her chest. "A gas leak at his apartment?"

"Safety first, Hannah. What kind of guy would Gabe be if he let you come over and exposed you to the fumes?"

"You're an asshole," she says, turning around.

I watch her stomp back up the sidewalk and into the building.

The next evening, I wait in the same spot. I lean back against my bike, ready for her when she comes to a frustrated halt in front of me. She's in a tight gray miniskirt, fitted white sweater, and sexy tights. She lets out a huff and just glares without a word. It takes one hell of an effort to keep a semi-straight face.

Finally, she says, "You poisoned him?"

"No." I straighten up to defend myself. "Giving someone who's lactose intolerant milk is not *poisoning* them. It's encouraging them to build a tolerance."

She takes a deep breath and lets out an exasperated groan, storming off.

By day three, I call in reinforcements—Chaz, my go-to man for fresh ideas. He does not disappoint. I don't even try and keep the smile off my face this time, seeing Hannah explode through the door. Her spiked heels click down the sidewalk, and my gaze rakes over her, starting from there. Those legs are bare again, all the way to the hem of a short blue-and-white-striped dress, partially covered with an oversize maroon scarf.

She walks straight over to me and starts batting at my arm. "Chickens!" she shrieks.

I laugh, turning away while she lets out her rage. Once she calms down, she takes a step back onto the curb. A section of hair falls from her messy bun, and she blows it out of her face.

Maybe it's the light inside from her outburst or the fact that I'm running out of schemes that don't include farm animals, but I sigh. "I'll back off."

She looks up from the cement between us, surprised. "What?"

"Go out with Preppy." I swing a leg over the seat of my bike. "It should only take you one real date to realize he's not worth the energy you're putting into him."

Hannah's face relaxes along with her stance. "Thank you, Cass."

I shrug, already regretting it. "Don't get fucking pregnant."

She backs away a few steps and smiles at me before spinning around and heading inside. My eyes fall shut as I take a deep breath. I might have just screwed myself, all for a smile.

# FALLEN REBEL

I'm sitting at the bar Wednesday night when my phone vibrates. It's a text from Hannah with a picture of her placing a pill on her tongue.

*Cheers.*

I check the crystal ball. She's sitting on her bed in yet another fuck-me outfit, staring at her phone. I snap a picture of the recently refilled whiskey tumbler in front of me and send it back. The fact that she's on birth control should ease the nagging feeling in my gut, but I find myself draining my glass and waving over the bartender for another.

The stool next to me fills with a redhead with legs for days. I'm drunk enough that my eyes linger wherever the hell they want, which happens to be everywhere.

"Hi," she says.

My attention finally makes it to her face, and when the bartender sets down another drink, I slide it over to her. I ignore the buzzing phone on the bar and tuck the orb back in my jacket pocket. A night off from Hannah duty might not be the worst thing to ever happen to me. In fact, it's exactly what I need.

We finish off a few rounds and then paw at each other in the back of an Uber. When we get inside her apartment building, I lift her up, pressing her against the back wall of the elevator. It takes two floors of grinding on her to notice the person hovering in the corner, but at this point, the doors are opening on her floor.

She tugs me down the hall by the bottom of my leather jacket and unlocks her apartment. I back her in, but after she tosses her purse on the table, she pulls her tongue out of my mouth.

"I'll be right back," she says.

My hand rakes through my hair as she disappears down the hall. "Fuck."

I adjust my dick and collapse on a couch that looks like it's seen its fair share of action. The apartment's small. Other than being on the fourth floor, I have no idea where I am or what part of town I'm in. Not that it matters.

Thanks to the booze, I almost miss the heat hit my chest until it starts burning hotter. My mind shoots to Hannah, and without considering the reason, I call up her image in the ball.

She's straddling Gabe's lap, the two of them making out on a black leather couch. I recognize his apartment from when I pretended to be from the gas company and convinced the owner to evacuate the building. It's big and open, and he only has a table lamp on instead of the track lights overhead.

I lie to myself that I'm watching to make sure there's no threat lingering in the shadows, but really, I'm interested to see this guy in action. Or lack thereof. He lets her run the show, keeping his hands on her thighs as she rocks onto her knees. She holds both sides of his face, kissing him. Her teeth tug at his bottom lip, and she pulls at the back of his head, wanting him, yet his hands stay planted. I almost yell instructions at him on how to give her what she's practically begging for, but my own redhead lands in my lap.

"What's that?" she asks. Her lips find my neck as soon as she finishes the question, so I doubt she cares about the answer.

I look back at Hannah's face, the light spreading outward from my chest and through the rest of me. Her cheeks are flushed, her eyes closed, and I can feel her. Teeth graze over my earlobe, and I let the ball bounce off the couch cushion. One hand jerks the girl's hips forward, holding her tight against my cock. The other reaches for the back of her neck. My fingers thread through her hair, and I pull her face to mine.

The energy inside me intensifies with Hannah front and center in my head. And it's her moaning into my mouth and desperately clawing at my shirt. It's me between her legs, thrusting to meet her hips. Me she wants.

"Shit." I move the girl off me and onto the couch. "I need a minute."

I nab the ball off the floor and head down the hallway until I find the bathroom. The door bangs shut behind me, and I scrub a hand over my face. *What the fuck?* I can't remember ever being this hard with my clothes on.

I brace myself on the counter over the sink in the tiny room made even smaller without windows.

Light still pumps through me when my phone vibrates. I fish it out of my pocket and read the two words Hannah sent.

*Find me.*

Since I already know where she is, the drop comes without thought. I land in a dark area off to the side of Gabe's apartment building. She paces the sidewalk not far from where I stand. I glance around, trying to find what has her so worked up, but we're alone.

"Hannah," I say, stepping out of the shadows.

She turns around and nails me with a glare. "You can feel me having sex, can't you?"

I stop moving, not sure how to safely respond. Most of my charges had sex—except a handful of super nerds and a few who took vows of celibacy, but even they were turned on from time to time. Adrenaline increases in both instances. I've never had a problem ignoring it though. Hell, I've never wanted to do anything *but* ignore it. At least, not until I imagined Hannah's pussy rubbing against my dick instead of Gabe's.

No answer proves enough for Hannah.

She marches toward me, pissed. "I can't be with anyone, knowing that." She shoves me in the chest without much effect other than chipping away at my patience. "This is all your fault."

When she tries for a second time, I catch her wrists. I resist the urge to tell her to calm down because it's me who needs to get a grip. The energy is cycling between us, out of my hands and into her and then right back to me as her pulse races under my thumbs. It sends my nervous system into overdrive, my breathing heavy and cock throbbing. My attention drifts down to her hot mouth, her full lips slightly parted.

I'm about to do something really stupid when I look up and see the resentment in her eyes. It's the same feeling I've always had for her, and it helps me see past the surge of power blinding me.

"I'm going to be miserable and alone for the rest of my life because of you." She jerks away, and I release my hold on her.

"Let me know once you hit a few thousand years, and I might give a shit."

I walk away, hearing her storm off the other way. Whatever this experiment with her was, it's over now. She can know what I am unless it complicates things. Until then, we can go back to how things have always been—me waiting for her to get the hell out of my way.

# TWELVE

## *HANNAH*

Weeks pass without a word from Cass. Every once in a while, I think I see him off in the distance when I'm coming out of class or walking back from the dining hall at night. And it probably is him. He wouldn't want anything to happen to his precious ticket into Heaven.

Knowing he has a direct connection to my sex life moves Gabe and me into the slow lane. Anytime my heart rate increases, I picture Cass. Not exactly ideal when trying to hook up with someone else. Of course, Gabe's understanding and sweet, never pushing the subject or asking for more between us. Only that makes me even angrier with myself for not just getting over it. It's not like Cass hasn't been there for every other time.

A few days before winter break, I take a time-out from studying for my last two finals and drive Terra to work. From the sounds of it, her social calendar is already filled for the two weeks she'll be in Rhode Island with family and friends.

"When do you leave?" she asks.

I shrug, careful in how I word my reply. "My last final's on Thursday."

"Any last-minute Christmas shopping you want to do before then?" She raises her eyebrow, looking at me out of the corner of her eye.

"Only for my adorable roommate."

She giggles, holding her hands above her head in the shape of a halo, and I smile.

At some point, she decided the reason I don't talk about my parents is because we don't get along. I've never lied but never freely offered information either.

Around the holidays, she poses vague questions, and I give vaguer responses. It works because she doesn't like the heavy stuff, and I hate the look of pity people give me when they know.

I pull to the curb outside the clothing store, and she scuttles up the sidewalk. On my way back to the dorms, I stop at a small boutique. We agreed to wait until she comes back from break to exchange gifts, but she'll probably change her mind, so I need to be prepared. After I buy the top she's been drooling over for weeks, I toss the bag in my backseat. I turn the ignition but only receive a *click, click, click.*

"No," I say, trying again.

*Click, click, click.*

I groan, dropping my forehead onto the steering wheel. Not knowing anything about cars other than where the gas goes, I dig out my phone and call Gabe.

He answers on the first ring. "Can't get enough of me, huh?"

"Something like that. My car won't start."

"I'm at work until seven," he says. "You want me to see if I can leave early?"

"No, it's fine. I'll see if anyone has jumper cables or knows how to work the little hood-latch thingy."

"My little mechanic." He chuckles. "Let me know if you don't have any luck, and I'll try to get out of here."

As I hang up, a knock on my window startles me. I look over at Cass staring down at me. I open my door, and he reaches down by my leg and pulls a lever, making my hood pop. I brace for his mood and get out to join him at the front of my car.

He props the hood open and wiggles cables around. "Try starting it again."

My car door dings when it opens, but nothing happens when I turn the key.

The hood drops shut, and he walks around to my side. "Battery's shot. Get your stuff. I'm taking you back to the dorms." His eyes dart across the parking lot to a man standing by a light post, and if possible, he grows more serious. "Let's go." He grabs my arm and pulls me out of the car.

"Stop it, Cass." I twist away once I get my footing. "I'll call a tow truck and wait for Gabe."

He closes the small amount of space between us, his eyes darker than I've seen them. His words come out almost as a growl. "Get the fuck on the bike, Hannah. Now."

"Fine," I hiss.

I gather my purse and the bag from the backseat. He slams the door and guides me around the car with his hand on my back. We're almost to his bike when a tug on my shirt slows me down, but then he's pushing me forward again.

Cass swings his leg over the bike. I loop the bags over my arm and climb on behind him. Like always, he tears out of the parking lot. It only occurs to me when we stop at a light that he never gave me time to put on the helmet.

He cuts the engine outside the dorms. "If you give me your car key, I'll get it taken care of."

I let go of his shoulder once my foot touches the concrete and switch arms with the bags. "It's fine. I'll call someone in the morning."

My phone goes off. I show him Gabe's name on the screen, and he smirks.

"Better get it," he says. "We'd hate for him to worry."

I walk away a few steps and answer.

"I just stopped by the dry cleaner for my cape. Do you need me to play superhero and come rescue you?"

"No, I found a ride back to the dorms, and I am just walking in."

"Damn. Good Samaritans are always stealing my thunder." He laughs. "Well, since I'm off, you want to grab dinner?"

"Sure. I'll see you soon."

When I turn around, Cass is watching me. His overpowering stare holds mine until my heart beats faster. He looks at his hands and stretches out his fingers, feeling the change. His eyes come back with a different look in them, but I only stay for a second longer. For once, I'm the one walking away.

Because I still don't want him in my life.

# THIRTEEN

## *HANNAH*

Christmas was *the* holiday in our house. My parents owned no decorations for Easter, Halloween, or Thanksgiving. But come the first day of December, the North Pole threw up all over the place. Fake snow everywhere, tinsel hanging in every doorway. Our cat wore an elf costume for twenty-four days in a row. And that was just on the inside. We needed extra circuits added so that we wouldn't constantly blow breakers with all the outside lights.

I remember how embarrassed I would be at the matching sweaters my mom coordinated for us and the giant Rudolph nose and antlers my dad wore anytime we left the house to do something holiday-related. Yet, come Christmas morning, I'm not only wearing a bright green sweater with Bigfoot in a Santa hat and red bikini, but a headband with antlers. At least I forgo the nose.

The dorms have been abandoned for winter break, except for a janitor I scared a few days ago. To make up for it, I carry down a plate of Christmas cookies to leave in his closet for the next time he works. I open the door to blackness and feel around on the wall for the light switch. Not finding it, I step farther into the darkness. Maybe it's a string you pull.

I balance the paper plate in one hand and check out the room using my phone screen as a flashlight. It lights up a person standing in the corner. I scream, backing toward the door, but I run into a hard chest as hands grab my arms. Cass moves me behind him, keeping a hand on me while his other illuminates the room. About the time his shoulders relax, I realize the person is a mop, leaning in the corner.

His hand falls away from my hip, and he turns around.

"Sorry," I say.

He shrugs, less annoyed than I anticipated. "I expected you to be jumpy today. You watched three horror movies before bed."

Another stupid tradition—watching scary movies with Christmas themes on Christmas Eve. That one was Dad's favorite. He'd wait until right before a jump scare and shout, *'Merry Christmas!'*

Mom would attack him with a pillow, beating him into submission.

Cass steps aside and holds out a hand, lighting a path so I can set down the cookies. On my way out, I hang a little wreath ornament on the handle.

"I can't believe you still do all this crap every year." He looks down at the front of my sweater. "I think that's my least favorite of the collection. You should wear the one that says, *'Go, Jesus. It's your birthday.'*"

I laugh, knowing the exact sweater he's referencing—my mom's proudest find—but then, thinking about it sends tears rolling down my cheeks.

"Shit, Hannah." He rubs the back of his neck. "I wasn't trying to be a dick."

"No." I shake my head, wiping a sleeve under my eyes. "It's just nice, talking to someone who knows about the crazy stuff we did. I thought I was the only one left to remember, but you were there for it all."

He half-smiles. "Cringing the entire time."

I take a deep breath, determined to regain my Kelley Christmas spirit. There are plenty of days for grieving, but today isn't one of them. "Well then, you know I have some eggnog to get through." At the bottom of the stairs, I spin around. "Would you like to watch me get drunk and lip-sync to Christmas music?"

Mad at him or not, being around someone who knew them makes everything feel a little better.

It only takes a second for him to shrug and walk over. "I've been doing it since you turned sixteen. Why stop now?"


Surrounded by every Christmas decoration I could squeeze into the space, we spend the afternoon drinking through seven different batches of eggnog. I only make it through one glass of each, but Cass has two and proceeds to polish off the one made with whiskey. He frowns at the empty pitcher, so I hang over the side of the bed and retrieve the rest of the bottle from underneath. Angels apparently have a much higher tolerance than mere mortal-angel hybrids.

"You went all out," he says, reading the label. "Top shelf."

I lie back on my pillow. "This is what the Kelley family trains for all year. We don't mess around."

"I know." He leans back against Terra's bed and messes with some of the fake snow covering the floor beside his leg. "I had to keep Brice from falling off the roof when he tangled his foot in a hundred feet of twinkle lights."

"Only once?" I ask in disbelief.

He brings the bottle to his lips, fighting off a smirk. "Once a year."

I smile. "That sounds about right." I roll onto my back and stare at the ceiling, thinking about all the amazing moments they gave me. "I worry, no matter how long they're gone, I'll never stop missing them this much."

Cass stays quiet long enough that I check to make sure he's still there. Our eyes meet, and I wait for the look I hate, but it never comes.

"I should go," he says, pushing off the floor.

I sit up, confused. "Do you have somewhere to be?"

"No." He stops with his hand on the doorknob covered in shiny purple wrapping paper. "But I thought I would try leaving before one of us is mad at the other."

"How are you getting home?" I ask, remembering he appeared out of thin air.

He tilts his head back and forth, deliberating, and then cocks an eyebrow. His hand falls to his side, and he comes back toward the bed. I hold my breath as his knee lands on the mattress between my legs. My mouth becomes his focus, and he inches closer.

"Cass…"

"Shut up, Hannah."

The whiskey on his breath ends up more intoxicating than the eggnog. Warm fingers skim over my jaw before they curl around the back of my neck, and I can't think straight anymore. I close my eyes, waiting for his lips to brush over mine, but the weight of him leaves the bed along with his touch. And I'm alone in a ridiculously overdecorated room.

I hide my face in my hands, taking a few deep breaths to clear my head. *What are you doing, Hannah?*

A buzz makes me peek through my fingers at my phone.

> *Thanks for saving me the cost of a ride. Stop drinking*
> *before you reach Brice circa eight years ago.*

The year we lost my dad for an evening. He turned up on a porch a few houses over, wrapped in garland. Apparently, he'd been all over the neighborhood, performing the Trans-Siberian Orchestra's version of "Carol of the Bells"—which is completely instrumental. He thrashed around and scared some kids. They held a neighborhood watch meeting over it the following week.

I drop back on the bed and smile after one of the best Christmases I've had in a long time. The first one I haven't spent alone in five years. Now I just need to make it through next month and the worst week of the year.

# Fourteen

## Cass

Rosdan frantically searches under couch cushions, tossing them everywhere in the once-tidy living room. He pulls at the back of his hair hard enough that it's a miracle the dark strands don't come out. "I know Alexandra had her binky before I laid her down."

Chaz's eyebrows pull together, and he shoots me a *what the fuck* look. I shrug. I don't speak nanny or anything baby-related and have no plans on learning. Ros throws his arms in the air when he finds a nipple-looking thing under the coffee table and runs out of the room.

"He needs to get laid," Chaz says. "A lot."

I chuckle and relax back in the oversize easy chair.

Rosdan's charge works in investment banking, giving him the funds for not only a full-time, live-in nanny, but also a house with three living rooms. Sorry, one's a family room because God forbid they watch a kids' movie on just any couch.

Chaz nods at the crystal ball glued to my hand. "How'd the chickens go over?"

"Beautifully. But I caved and stopped screwing with her."

He steeples his fingers and brings them to his dimpled chin, mimicking Rosdan whenever he's overly serious. "Now, why would you do that?"

Rosdan reappears, sparing me from Chaz's inquisition. He drops onto the cushion-less couch and heaves out a sigh. "We can talk now."

"So, you had another attack?" I ask.

He nods and wipes his hands over his face. "A few days ago. It went after Mark at work. He took the stairs instead of the elevator as part of his New Year's resolution. The demon portaled in on one of the landings."

I roll my globe over the arm of the chair, my eyes following it back and forth. The day Hannah's car wouldn't start in the empty parking lot, I caught a demon watching us. No one else was around when he showed up, same with the alley. My other hand swipes over the ball, bringing up Hannah. She's sitting in class, surrounded by fifty other students.

"Kasdaye."

I look up at my name.

Chaz leans forward in his chair across from me. "What are you thinking?"

"They're only targeting them when they're alone."

He thinks for a second, then nods. "That adds up with the attack on mine. He was by himself in the locker room at the gym."

"And when they went after Alistair walking home from school." Rosdan yanks at the back of his hair again. "But why? What do demons want with a Nephilim? They don't have their powers, and most rituals using their blood need a bigger astrological event than a full moon. Right, Cass?"

I nod, my attention drifting back toward the ball. "And there won't be anything strong enough for a few months."

Hannah leans on her hand, propped up by an elbow. I keep looking at her like if I stare long enough, I'll discover whatever they want with her. Not her powers. Not her blood.

"What if they want to take us out?" Chaz taps his finger on his leg. "It only takes one charge for each of us and no more Fallen Watchers."

Rosdan lets out a long sigh. "Then they could use Nephilim blood anytime they want, no matter how small the ritual."

"No more risk," I finish out our collective train of thought.

We all sit quietly, searching for holes in the logic. But it makes the most sense out of anything we've come up with so far.

All three of us reach for our phones within seconds to text Samy. One of the nice things about knowing each other our entire existences is the predictability aspect.

"I'll be the buddy," Chaz says. "Ros, act concerned and let him know what's up. And, Cass … be Cass."

I'm already hitting send on my message, doing just that.

> *I'm done fucking around. Get your shit together and call me, or I'm going angelic bounty hunter on your ass.*

Rosdan pockets his phone. "You two had better go. Alistair's new carpool will be dropping him off from school soon."

Chaz snorts and jumps up. He pulls Ros in for a hug, slapping him on the back. "You're the best mommy out of all of us, Armaros." Knowing better than to try heartfelt embraces with me, he gives a salute. "Let me know when you decide to take charge of your charge again."

I flip him off. "Stop worrying about my charge and call your own, Blondie."

He winks and holds his phone to his ear. Triggering a charge's adrenaline so we can drop wherever we need to go is the most efficient form of travel for us. We scrub the incident from their mind the first chance we get. Although one of the rare perks of Hannah knowing: I won't have to this time.

His charge answers, and Chaz's face grows serious. He uses a low, gravelly voice to say, "I've been watching you, Avery. At night, when you think you're alone in your room." He heads toward the kitchen, and not long after he walks around the corner, his voice stops.

"And people think I'm an ass," I say, pulling up Hannah's number.

"How's that going?" Rosdan asks. "With her knowing our big, bad secret."

I shake my head, staring at her name on my screen. "Half the time, I want to grab her face and wipe it all away."

"And the other half?"

I give a half-shrug and walk away. "We'll talk soon, man."

The light centers in my chest before Hannah answers.

"Cass?" She sounds confused, surrounded by the bustle of a busy hallway.

"Glad you figured out how caller ID works."

"You've never called me before."

I lick my lips to keep from smiling even though she can't see me. "I have. You just don't remember."

Silence.

"Hannah?"

My extremities warm.

"Why wouldn't I remember?"

"Because I can wipe your memories." And I drop, my feet landing in the living room of my apartment. "Thanks, sweetheart. I gotta go."

I end the call and chuckle, heading to take a shower. Something tells me my powers will be in the on position for quite a while.

I'm prepared for the third week in January to be rough. It contains four of the worst days of the entire year, all back to back. Hannah's mom, Fiona, kicks us off with her birthday. She met Brice the next day. The one after is their wedding anniversary and then day four brings us to Brice's birthday. We make it through the first three days with less moments of panic than the previous years. Granted, I only sleep an hour a night, and Hannah's not far ahead of me.

She's in class on day four while I prematurely celebrate being done with this shit until the day they died in September. The ball sits on the bar while I explain what a day originally meant to a man I've dubbed Carl, who's passed out on the stool next to mine.

"The term's meant to qualify the time between two events. If I say, 'You were a sex god back in the day,' I wouldn't mean that you were a sex god for twenty-four hours. I'd mean you were a sex god in the period between when you started being one and stopped." I sip my beer and look over at him, sweaty and unkempt and drooling on the bar top. "My point is, Carl, the time between sculpting the universe and creating man was eons. Not a literal day. And there were a lot of resets back then that you never hear about. You wouldn't believe the number if I told you."

Sunlight on the back wall distracts me from my companion. I look behind me at the front entrance, and in walks the last person I expected. Hannah stands there, her hair wet from the snow. Blame the alcohol, but I double-check with the orb, verifying it's really her. With a close-up of her face, I see she's crying.

I slide off my stool. "See ya later, Carl."

She notices me coming and swipes away the tears on her cheeks. "Hey, what are you doing here?"

"It's the closest bar to your lecture hall, Hannah. What are you doing here?"

Her laugh sounds sad as she glances around at the tacky decorations on the walls. "It's the closest bar to my lecture hall." She looks down at her snow-covered boots, crying again. "Thanks to statistics class, I now know the exact odds of being hit by lightning." She forces a smile. "And dying in a plane crash."

*Shitty timing.*

I want to tell her none of it matters because they were destined to die. If they weren't, I would have felt Brice before it happened rather than after, when our bond broke. But that's not what she needs right now.

I keep my eyes on her while craning my neck around enough so that the bartender can hear me. "Can we get a couple of shots over here?"

"What do you want?" he says.

My eyebrows rise at Hannah. "Lady's choice."

She doesn't even think it over, answering, "Tequila. And keep them coming."


Hannah was playing it conservative with the eggnog on Christmas but not today. Today, she came to forget.

As an angel, I can't fully understand human grief. I can feel loss, but I'll never have to come to grips with my mortality. And that's what the death of a loved one does to man. It reminds them that what they know will end one day, and they can't stop it from happening.

I only let her get to the point of giggly before I cut her off and haul her ass back to the dorms. She used to laugh a lot. Her nose wrinkles when she starts, and if she's not careful, she snorts. We're walking down the hallway when it happens. It makes her laugh harder, and she stumbles into me. I hold on to her until we reach her room.

She leans against the wall and hands me her keys. "I'm not even going to try it."

I smile, shaking my head as I unlock the door.

"You should smile more." She studies me through her lashes. "I might like you more if you did."

Our gaze holds for a second before I say, "I'll get right on that."

I follow her in and shut the door behind me, not sure how long I need to stay. Tipsy and alone makes for a pretty easy target if any demons are waiting for their chance.

"When's Terra get back from class?" I ask.

"Soon." She tosses her bag on the bed and slips off her shoes. Her mood's heavy again when she turns around. She stands in front of her bed and stares at the floor, happy Hannah fading to black in front of me. "If I ask you something, will you swear to answer honestly?"

"I don't make promises," I tell her. "But I'm probably too drunk to lie to you at this point."

Her eyes stay lowered, voice quiet. "Why didn't you make me forget what happened in the alley?"

"The light alters the brain enough. Add it on top of a concussion, and I could have left you permanently damaged."

She nods like she understands, but her eyebrows pull together. "But I'm fine now. What's stopping you from making me forget who you are?"

"Where are you going with this?" I ask, a bite to my tone. I find the question grating, and I've entertained her long enough.

"Wouldn't it be easier for both of us if I went back to not knowing who you were?"

"Is that what you want?" I snap. After all the tiptoeing around I've done, she doesn't even *want* the fucking memories? "Because we can. Just say the word, and I'll erase every memory of us until it's like we never met."

She doesn't answer, staring at her socks, and anything I have resembling patience is gone. I close the space between us and take her face in my hands, like I should have done that night in front of Gabe's.

"Say it," I command, tilting her head back.

She looks up then, her eyes wide, and light slams into me. Mixed with tequila, it destroys any chance of rational thought. Hot and intense as it burns through me. Before I can stop myself, my lips crash down onto hers. She gasps, sending another pulse through me, and I thrust my tongue into her mouth, needing more. More of her, more of the light—all of it. Then she starts grasping at the back of my hair, dragging me deeper. I can't breathe without her filling my lungs or move without the chill of her skin on mine. I'm drowning. Inside, outside—she's everywhere. Inescapable.

I break away from her, unable to stand it anymore. Without so much as looking at her, I walk out.

Even if she'd asked, I wouldn't have taken the memories away from her. I want her to remember. I want her to remember every second between us.

If I have to be miserable because of her, then I want her to be fucking miserable with me.

# FIFTEEN

## *HANNAH*

My mind's scattered around the room when Cass storms out. I stand, shaking, my lips still warm from his. For the past four days, all I've felt is wounded. Hurting in ways I doubt will ever heal. But just then, I wasn't thinking about any of it. I wasn't feeling *any* of it. And I need him to make it stop again.

Without bothering to put shoes on, I yank the door open and run after him. I'm not even sure if he's still in the building or already back to wherever he goes when he's not with me. Then, at the bottom of the stairs, I spot him walking across the common area.

Catching up with him, I touch his arm. "Cass."

He jerks around, his eyes dark and feral. Before I can take a breath, he's pushing me into the janitor's closet. I can't see anything, but it doesn't matter. His lips are on mine again, kissing me hard. I grab at him, whatever I can to get him closer. He backs me into the wall, pinning me there with his body, and I wrap my arms around his neck.

"You want to forget me, Hannah?" He practically growls in my ear while his feverish hand slips under my shirt. It stays flush with my skin, sliding under the top of my leggings and panties. "Or do you want something else?"

My head falls back as he pushes between my thighs, and his palm presses against my clit.

"Is it this?" he says. His fingers stroke through me before dipping inside my wet pussy, and I bite my lip to stifle a moan. They pump in and out of me, faster and harder, his other hand tangling in my hair. "Tell me, Hannah. Tell me what you really want."

My heart races, and we both know what I want.

"Make me forget everything *but* you."

I barely get the words out, and Cass's mouth descends on mine, his tongue demanding. I feel the heat through his clothes, his mouth, his hands. It's almost too much, but it keeps everything else away while he does exactly what I asked him to do.

He's rough with me, not treating me like something fragile he can break. Or maybe he's trying to break me, and I just don't care. Teeth scrape over my skin, stubble scratches my jaw, his palm rubs in hard circles against my pulsing clit. As my breathing grows erratic, he grunts and thrusts his erection against my hip.

He rocks faster, keeping pace with his fingers, pulling me apart from the inside. I feel the delicious ache building, which means Cass feels it too. His arm slides around me, holding me against him. Just when I'm tumbling over the edge, he bites down on my shoulder.

I cry out as he marks me, and my legs give out as I surrender to every sensation coursing through me.

His grip on me tightens, fingers pumping, then they suddenly drag all the way out. He pushes me up the wall, hooking my legs around him so he can use me the way I used him. The friction of his hard cock grinding on my sensitive clit nears torturous, echoing through my body. I dig my nails into his scalp, and he unleashes a growl.

"Fuck," he grunts out. "Fuck, Hannah."

His face buries in my neck as the fingers clenching the backs of my thighs burn hotter. He tenses with one last thrust and groans, sending another shudder through me when he comes.

Still pressed into me, his chest heaves against mine until I take a deep breath. The second my pulse begins to slow, he steps back enough that I slide down the wall.

"Any other itches you want me to scratch?" he asks, his voice harsh. "Or are you good for a while?"

It would sting if it wasn't true. He's right, though; that's all this was—I needed something, and he gave it to me. But he also took what he wanted in return.

"Are you?" I challenge.

The heat of his breath touches my face, and a soft glow illuminates the space between us. His heated gaze hovers on my mouth before his dark eyes flick up to mine. Even with my body still trembling from him, I hold his stare, well aware of how to play the game by now. One side of his mouth curls up, and all at once, the light disappears along with the warmth of him in front of me.

I pull the string for the light, hanging from the ceiling. Once again, I'm alone and feeling everything.


Gabe and I hook up a few days later.


I don't see Cass for over a month.

The eye roll is back when Terra sees the skirt that stops above my knee and the top that only hugs most of my chest. "Where's get-some Hannah? I liked her."

"She's going to a nice restaurant, not the backseat of a guy's car."

I check the mirror as I pull my hair up. Her reflection pops up behind mine and starts pulling out strands. My hands fall to my sides, letting her finish.

"So, what are you going to tell Gabe?" she asks, spinning me around so she can see better.

I sigh for what seems like forever. Gabe wants to take our casual relationship and make it official. It shouldn't be an issue in the least, considering the biggest flaw I've found is that he's perfect. He's respectful and considerate and giving and humble. Yet anytime I try to imagine a future with him, all I see is the constant interference of a certain asshole angel who's gone underground for the past five weeks. No one deserves to deal with that baggage for the rest of their life.

Terra steps back, admiring her artistry. "There. Don't walk too fast, or the breeze will ruin it."

"I'll keep it at a leisurely stroll. As for Gabe, I think I'm going to say yes."

Her face pulls back in an excited grin, eyes wide and strained, and she grabs my hands.

"But," I say before she erupts into a shrill squeal, "on a trial basis. He works all the time, and I plan on taking summer classes, so I can graduate early."

Her face falls at the last part. "Oh, right." She stomps across the room. "I forgot you hate me and never want to see me again."

I nod. "It's true. I've been trying to find the best way to tell you for years."

She sticks her tongue out at me. "Well, a yes is a yes. You need to have sex on a regular basis before you're too old to have a quickie in the back of a bar."

"Words to live by." I grab my purse on my way out. "And just so you know, the only reason I hate you is because you're so much prettier than me."

"That's a good reason," she calls after me.

Gabe's waiting at the curb, car door open. He gives a low bow and sweeps his arm off to the side. "M'lady."

I smile as he straightens up. "I see we're going with cheesy and over the top tonight."

"Only the best for you." He folds his arms around me and grazes the tip of his nose over mine. He kisses me, slow and purposeful. That's another one for the win column. He kisses like he's savoring every single moment his lips are touching mine. Completely swoon-worthy.

Gabe tucks the carefully sculpted hair behind my ear. "Ready to go?"

I nod, and he steps aside, shutting the door after I climb in.

When we get to the restaurant, it's crowded, everyone piling in for a Saturday night date. Gabe keeps his hand on my back as we follow the hostess to our table, then pulls out my chair without a thought.

He kisses me on the top of my head on his way to his own chair. "So, you going to break my heart right now or wait until after you've ordered the most expensive dessert on the menu?"

I purse my lips and flip open the menu, scanning the dessert list. "I'm not a huge fan of tiramisu."

He's serious when I lower the menu. "Be with me, Hannah."

It's the kind of request that crawls into your chest and warms you from the inside out, and the reasons not to seem unimportant.

I start to answer but cut off at what sounds like an entire tray worth of dishes crashing across the restaurant. I twist around in my chair, expecting to find Cass once again sabotaging my life. All I see are two waiters scooping down to collect shards of plates. I check the rest of the dining area. *He has to be here.*

A hand on mine brings my attention back to Gabe, a patient smile on his face as he waits. My mind's still on Cass, but I nod at him.

His entire body relaxes, and he grins. "Yeah?"

I smile. "But I still don't want tiramisu. Ever."

He laughs, his grip on my hand tightening. "We'll deal with your poor palate another time."

During dinner, I check around the restaurant a few times. The feeling of being watched lingers, but it fades by the time Gabe orders every dessert on the list, *except* for tiramisu. We choose what we want, and he sends the rest to the surrounding tables.

When we go to leave, the front of the restaurant's still packed with people waiting to be seated. Gabe takes my hand, leading me the other way, farther into the restaurant.

"Where are we going?" I ask.

"I worked here a few summers ago. There's a side exit through the kitchen we can take rather than fighting the mob." He looks around while pushing open a swinging door.

I follow him through an area where several servers fill glasses and make salads. As we cut through the kitchen, he nods at someone behind a counter. They seem unbothered by our presence, giving a nod back and wiping their hands on their apron. We walk between high wire racks filled with dry goods before we reach a door. He pushes the metal bar across the middle, and we step out into an alley.

"See," he says, pulling me to his side. "It's the super-secret path."

I lean into him but straighten up as we near an abandoned car parked next to one of the brick walls on either side of us. "What's that smell?"

He shrugs. "Smells like an alley to me."

I stop, the scent now so heavy that I can't *not* recognize it. *Sulfur.* My mind flashes to another alley where it hung in the air, the rest of the memories not far behind.

Gabe's arm slips from around me, and he turns back. "Hannah?"

A sick feeling creeps over me when a man steps out of a shadow by the car. He's practically a shadow himself, his movements cagey, eyes darting around like he's waiting for something.

*Was he there a second ago?*

The jumpy gaze settles on me, and a chill shoots down my spine. I tug on Gabe's hand, trying to pull him back in the direction we came from, but he sees the man and steps between us.

"Do you need something?" His voice stays calm as the man starts toward us, eyes never leaving me.

I let go of Gabe, my feet pedaling me backward on pure instinct. "Cass."

Other than the terrified pounding inside my chest, everything stills for a moment. The man does another sweep of the area, but when nothing happens, an unsettling smile spreads across his face. In a flash, he's throwing Gabe across the alley. His body bounces off a brick wall and lands on the hood of the car, denting the metal.

Just as I look back at the man, he moves toward me too fast. Before I can scream, everything goes white. Heat envelops me, my feet not on solid ground anymore. It's over in a second. The world comes back, and I'm on a sidewalk in front of a pawnshop.

# FALLEN REBEL

*Cass.*

I regain my bearings, recognizing the street, and take off at a run back to the restaurant. He left me only a block away, so it doesn't take me long. I dash around the corner into the alley but freeze within a few steps. Sparks crackle from both of Cass's palms, his back to me, but it's the man in front of him that sends dread streaking through me. Blackness swirls around him as he holds what looks like a ball of fire in his hand.

Since he faces me, I earn the man's attention right away. Cass checks over his shoulder. His fiery eyes lock on me right before both he and the man disappear. I've barely processed them vanishing when something slams into me from behind. It knocks me to the ground, but by the time I look back, nothing's there. A crash down the alleyway sends my head back in the other direction. Cass stumbles out from near a dumpster, the man and his fire hand nowhere in sight. He stops a few feet away and stares down at me.

"Goddamn it, Hannah."

I scramble to my feet and run to him, not caring that he's still cursing me under his breath.

He catches my face in his hands, searching it over. "Are you hurt?"

I shake my head, tears blurring my vision.

Letting out a pent-up breath, he pulls me toward him. He holds me tight against his chest, and I hide my face in his shirt. When I throw my arms around his middle, he jerks back, sucking in air. There's a giant hole on the left side of his shirt, singed around the edges.

I gasp, seeing the ripped and burned flesh beneath. "Oh my God, Cass."

"It's fine," he says dismissively. "Immortal being, remember? Your sweater on the other hand, not so much."

He tugs at the hem of my shirt. I look down at my top, covered in his blood. He shrugs out of his leather jacket and drapes it over my shoulders. As I slide my arms in, he steps aside, and I see the car behind him.

*Gabe.*

"Oh no." I sprint down the alley, hating myself for not remembering him sooner.

He's still on the hood where he landed, not moving. Cass snags my arm, stopping me a few feet away. His hand runs down to mine, and he steps in front of me to press his fingers to Gabe's neck.

"He's alive." He checks around us, his grip tightening. "We need to get you out of here. I'll come back for him."

I shake my head and start to back away. "No. He needs an ambulance."

"Yeah, I'm not doing this with you."

He jerks me back toward him. Heat, blinding white light, and I'm not in the alley anymore. I let out a frustrated groan, glancing around the dark room. My eyes adjust enough so that I can find a lamp and switch it on. All it takes is the empty whiskey bottle on the coffee table for me to figure out where I am.

# SIXTEEN

## CASS

I lug Gabe's ass into the emergency room, claiming I found him. Dropping Hannah at my apartment made her angry enough that it sped my healing, so I only need to explain the hole in my shirt rather than the gaping wound the fireball left me.

By the time I put him down on a gurney, he's coming around. They clear him of any head injuries, but he needs surgery for a broken arm. While waiting for a surgeon, they set him up in a room. I hang around until the last nurse walks out, closing the door behind her, and text Hannah. I've been saving a specific piece of information for a time like this.

> *By the way, that was a demon that attacked you.*

It only takes a minute to feel her, and I drop in beside Preppy's bed. Not giving him time to panic, I take his face in my hands, the light relaxing him until his eyes glaze over.

"You were mugged at that stupid park with the lake you like so much. It was dark, so you didn't get a good look at the guy."

His eyebrows pull together. "What about my girlfriend, Hannah?"

*The fuck he just say?*

It takes a lot of effort to keep the edge out of my tone to keep him under. "Hannah's safe at the dorms. You'd already dropped her off."

A doofy smile appears as his brain fills in what happened *when* he dropped her off. I consider suggesting they ended the night with a firm handshake but feel the power fading fast.

"You won't remember anything from the alley or seeing me or talking to me. Understood?"

He nods, and before I lose the ability to drop back to my apartment, I let go of him. He's the only reason any of tonight even happened. If I wasn't trying to sort out false positives whenever Hannah went out with him, I wouldn't have missed her being in actual fucking danger. But I'm not letting him get in the way anymore. Hannah either. Chaz was right. It's time I take charge of my charge.

When I land in my living room, it's dark, except for a lamp and a glow from the hallway. I follow it to my bedroom. A wedge of light shines through the partially open bathroom door. The shower runs, steam creeping out. I guess Hannah's made herself at home.

The burned-to-shit shirt lands on the floor, and I stretch out on the bed. My eyes fall shut, and I relax in what feels like the first time in weeks.

At least with her here, I don't have to worry about any attacks. After Lydia had let herself in angel-style, I dug through the spells we'd collected over the years. This place has been on lockdown since. Nothing from Heaven or Hell can make it in. Other than me.

The water cuts off, and the shower curtain drags back. I force my eyes open and turn my head toward the door. Hannah faces away from me, towel secured around her while she dries her hair with another. She doesn't notice me sprawled out on the bed when she comes out and starts digging through my drawers.

"Looking for something?"

She jumps, and I stretch out my fingers. I'll never get enough of that. Divine light, that is. Hannah, on the other hand, has her limits.

"Jesus," she says.

"Kasdaye actually."

She pulls out another drawer. "I need something to wear without angel blood all over it."

I haul myself off the mattress to find her a T-shirt and a pair of gym shorts.

She takes them from me, her head cocking to the side as I lie back down. "You need to be in here?"

"My bedroom, Hannah."

She huffs and walks back into the bathroom, leaving the door mostly open. "Is Gabe okay?"

I pull out my phone to text Chaz and Rosdan about the attack. Samy too, because, pissed at him or not, he needs to stay in the loop.

"Preppy's going to be just fine. I told him he dropped you off and was mugged at the park."

Her shadow casts over me and the bed, and I look over as she walks out. Fuck if she doesn't look hot, wearing my clothes. If I were the type to repeat mistakes, I would be only one burst of light away from pinning her against a wall again.

She stops next to the bed and puts her hands on her hips.

"What now?" I ask, staring at her hovering over me.

She marches out without a word. It's annoying when she does it. I pull a pillow over my face and groan into it. Being around her is just as stressful as not being around her.

I get out there, and she's already standing in the middle of the living room, arms crossed. Having a feeling I'll deserve one in a few minutes, I detour to the kitchen for a beer.

"Demons?" she asks when I reappear.

I twist the top off and take a long drink, appreciating the slow build inside me. "Angels and demons. They go hand in hand."

"Is that who attacked me last time too?"

I nod. "But if it makes you feel any better, you're not the only one they're trying to kill."

"Kill?" she shrieks.

Maybe I should have left that part out.

She hides her face in her hands, taking a few deep breaths to calm down. All of a sudden, she lifts her head. "Wait, why aren't you hurt anymore?"

I smirk. "You really don't understand how all this works, do you?"

She steps in front of me, looking at my abs where the fireball ricocheted off me. "Your powers can heal you."

Her hand reaches out to touch me, but I catch it. "I don't think your boyfriend would appreciate you putting your hands all over me."

She looks up, not pulling away from me. "How do you know about that?"

"He told me while I was wiping his memories." I let go of her hand and go to the couch.

Her eyes wander the room for a minute, and she disappears into the kitchen. Cupboard doors bang around for a while, and then she comes back with two glasses and a bottle of whiskey. She buys my attention by pouring a glass and trading it for my empty beer bottle.

"Why are the demons attacking me?"

"We think they want to turn all the Watchers human, so they can use Nephilim blood whenever they want. They wait until you're unprotected and try to kill you before we get to you."

She nods, filling her own glass. "So, they'll keep coming after me. Possibly for the rest of my life."

I relax back and shake my head. "Unlikely. Demons have a short attention span."

"How long then?"

"Two, three decades?"

I'm warm, but she keeps a poker face.

"And the only way I'm completely safe is if I'm with you."

It's not a question, but I answer it anyway. "Or if you're here. Which means—"

"We need to be together as much as possible, or I die and you never reenter Heaven."

We're on the same page about something for once. *Amazing.*

I drain my whiskey in one swallow and immediately start pouring another. "At least until I figure something else out. We thought they were only targeting Nephilim when you were alone, but after tonight, I'm not so sure. We might be able to throw together a spell to help hide you, but it will take time."

And chanting. It's all about the chanting.

Hannah brings the rim of the glass to her lips. "I need you to do me a favor." She finishes her drink and grimaces as she sits down on the couch beside me, pulling her legs between us. "The only reason Gabe got hurt tonight is because of me. I don't want him to be in that kind of danger again, so I need you to make him forget we're dating."

My eyebrows shoot up, as I was not expecting the "favor" to be breaking Preppy's heart for her. Her eyes drop to the empty glass in her hand, so I bury the urge to act like a complete asshole about it.

"Are you sure?"

She nods, looking back at me. "I only said yes at dinner. Plus, who wants to be with a girl who spends all her time with another guy?"

If I'm not mistaken, a brief moment of relief flashes over her face before she sighs. "Any chance you'll let me sleep at the dorms tonight?"

"Take the bed," I say, standing up. "I need to move Preppy's car to the park before anyone finds it at the restaurant."

"Wait. I'll come with you."

Before I can tell her no, she runs to the bedroom. While I listen to her rifling through my shit again, I drain my drink and pull on a hoodie. I'm about to the door when she finally reemerges in my leather jacket, a pair of sweatpants with the legs rolled up, and her shoes.

"Let's go." Her hand swipes over the back of her neck, pulling the hair out of the collar of my jacket.

It's not worth the effort of arguing, so I head back toward her. If she's coming, we're at least taking advantage of the Hannah Expressway and saving ourselves time.

"What are you doing?" she asks.

I scoop her up, throwing her over my shoulder.
"Cass!"
And we drop.

Sometime in the middle of the night, I jolt awake on the couch. Power pounds through me. I reach for the ball on my chest, the need to see Hannah deafening. Then I remember it's not there because she's in my bedroom. In a blink, so am I. She's sitting in bed, sobbing into her hands.

*Nightmare.*

I give myself a second to recover before walking farther into the room. The floor creaks as I reach the bed, startling her until she realizes it's me. She throws off the blankets and pushes onto her knees. As soon as I'm close enough, her arms lock around my neck.

"You're okay," I say. "It was just a dream."

The hold on me tightens, her face burying in my neck, and I secure my arm around her. Of all the times I've witnessed her wake up from a dream, it's the first time I've ever really been there.

Once the light begins to fade and her breathing evens out, I lean down so her knees touch the mattress. She lets go and sits back on her heels, wiping away the tears. I wait until she's back under the blanket before leaving.

"Cass."

I pause in the doorway.

"I know nothing can get in, but will you stay anyway?"

My hand rakes through my hair as I change direction. She shifts over, and I settle in next to her, stretching out on my back. Just when I think I can fall asleep, cold feet hit my leg. Hannah squirms around, readjusting, then she pulls all the blankets off me and flips from one side to the other every few minutes. After her third sigh, I reach over and drag her over to me.

"Cass! What are you doing?"

I've never even let someone else sleep in my bed, and now I'm about to fucking cuddle with someone in it.

My arm slides under her, and I pin her against my side, so she can't move anymore. At first, she acts like she's going to protest, but soon she relaxes against me.

"You're so warm."

Her arm drapes over my stomach, and she snuggles into me. She smells like my body wash and shampoo, but underneath it is Hannah and the faintest hint of flowers. After her breathing slows, I let my eyes fall shut. And then I sleep the same way I always do—with her on my chest.

# SEVENTEEN

## *HANNAH*

I wake up, too warm with Cass's arm around me and his chest pressed against my back. I try to move away, but his hold on me tightens.

"Stop moving," he demands, pulling me closer.

His leg hooks over mine, further emphasizing the point, and he actually nuzzles against the back of my neck. Big, bad, broody Cass spooning me would be funny if he wasn't like an electric blanket. This time, when I pry his arm away from me, he lets go and rolls onto his back. I scoot over to the edge of the bed and find my phone on the nightstand.

Three missed calls from Gabe and twice as many texts. *Shit.* I read through them, all matching what Cass told him had happened—he was mugged after he dropped me off. The last one lets me know they're releasing him this afternoon, and he wants to see me. I set my phone back down, not answering. It's better to wait until after Cass erases the memory of me saying yes to dating him. Saddest part is, at only one day, he will still be my third-longest relationship.

I roll over as Cass turns to face me again, hugging his pillow. It's the most peaceful I've ever seen him, his features and body relaxed, breathing slow and even. My eyes drift down to the smooth skin on his side. Hours ago, it was torn open and burned from when he saved me. Now it's healed because of powers I somehow control.

I run my fingers over the spot, finally beginning to understand the true connection between Nephilim and Watcher.

We need each other.

Cass's gaze waits for me when I look up, and my hand falls to the mattress between us. The softness stays in his face a little longer before the edge creeps back in.

"You're a pain in the ass to sleep with," he says, getting out of bed. "Don't ever expect me to do it again."

He slams the bathroom door behind him. Big, bad, broody Cass is back, and as strange as it sounds, I think I missed him.

When he reemerges, his hair's dripping wet from his shower, and a towel haphazardly hangs low on his hips with his prominent V on display. I pretend not to notice how incredibly hot he looks, but he knows the second my heart rate increases. A dimple appears as he swipes a shirt out of a laundry basket.

*Asshole.*

He heads back into the bathroom and steps around the door, leaving it open. "What do you want me to tell Preppy when I go see him? That his gee-Mary-Sue-you're-the-keenest bullshit makes you want to hurl yourself off a cliff?"

I get out of bed and search through the same basket for something I can wear until he takes me back to the dorms. "What's your problem with him anyway?"

His head pops out. "You want the list?"

I shake my head, and he disappears again.

"I guess tell him, instead of saying yes, I said I need to concentrate on school."

He steps out, fully dressed and dragging a hoodie over his head. I pass him on my way in to change. I start to shut the door, but his hand catches it.

"You want to come with me?"


If I thought breaking up with someone would be awkward, watching someone else do it for you is way worse. Cass sticks to the script, albeit with a shit-eating grin on his face the entire time.

Once he finishes, we leave Gabe still in a daze. Cass grabs my hand, tugging me toward him. He wraps his arm around me and leans down until his lips are at my ear.

"Demon," he whispers.

A rush of anxiety shocks through my chest at the word, and everything goes white. He keeps ahold of me as I blink a few times and realize we're back in his living room.

"Sorry," he says, staring down at me. "We needed to get out of there before Preppy came out of it."

I nod and fake a smile, taking a step backward. "It's fine."

He reaches into his hoodie pocket for a cigarette and his lighter. "We'll take the bike to the dorms to grab your stuff."

I'm right behind him when he heads toward the bedroom. "And why do we need to grab my stuff?"

Cigarette lit and balanced between his lips, he grabs his leather jacket off the dresser. "Would you prefer I stay with you and Terra at the dorms?"

"Cass, I'm not moving in with you."

"You're right. You're not. But until I know they aren't coming after you every time I'm not around you, we're not taking any chances."

I want to argue, but if the demons do keep attacking, I can't risk putting Terra or anyone else in the same kind of danger I did Gabe. Not anyone who doesn't heal the second I hyperventilate anyway.

"It's only for a few days." He tosses the jacket at me and walks out.

At least he says things before leaving now.

I catch up and follow him to the stairwell at the end of the hall. At the first landing, his hand touches my lower back, guiding me around the corner to the next set of stairs. I might not have a direct line to his adrenaline responses, but if I have to guess, the stairs make Cass nervous.

Once I crawl onto the motorcycle behind him, he seems to relax. I slide my hands into the front pocket of his hoodie without invitation this time. He doesn't seem to mind, speeding out of the parking lot.

We only stay at the dorms long enough for me to pack a bag, then it's back to the apartment where we spend the rest of the day no more than a room apart from each other. For dinner, we finally eat that pizza we were supposed to have the day he told me who he was.

We sit at the kitchen counter in our usual silence until I ask, "Do you have wings?"

He picks up his pizza like he doesn't plan on answering.

Fair, since I've bothered him with random angel questions all day. Most he shrugged off or spit out a sarcastic response to.

But he pauses with the slice halfway to his mouth. "Yes."

"Can I see them?"

He considers it, his eyes dragging down my body. "Can I see your tits?"

I squint at him, and he smirks.

"Then no, you can't see them."

After we finish, we lounge around in the living room—him reading, me getting a jump-start on studying for midterms. God, I really must be boring to follow around. School, studying, and that's about it. The last two summers, I worked at a pet rescue, but I doubt that was very entertaining to watch. All I did was give dogs baths. Maybe instead of summer classes or working, I should do something this year.

"If you could go anywhere, where would you go?" I ask.

He answers right away, never losing focus on the page. "Home."

"I meant, in the world."

Still reading. "Are we going together?"

"Yes."

"There's a dam in Switzerland where you can bungee jump from over seven hundred feet." He looks at me then and says, "I want to throw you off it."

Fighting off a smile, he returns to his book. I sigh, putting away my textbook, and shove his legs out of the way to go take a shower, never bothering to ask if he's kidding. He probably wouldn't answer anyway, and on the off chance he did, I would more than likely wish he hadn't.

Since he hasn't told me not to, I use Cass's bathroom because it's bigger. I brought my own shampoo and soap from the dorms, but as I pull on my tank top and a pair of shorts, I swear I still smell like him.

By the time I come out, it's after midnight. He's stretched out on the couch, asleep with the book resting on his chest. I throw a blanket over him and shut off the lights before I retreat back to the bedroom and go to sleep.

Just like last night, the blackness that encircled the demon appears. It grows and creeps until it surrounds me. I open my mouth to scream, but it fills my lungs, suffocating me. I'm gasping when I wake up, clutching my heaving chest. Cass is already on his way over to the bed.

He rubs the back of his neck and puts his knee on the mattress. "Move over."

I do, but after he lies down, he slides me against his side. My head rests on his chest, and he folds his arms around me, the heat of his skin lulling me to sleep.

Even if he did throw me off that dam in Switzerland, he'd catch me before I hit the bottom. We both know it.

Every day, Cass walks me to my classes and waits there for me to come out. We eat breakfast together and lunch and dinner. In the evenings, he reads, and I study until one of us annoys the other so much that we can't stand to be near each other anymore. Our new arrangement is quite the adjustment for two people who have no one to answer to but themselves. Doors slam, I refuse to talk to him, he walks out. But even after all that, every night ends the same way—with him being the only thing that keeps the nightmares away.

On Thursday afternoon, he meets me outside my ethics lecture with a coffee. I graciously accept, not even testing the temperature before taking a sip. Even though spring break is only a week away, no one told the weather we'd moved on past January. My free hand pulls into the sleeves of the leather jacket as we walk to his motorcycle, which Cass insists it's warm enough out to ride. He climbs on while I drain the rest of my drink and already has the engine running when I get back from throwing it away. Cass, as patient as always.

We pull out of the parking lot, going the wrong way for his apartment. It takes me until we're only a block away to realize where he's heading. He parks at the curb in front of the dorms, and I squeeze him tighter before climbing off.

"Trial basis," he says, swinging his leg over the seat. "And I'm inside with you whenever Terra isn't."

He takes the helmet from me, and I smile, backing up the sidewalk. "Thank you, Cass."

I get a sighed, "Whatever." The Cass equivalent to *you're welcome.*

Walking from the top of the open stairway to my room, I'm the most stressed I've been over the past few days. The empty hallway threatens a similar setup as the alley, walls blocking me in. I fight the urge to run the last few steps, like I used to after shutting off the lights in the basement, and make it without anything appearing out of thin air.

I walk in to see my bags are already on the bed and a shirtless guy is in Terra's. At least nothing's changed there. I don't pay attention to him on my way to the window. Cass is still waiting where I left him, where he'll stay until he comes inside.

Terra walks in a minute later. Her guy has already found his shirt and left, but she doesn't seem to care. She squeals and jumps at me, wrapping her arms around me like I've been gone for a year, not a few days. I hug her back, having missed her just as much. We spend the next hour catching up. Not that either of us have done much of anything since I texted her about staying off-campus to help a friend. Technically true. I was helping my friends not die.

When her work reminder goes off, she pouts out her lower lip. "I wish I didn't have to leave. Promise you'll be here when I get back and won't have gone to find a new best friend you want to live with forever?"

I laugh and nod. "I'll be here, waiting for you."

She gives me one more hug and grabs her coat on the way out. Less than a minute later, Cass lets himself in. Really, I'm surprised it took that long. He shuts the door behind him, phone to his ear. I fold my legs up on the bed and watch him pace.

"Yeah … Nope … Fuck off … Fine." He shoves his phone in his pocket. "None of the others have had a demon attack since yours."

"Where are the others?" I ask.

Outside of when he originally told me about the Watchers, he's never mentioned them.

He drops down on the floor and leans back against my bed in front of me. "Chaz is close to where you were in Colorado, Rosdan is in Seattle, and Samy's supposed to be somewhere in West Virginia, but who the fuck knows anymore."

"All of the Nephilim live in the United States?"

I can only see the side of his face, but a dimple appears. "A few hundred years ago, we all 'suggested' our charges come to America. It took a few decades to get them all here, but it made everything much easier. For a few years, Ros and I were in the same colony."

An image of Cass in colonial era clothing enters my mind, but I dismiss it, not ready to dive into the weirdness.

"Which one were you just talking to?"

"Chaz." He looks back over his shoulder at me. "He was asking me to sneak a picture of your ass and send it to him."

His side of the conversation replays in my head. I stop myself from asking which was his answer.

He spreads out on the floor when I pull out my review notes. An hour ticks by without so much as a sound from him. I assume he's asleep until he starts tossing the crystal ball in the air. It pops up and disappears a dozen times at least, my focus lost each and every time. I lean over far enough so that the next time he throws it, I can intercept.

"It's a crystal ball, Hannah. You think I can't see you in it?"

He sits up fast, surprising me, and my pounding heart follows close behind. The few inches of space between us warms. Cass shuts his eyes, a torn expression on his face. And that's when Terra walks in, her mouth falling open at the sight of us. Cass's eyes open as I sit back on the bed, away from him.

"What are you doing back already?"

"I, uh…" She watches Cass pushing off the floor, and with his back to her, she mouths, *Oh. My. God.* When he turns around, she smiles and cocks her head to the side. "I found someone to cover the rest of my shift, so we can go to dinner since you've been so busy lately. Hi, I'm Terra." She seamlessly transitions into introducing herself, holding out her hand to Cass, who doesn't bother even faking a pleasant expression.

"This is Cass," I say, scrambling to my feet. "He's my…"

*Watcher?*

*Guardian Angel?*

"Friend from high school." He looks over, eyes narrowed at me. "Just moved to town."

"Right." Terra looks back and forth between us. "Well, would you like to come to dinner with us? Or if I'm interrupting something, I could—"

"No. He was just leaving, right?"

His jaw tenses as he moves toward the door. "Nice to meet you…"

"Terra," she says. "If you don't have any plans tomorrow night, the bar on McKinley hosts a great St. Patrick's Day party. You should come. Hannah's my date, but I'd be willing to share."

"I'll think about it."

"See you soon," she calls after him as he walks out, then her head whips around, crazy eyes on me. "Spill."

Once again, I choose my words very carefully. "It's nothing to be excited about. He's known me for a long time and helped me through some stuff."

"Is he why you aren't with Gabe?"

I shake my head, not wanting to say anything more that may lead to an actual lie.

Her lips purse as she studies me, but then she shrugs. "Well, I hope he comes tomorrow night. He's fun to look at." She holds her arm out for me. "Shall we go eat fried food we'll instantly regret?"

And that's exactly what we do. Eat and regret. We stay at the restaurant, drinking milkshakes like we're in a fifties' soda shop after school, giggling about nothing. It's one of the most normal moments I've had in a while, and I need it.

When we finally make it back to the dorms, I shower and get ready for bed. Terra's already asleep. I check out the window. Cass is leaning against his bike, and a part of me I didn't even realize was tense relaxes. I crawl into my bed for the first time in almost a week, snuggling down under the covers.

It's harsher this time, the blackness somehow even more void of light. The spirals branch out, each one stretching sharp points toward me. They slice at my skin until blood runs down my arms, dripping from my fingertips. One wraps around my neck, squeezing until I can't breathe.

A warm hand slips around me, drawing me out of the dream. I wake in a panic, and Cass is there. He's lying on his side between me and the wall, pulling my body closer to his. I press my forehead against his chest and bite back a sob. I focus on each of his long, slow breaths until mine match. As my heartbeat calms, he readjusts, resting his chin on top of my head and his arm over my hip. It doesn't take long for me to relax against him. Safe from everything.

# EIGHTEEN

## CASS

The ball shows Hannah on her bed, out of the line of fire, while Terra strews clothes around their room. Her roommate's in a lime-green bra, her tits bouncing around with each item she flings.

She hit on me once at a party last year, cornering me in her miniskirt and low-cut top. As tempting as her offer was, I managed to keep it in my pants. It took me a week to time Hannah's adrenaline right, so I could make Terra forget my face.

An hour later, they finally deem themselves worthy of a bar full of horny college guys, drunk in the name of a holiday that's deeply rooted in the spreading of Christianity across Ireland. The guy's name wasn't even Patrick, for Christ's sake. He went through some heavy shit, though, and after hearing his story, I wanted to get black-out drunk to forget, so the holiday makes sense in that regard.

I have no plans on going inside when they get to the bar. It's crowded and loud, and Hannah and I have practically been on top of each other for five days straight. If I don't get some space from her, I'll wind up doing the demons' job for them. Whatever happens inside, I can monitor perfectly fine through the ball. But by the time Hannah's two shots in, I'm overanalyzing every shift in the shadows, convinced a portal's opening, and waiting for the light.

*Shit.*

I have no plans on joining them when I get inside the bar. I walk around the edge, avoiding the booth where they sit and head toward the bar for a drink. All the barstools are taken but one down at the far end, and I immediately know why it stays empty. I slide into it and slap the man next to me on the shoulder. His dirty gray hair, rip in the sleeve of his green coat, and his cheek flat against the bar top are more than enough for me to recognize my good ol' buddy Carl.

Eventually, the bartender makes his way down. I order us a round and wait for him to walk away before I finish clearing up a few misconceptions about the holiday we're celebrating.

"There were never any snakes in Ireland for Saint non-Patrick to banish. It was a metaphor for the Druids, whose magic is one of the most useful tools humanity ever received, by the way. My brother Samy had a hand in teaching man that one."

My phone vibrates, and I look down at Hannah's text.

*Where are you?*

I pull the ball out under the bar to check on her. She's looking around, all alone at the booth. It doesn't take me long to find Terra by the pool tables with a guy pushed against her backside as he teaches her how to shoot. Not wanting a repeat of the Halloween party where Hannah sneaks out on her own, I stand up off my stool.

"Hate to do this again, Carl." I drain the last of my drink and take his untouched one with me to the other side of the bar.

A guy's standing next to the booth, delivering a lame pick-up line when I get over there. Something about her not needing to wear any green because of the intensity of the color in her incredible eyes. Except she is wearing green, a shamrock in the middle of her tight white tank top that peeks out from under a green plaid shirt. I slide in across from her and wave him off. He stops mid-sentence, looking at her for confirmation on whether or not he should leave her alone with me. She gives him a small smile and then glares at me as he wanders away.

"Thanks," she says, the sarcasm unmissable. "A text with your location would have sufficed though."

"Why aren't you over there, learning how to handle a stick?"

She shrugs, peeling off the label on her beer bottle. "I already know how to shoot pool."

I rest my arm on the seat back and crane my neck around to see the pool tables. Terra laughs while the guy next to her watches her hand slowly gliding up and down the stick.

"I really don't think that's the point."

A brunette walks by in shorts that are in no way long enough to be called shorts, a green crop top with rainbow suspenders, and a top hat. She smiles, her eyes traveling over me while mine do the same to her.

"You can go if you want."

I look at Hannah. "What?"

"I won't leave without telling you." She shifts and looks away. "I think you're right though. I should go play pool." As she gets out of the booth, her hand drops down to the seat, grabbing my leather jacket. She pulls it on and pushes through the sea of green.

I watch Terra pull her in for a hug and introduce her to the three guys at the table with her. She flashes a smile at them, lingering on the closest, who angles his body toward her, immediately engaging.

Carl's unsurprisingly where I left him. I set his now-empty drink back in front of him and have barely sat down when rainbow suspenders enter my peripheral. The brunette pretends not to see me, slipping between my stool and the one on the other side that's also occupied. Not the one with Carl in it, although he would have appreciated her brushing up on him.

She looks over, waiting for the bartender. "Where's your green?"

I lick my lips and bust out the dimples. "What happens if I'm not wearing any? I always seem to forget."

"Hmm." She touches a finger to her chin. "I think I either pinch you or give you something of mine that's green."

"I like the second option. But the real question is, do I get to decide what you give me?"

It's her panties. I'm going to ask for her panties, and she's going to take me to the men's room and give them to me. Her hand brushes over my thigh, teeth dent her bottom lip, and fuck if it's not the worst time for my chest to warm.

I let out an exasperated sigh and check over my shoulder. Hannah's still talking to the guy. He leans even closer, no doubt making up some bullshit about how he's having trouble hearing her because of the noise. As he talks in her ear, he touches the sleeve of the leather jacket. My leather jacket that smells like me.

"It depends on what you want." The brunette's answer to the question I forgot I'd asked brings my attention back to her. "I have on five things that are green."

"Top hat, suspenders, and shirt are obvious."

She runs her hand through my hair, not shy at all. Then the heat creeps down my arm. The muscles in my jaw tense, and I look at Hannah again. Dude tucks a piece of her hair behind her ear and puts his hand back down on the pool table so that he overlaps her fingers.

"The other two are hidden."

Like a tennis match, I'm back to the brunette. Her top exposes enough of her shoulder so that I can see her green strap running parallel to the suspenders.

"Your bra."

My thumb slips beneath the strap and slowly slides down until I reach the neck of her shirt. She's straddling my leg now, a hard thigh on each side, so of course, the light shoots the rest of the way down into my hand. I stretch my fingers as the power boils below the surface. It almost feels off, like there's an edge to it, and I have to fight against the urge to find out what's going on behind me.

"One more," the brunette says.

In a hurry to finish the game, I hook my finger in the belt loop of her shorts. I tug her toward me, and a rough surge of energy hits, forcing my head back around. My eyes lock with Hannah's, her attention fully on me and not the jabroni laughing and resting his hand on her hip. A palm touches the side of my face, bringing on another harsh wave, and then Hannah looks away. She laughs along with whatever the comedian said. Even from across the bar, I know it's fake.

The brunette pulls on my face until I'm looking at her. "Do you need a hint?"

*God fucking help me.*

My hand presses gently against her stomach, prompting her to take a step back. "You know what? I just remembered." I lift enough of my hoodie to show her my green T-shirt. "I guess I don't need anything from you after all." I scrape the stool back and walk away.

Terra spots me and practically leaps in front of me. "Show me your green."

I prove myself, earning a smile.

"Very well. You may talk to her." She bounds back over by the jukebox where a girl dressed in the same white tank top with a lime-green bra showing through waits for her.

I step behind Hannah. "Can we leave soon?"

"Hey." The guy sticks the hand that, until a second ago, was touching her in my direction. "I'm—"

"Cool," I say, my tone perfectly conveying my mood. "Now let me talk to Hannah."

He doesn't obediently run away like the one from earlier. But when she focuses on me, he backs off toward the rest of his group over by Terra, his eyes on us the entire time.

"Shouldn't you be finding the pot of gold at the end of that girl's suspenders?" She delivers the line with such disdain that I almost smile.

Judgmental Hannah isn't someone I've met. I may be rubbing off on her.

"Someone keeps interrupting me." I skim my fingertips over the back of her hand, giving off enough light to spark against her skin. "It makes it a little hard to focus."

Her cheeks are flushed from the alcohol, but they brighten even more. "I guess we're even then since you ran off a guy earlier."

I tip my head toward the jukebox. "Two guys."

She glances back at the guy who, a minute ago, only had eyes for her, just as he shoves his tongue down another girl's throat.

How does she keep attracting these assholes? But Hannah's expression stays indifferent.

"Probably for the best since we both know I'm going home with you at the end of the night anyway." Her gaze returns to me. "Let me tell Terra we're leaving?"

If only it were that easy.

Terra insists we stay until her song plays on the jukebox and we've taken green Jell-O shots with her, and then she drags Hannah into the restroom. It reminds me of the parties she used to go to before her parents died, minus the underage drinking. Except, back then, it was Hannah smiling like a lunatic and pulling people around the room by the arm.

They eventually reappear, and I think we might finally be able to go when Preppy pops up out of fucking nowhere. He's sporting a sling on his arm, which immediately earns him pity from half a dozen drunk girls who ascend on him like he's an injured puppy. Although the only one he seems interested in is the one standing next to me.

"Jesus," I mumble as he walks toward us.

"I hoped you'd still be here." His grin fades, his attention drifting over to me, and he stops. "I remember you."

His comment causes Hannah to panic. The power hits me so hard that I grab on to the pool table to keep it under control.

"Yeah," I say through clenched teeth. "From the park. Flat tire, right?"

"Right."

She calms down, realizing he remembers me from their first date, not their last.

He looks at the space between Hannah and me, fucking analyzing it before he smiles at her. This guy irritates me to no end.

"The doctor cleared me to go to Florida for spring break. Do you still want me to bring along those headphones for you?"

"Florida?" I ask.

She looks at me, but I stay locked in on Gabe, who keeps his eyes on her.

"Terra's friend Jesse and I are crashing their trip," he says. "It'll be the four of us for an entire week of sun and beach."

I check out of the conversation then, all my effort pouring into not carrying Hannah's ass out of the bar. She's explaining to Preppy that we need to leave when I stalk away. She follows, neither of us saying a word on our way through the crowd.

Out the door, I keep going across the parking lot, my temper barely in check. Hannah's feet crunch gravel behind me until I reach my bike. The sound stops, and so do I, whipping back around.

"I was going to tell you," she says from several feet away. "We go somewhere every year, and I know, with the demons, it might be a little more difficult, but—"

"Fucking Florida?" My palms glow when she flinches at my tone. "For starters, why? Also, no fucking way. I'm already risking everything by leaving you unattended in class and at the dorms with Terra. Now I'm supposed to watch from a distance for an entire week?"

"No."

"Then how do you think it's going to work?"

She fidgets with her zipper, not wanting to look at me. "We have enough room for one more person. And you've already met Terra, so I thought you'd just come with us."

I laugh once at the idea. "I'm not going on vacation with you and Preppy." I hand her the helmet, watching the parking lot. "Let's go. I don't like being out here in the open."

She starts to reach for the helmet, but her hand drops away. "No."

"What do you mean, no? Get on the bike."

Her arms cross over her chest, her chin lifting to challenge me. With my mood worsening by the second, I take a step toward her, ready to drop us back to the dorms, but the light fades at a rapid rate until it's barely a twinge. I watch her chest rise, each breath slower than the last.

"Fine." I lean back against the seat of my bike. "Go back inside and wait for Terra then. Just don't expect me to come running anymore when you have nightmares."

I get a little more of a ripple, and she turns around and stomps across the parking lot.

"We're still not going to Florida," I call after her.

She turns around and flips me off.

I chuckle, not bothered by her tantrum in the least. We both know when she wakes up terrified, she'll want me there. We both also know there's no fucking way in hell we're going to Florida.

Hannah doesn't have any more nightmares.

And the Saturday after midterms, I meet her in the parking lot with my suitcase.

Damn it.

# NINETEEN

## CASS

The car ride.

*Holy shit*, the car ride.

Terra's friend Jesse, a six-foot-six monster of a guy with a mess of blond hair and a constant smile, drives us down in his Jeep. She sits up front with him. I'm half-convinced it's because she wants to see how everything plays out with Preppy, Hannah, and me squeezed together in the backseat. In that order.

Within the first thirty minutes, Preppy tries to put his arm around Hannah, and his hand brushes my shoulder. She shifts closer to me, trying to avoid him.

Unable to help myself, I lean over and whisper in her ear, "How's that 'I need to concentrate on school' excuse working out for you?"

She sets her jaw and looks away from me. We're still not on the best of terms since our fight last week at the bar, tolerating each other but not much more. What's that saying? *One step forward, two steps back*? With Hannah and me, it's more like one step sideways, run backward for a quarter of a mile.

Not wanting to chance any of the mortals falling asleep behind the wheel, I take over driving in the middle of the night. Terra promises to stay awake and keep me company. Thank God that only lasts about twenty minutes.

I watch Hannah through the mirror. She doesn't sleep much, mostly staring out the window and listening to the noise I still refuse to call music in a pair of headphones she bought. Every now and then, our gazes cross in the mirror. It only lasts a few seconds before one of us looks away. I'm starting to wonder if it will ever get easier with her or if we'll be battling over every little thing for the rest of her life.

By morning, Jesse's rested enough to finish out the trip. I settle back in beside Hannah and end up sleeping more than I have in the past week. Only, when I wake up, Gabe's fucking hand is touching me again.

After twenty miserable hours in a cramped space with people I either don't know, can't stand, or keep receiving icy stares from, we arrive at our hotel in Daytona Beach.

*One day down, five to go.*

From our first step out of the vehicle, it's a constant parade of skimpy swimwear and easily acquired alcohol. Neither of those I ever thought I would complain about—except, after a while of bouncing between beach parties, keeping track of Hannah becomes exhausting. She's in a sexy red bikini top and jean shorts that show off those legs, so my eyes have no problem staying on her, but she easily disappears unless I'm right next to her. At first, she throws daggers at me if I get too close. But as the crowd gets liquored up and rowdy, she checks over her shoulder more often, making sure I'm there.

We're following Terra past a DJ's stage when the feeling comes on fast.

I touch Hannah's arm, and she turns. "You okay?"

Her eyebrows pull together, and she nods.

*Fuck.* My eyes frantically scan over the hundreds of heads gathered in the area, looking for any sign of a portal, then they shift to the stage.

The platform beside us stands four feet off the sand, the turntable on one half. Three couples are dry-humping to music on the other. One oily guy pulls his sunglasses down, checking out the rack of another oily guy's girl. The girl quickly brings it to the attention of oily guy number two.

I reach for Hannah's arm just as one oily guy charges for the other and tug her back toward me, her chest hitting mine. A second later, the men crash off the stage onto the ground where she would have been standing. They're both throwing furious punches, other people jumping at the chance to join in. As I tuck her against my side and move us farther away from the brawl, Jesse does the same with Terra on the other side.

Once we clear the crowd, the sensation subsides, and I let her go. She stays close, though, her arm still touching mine while she searches around for Terra.

"She's with Jesse," I say. "You ready to go back to the hotel?"

She nods, studying me. "How did you know?"

"Built-in danger detector, Hannah."

"I meant, how did you know they would fall off the stage?"

Not having a clue how to explain it, I shrug. "I see how one action will lead to the next and domino from there."

One side of her mouth turns up in the closest thing to a smile she's given me since before the bar. "If I didn't know better, I'd make a joke about you using a crystal ball to predict the future."

I shake my head as I walk away. At least she's talking to me again.

After the beach beatdown, Hannah's interest in the party scene vanishes. She spends the next few days exploring museums, art galleries, historical places, and everywhere else that sparks an interest in her.

The glacier between us gradually begins to melt, and the outings might even classify as enjoyable, if not for the hundred-and-eighty-pound Beaver Cleaver that accompanies us on every one.

On the third day, Gabe hijacks her plans to visit the ruins of something, asking her to go to the mall. Because why learn about history when you can find designer sunglasses at fifty percent off?

"You look too gorgeous in them for me to decide," says Gabe. "Buy both."

"I don't need two pairs of sunglasses." She switches back to the darker frames for the fourth time and turns to me. "What do you think?"

I'm playing with a display, and I don't even glance at her. "I think you don't need either because they're ridiculously overpriced, and you'll lose them before we go home."

Just as I look, she takes them off. "You're right."

Much to Gabe's dismay, both pairs go back on the counter. "But they're on sale."

"So are these." I pick a cheap pair of black ones with gold-winged tips and put them on her. "Marked down to five ninety-nine from twelve."

Her nose wrinkles, and she laughs. "They'll look great with the helmet and leather jacket."

I smile as she pulls them off. She's wrong. They'll look hideous. But I make sure she buys them anyway.

Our next stop is a clothing store that smells like every high school boy on his first date. Gabe pushes for Hannah to try on outfits, and she finally agrees, taking a few to the changing room. After she disappears, he takes an armful of shirts into the dressing room on the other side of the store.

Other than a cashier distracted by her phone behind the counter, no one else is around. And I have one of the better ideas of my entire existence.

I check under the two doors, finding feet under the second one. "Hannah."

As soon as the handle turns, I push my way into the dressing room with her. She's fully dressed, the clothes just hanging on the hook, untouched.

"What—"

My hand cups over her mouth as I shoulder the door shut. "We're getting out of here before he comes out of the dressing room."

She pulls my hand away, and I expect her to object, but she grabs her bags off the bench in the corner. I don't move out of the way when she reaches past me for the handle.

"We're not walking out of here."

I lunge at her, catching her as she jumps backward. Everything but Hannah drops away until we're at the ruins she originally wanted to visit. Now our vacation can continue without unwanted interruptions.

Late in the afternoon, we walk through the lobby of the hotel and run into a waiting Gabe.

"What the hell, Hannah?" he says, storming toward us.

"I wasn't feeling good," I say. "And her phone died, so she couldn't text you."

She holds out her phone, showing him the black screen. Part of me wishes her thumb would bump the button, lighting it up, but she puts it down too fast. Even if he wanted to try to poke holes in our story, Terra steps out of the elevator with Jesse and squeals on her way toward us.

"Guess what!" She grabs Hannah's hand, swinging it back and forth. "We're doing a bonfire tonight on the beach."

Hannah glances up, expecting me to tell her no, which is exactly what I want to do. Dark, isolated, and an entire ocean's worth of room for a demon to lurk in—it sounds like a disaster waiting to happen. And yet, I discreetly nod at her. Maybe it's the humidity messing with my head or the fact that we're getting along for more than thirty-minute intervals.

She smiles at me as Terra drags her toward the elevators, not waiting for the rest of us.

When I get to my room, I stretch out on the bed. I can hear the two of them through the wall in Hannah's room. Terra's always been loud. She's the reason I stopped using the spell that allows me to listen through the crystal ball. Nothing said ever proved useful anyway, so it was more like putting on the TV for background noise.

After a while, I go take a shower. I come out, towel wrapped around my waist, and it's quiet. I grab a shirt from my bag, but before I pull it on, a knock comes from the door between our rooms. I rake a hand through my hair, swinging it open.

"Oh." Hannah looks away from my bare chest. "Sorry. I was going to see if you were ready to go to the lobby for dinner."

"Give me a minute."

She hovers between the rooms while I head back into the bathroom with my clothes. She's in tight black jeans with rips at the knee and a short-sleeve shirt that hangs off her shoulder.

"Is that what you're wearing tonight?" I ask.

"Why? What's wrong with it?"

"Nothing." I'm still yanking the shirt over my head as I walk out. "But you'll be cold the second the sun goes down." I dig out a sweatshirt and toss it at her.

"Thanks," she says, draping it over her arm.

"I'll add it to the list of shit I'll never see again."

"If you mean your jacket, you can have it back anytime you want. You just have to ask."

Before I can do just that, someone knocks from the hallway on her side. I flip off the lights in my room and follow her into hers. Hannah opens her door to Gabe, who's standing there with a sweatshirt in his hand. His attention goes to the one she already has and then straight to me behind her. I give him a smug grin, really enjoying being in his way again.

Rather than leave Hannah and me alone while he goes back to his room, he totes the damn thing around with him the rest of the night. We eat dinner at a crowded place that only serves chicken wings. The goal of everyone there is to talk louder than everyone else around them. Gabe slides into one side of the booth, and just to push his buttons, I scoot in right next to him. Sabotage is so much more fun up close and personal.

The beach is a harsh contrast to the restaurant. Every hundred feet or so are small groups of people gathered around a fire ring, but the ocean seems to swallow up every noise outside of a laugh here and there. One interesting thing unchanged about man since the beginning is their weird sense of camaraderie surrounding certain activities. Harvest has always been a big one and anything to do with fire another. Perhaps it's the sense of power controlling something so destructive.

We light ours as the sun sets and spread out towels on the sand to sit on. Jesse starts pulling bottles of beer out of Terra's oversize bag and passes them around.

"I'm good for now," Gabe says. "I was thinking about going for a walk down the beach." He pauses, and I wait for it. "You want to come, Hannah?"

Her attention stays on the waves rolling onto the shore. She's close enough that I nudge her shoe with mine. She looks at me first and then Gabe. "No, thanks though."

He hesitates, reconsidering his plan, but she goes back to watching the water, so he gives a small, defeated smile and wanders off. Fuck, I almost feel bad for the guy. If not for demons and me, he probably could have had a chance at a white-picket-fence ending with her.

"I'm going to meet our neighbors." Jesse collects a few extra beers to distribute.

"I'll come." Terra dusts off the backs of her legs as she stands up off the sand. "You two want to be sociable for once?"

We both shake our heads, and then it's just us and the fire. As night takes over, I lean back on my palms and look up at the sky, trying to see any changes from the last time. A complete impossibility, but it never stops me. It doesn't take long for Hannah to move over next to me, bringing a blanket with her. She wraps herself up before offering me enough to cover my leg closest to her.

"Hannah Grace Kelley, always thinking of others."

"Hey, you come with a built-in heating system. You'll be fine." She pulls her legs under the blanket and stares up with me. "What's that star called?"

Given the vicinity in which she points, I assume she means the brightest one. "Regulus."

"And that one?"

"Alioth."

"What about—"

"Is this what you plan on doing all night? Because I can drop your ass at the planetarium at any time."

Her hand disappears back under the blanket. "You stare at the sky like my mom used to stare at the ocean."

"How's that?" I ask, sitting up.

"Like it brings you peace."

The last time I saw Samy, he mentioned something similar but said it made me look alive. Then he slapped me on the back and told me to stop looking up and find something down here that could do the same. Whatever the fuck that meant.

Hannah's watching the ocean again, her eyebrows pulled together.

"You figuring out the meaning of life?" I ask.

She shakes her head. "I'm thinking about the last time I was on the beach at night."

*Fuck.*

The blanket falls off her shoulder as she picks at the fringe running along one side. "Were you at my parents' funeral?"

I swallow hard, already knowing where this train is heading, and fuck if I don't want to get off it. "I was close by but not there."

She nods. For a second, I think she might drop it, but then she says, "And when I went to California after?"

She looks at me through her eyelashes, and I don't need to answer her. It already hangs in the air between us. What happened after she spread her parents' ashes into the ocean. When she walked into the dark water with the urn. How she swam out, and then she just … stopped.

It was the moment I almost lost everything.

"You pulled me out of the water," she says. "You pulled me out, and then you made me forget you."

"I'm sorry I didn't make you forget the entire fucking thing."

"Why didn't you?" she asks, not missing a beat.

I avoid her eyes and shrug. "Because when I got to you, you were fighting. At the last second, you changed your mind and wanted to live. You needed to remember what it felt like to lose everything and still find a reason to survive." I hesitate, forcing myself to look at her. "*I needed you to remember, so I wouldn't have to find out what it felt like for myself.*"

It happens fast. She leans in and gently presses her lips to mine, then she's already pulling away. "I'm sorry. I—"

"Stop talking." My fingers wrap around the nape of her neck, bringing her mouth back to mine.

It's all Hannah at first. Her soft lips and warm skin burn through me before I even sense any light. And it's fucking incredible. Her lips part, and I brush my tongue against hers. Light pulses through me then in a familiar rhythm. I move my hand to the front of her neck. The same cadence beats under my palm, slowly gaining speed. It's never occurred to me the two would match, but it makes nothing but sense.

Her hand runs through my hair, the other on my cheek. She pulls me closer, wanting me as much as I want her. I start to move her onto my lap, but a voice breaks through the waves.

"Hannah," Terra calls.

Her lips leave mine when she looks away, and I hang my head, knowing they won't be coming back.

"I should go." She gets up, taking the blanket with her. A few feet away, she stops but doesn't turn around. "Cass." Not even a glance over her shoulder. "Thank you."

The two words hit harder than I thought two words ever could, ripping their way far enough into me that they'll never leave. I'm watching when she reaches the next fire down the beach, and I'm watching as Terra pulls her over to join the group, and I'm watching each and every time she glances over her shoulder, looking for me. And I feel her when she finds me sitting where she left me. The girl I thought was an obstacle between me and everything I could ever want. But that's not Hannah anymore, and maybe it never was. She's so much more. She might actually be the everything I stand to lose.

# TWENTY

## *HANNAH*

Unsurprisingly, Cass and I don't talk about the kiss on the beach. Not while walking down the hall of the hotel or before he cuts through my room to his and shuts the adjoining door. In fact, we barely talk at all other than him asking if I want syrup for my pancakes at breakfast. But this is what we do. We hit a point of vulnerability neither of us is comfortable with, blur the line between us, and then avoid each other until our situation forces us back together.

It's a merry-go-round. The longer we're on it, the faster it spins. What worries me is what happens when one of us falls off.

Since it's our last full day in Florida, we all spend it on the beach together. We find a quieter area away from the madness still going on in certain parts. Jesse brings his football and makes the poor life choice of trying to teach Terra and me how to play. Every time she gets the ball, she just starts running, not even caring if it's in the right direction. I'm not any better. He throws me the ball, and I duck, letting it bounce across the sand on the other side of me.

"Seriously, Kelley?" he shouts, tossing his hands in the air.

A laugh comes from behind me, and I spin around to see Cass shaking his head while reading. He's stretched out on a towel next to Terra's "shit," which she ordered him to watch.

"You're wasting your time," he says when Jesse jogs by to retrieve the ball. "They kicked her off the volleyball team in junior high for the same reason."

"What?" I push away the hair the breeze keeps blowing in my face. "Mom said they politely asked me to resign because the team was full."

"Don't listen to him." Jesse stops in front of me. "He's just trying to get in your head. You got this."

As he backpedals away, Cass looks up from the book, focusing on me.

"Ready?" Jesse shouts from about fifty feet down the beach.

I nod, and his arm pulls back. The ball spirals toward me, and proving his confidence in me is completely misplaced, I wince and close my eyes. They fly back open at a loud smack, Cass's hands only a few inches from my face with the ball in them. He stares down at me, eyebrow raised.

I swipe the ball from his hands. "Danger detector go off?"

"Nope. That one was just obvious."

I laugh, and a dimple appears along with his half-smile. For a second, the spinning doesn't feel so bad. It almost seems like it slows down a little.

We lounge around the rest of the afternoon, finally going back to the hotel to clean up for dinner. I'm not surprised to see Gabe in the hall when someone knocks after my shower. He's been relatively reserved around me since the bonfire last night. Part of me thinks he saw me with Cass.

"You ready to go downstairs?" he asks.

"Yeah, let me grab Cass."

He catches my arm as I turn. "Is he the real reason we're not together, Hannah?"

I adamantly shake my head. "No."

"Then why? Because I don't buy the school excuse. Anytime we talked about it, we—"

The door between our rooms opens. Cass's eyes lock on Gabe's hand on my arm, his jaw tense when he looks at me.

Gabe's hand falls away, and he gives a sad smile. "I'll meet you in the lobby."

He turns down the hall, head hung, and I start after him.

"Hannah." Cass's voice stops me, softer than usual. "Let him go."

I spin around in the doorway. "I can't let him think I dumped him for you."

Something passes over his face, and he rubs a hand over the back of his neck. "Fine, go nurse the puppy. Just stay on this floor." He walks back into his room, slamming the door behind him.

I let out an exasperated groan.

This needs to end now.

Gabe's just stepping onto the elevator when I catch him. I grab him by his uninjured arm and haul him back to my room. He follows, not even asking why. Whatever he thinks is about to happen is probably the furthest thing from reality because my reality has become too unbelievable to believe.

*Fuck, I need a therapist.*

"Sit," I say, pointing at my bed.

Gabe complies, but as I knock on the door joining the rooms, he warily says, "Hannah?"

Cass jerks the door open, his eyes going straight to Gabe on my bed. They shift to me, stormy and intimidating. "What the fuck do you want, Hannah?"

"Tell him he realized we are better off as friends."

The annoyance vanishes from his face, and his stance loosens. "You're sure?"

"What are you guys—"

"Shut it, Preppy," Cass cuts Gabe off, still searching my face for confirmation. "This is really what you want?"

I nod. "I don't know why I didn't think of it sooner."

Cass leans in the doorway, fully at ease. Then he jumps at me, and even though I should see it coming by now, I flinch. He smiles on his way past me, palms glowing.

"There has to be a better way to do that," I mumble.

"There is," he says over his shoulder. He lowers and grabs Gabe's face in his hands. Gabe's body relaxes, eyes losing focus, and Cass's voice becomes soothing. "You and Hannah are better off as friends. Even if she climbs on top of you and rips her shirt off, you just don't feel that way about her anymore."

Gabe nods, moving Cass's hands with his head. "She has great tits though."

*Oh my God.*

My face burns red, and I hide it in my hands, really wishing I had left the room.

"Yes, she does," Cass speaks slowly, like he's struggling. "But you don't remember ever seeing them. And you never want to see them. Now, go to the lobby and wait for us down there. You won't remember talking to me."

I peek through my fingers as Cass releases him and straightens up. Gabe shakes his head, stands like nothing happened, and walks out, not even looking at me. And so ends the heavily edited and mostly rewritten love story of Hannah and Gabe. Directed in part by none other than Cass Daye.

Cass smirks on his way into his room. He reappears a few seconds later, closing the door behind him, and tosses me the same sweatshirt from last night. "Let's go. Something tells me Gabe's waiting for us in the lobby."

He is, along with the other two. Terra loops her arm through mine on the way to Jesse's Jeep and leans into my ear. "Jesse wants to go go-karting after we eat, so help me figure out something else."

I nod, agreeing, and she breaks away from me, so we aren't caught conspiring. Cass waits for me to get in first, but different-colored lights blinking off in the distance divert my attention.

Cass nudges me. "Hannah, get in."

"I think I know what we should do tonight after dinner."

He shrugs, not interested until my head tips toward the lights. His eyes follow, and the second he realizes what he's looking at, they shoot back to me. "Hannah…"

"Sound like fun, Cass?" I ask.

He stares down at me, his voice husky when he says, "Baby, you have no fucking idea."

Cass never experienced the excitement of birthday parties growing up because he never *grew up*. But walking onto the carnival midway is his equivalent. His entire face lights up, the flashing signs reflecting in his eyes. I can practically see him drawing out a map in his head of where he wants to go and what he wants to do.

"Hannah and I are going for funnel cake," Terra says.

His hand slides into mine. "No, you're not." He pulls me away from the group, dragging me behind him until we stop in front of a roller coaster. He turns around and puts his other hand on my waist. "Please, Hannah."

I laugh, already regretting this. I hate thrill rides. But I can't back out now, especially not with his eyes pleading me not to say no.

A rush of anxiety washes over me, and he smiles, not needing any more of an answer from me.

Everyone else joins us by the time we get tickets. Since Gabe's arm is still in a sling, he leans against the metal railing while the rest of us get in line. Considering how terrible we were at protecting each other in the haunted house, Terra has no problem going with Jesse. Not that I think Cass would have given her any other choice. He hasn't lost contact with me for more than a few seconds at a time, a small pulse releasing every now and then that only amps up my heart rate more.

When we climb into the car, my breaths come faster, and his eyes are on me.

"You okay?" he asks, lowering the bar over us.

I swallow and nod, and, *God*, I really hate roller coasters. The cars lurch forward, and Terra shrieks behind us. We ratchet higher and higher at a harsh angle. The pull of gravity reminds me that this is not what I'm meant to do. Humans don't fly. We fall. We fall hard and break and die and—

"Breathe." Cass's lips are at my ear, his hand scorching on the inside of my bare thigh. It stays there. His fingers flex, tightening, crackling against my skin as we inch ever closer to the top.

I force a few ragged breaths, anticipating the upcoming plunge. Then everything grows eerily quiet. The air around us changes, not the same as everyone else's. Like it's moving at a different speed. We should be careening down the track, but we hover at the peak. I look over, and Cass smiles. Just as I realize he's slowing down the world around us, it all rushes back.

We fall.

The cars rattle as we drop and clank on the rise. Hair whips across my face, and Cass's free hand finds mine, his eyes never leaving me. Even though my heart pounds with every jolt of the ride, it smooths out too soon, slowing. He lets go of me once we creep to a stop and pushes my hair back. His hand lingers, brushing a thumb over my bottom lip until Jesse laughs, walking by our car, and Cass pulls away.

The other three are waiting for us, already discussing where they want to go next. Cass doesn't pay attention though. His sights are set on what looks like a Ferris wheel on crack. Cages rock and spin while rotating up and down a towering oval. His hand on my lower back guides me forward.

"That one," he whispers.

Everyone else goes to get Terra her funnel cake while we wait in line for The Zipper. The line's not long, and soon enough, we're climbing into our own metal enclosure. Cass slams the door shut, which brings the bar down across our laps. Our cage swings as the ride rotates to let passengers into the next car.

I sigh, already feeling anxious. "Are you enjoying my torture?"

"Trust me. The roller coaster was just as torturous for me."

"What? How is that even possible?"

He yanks me closer on the seat, angling his upper body toward me. "Because, the entire time, all I fucking wanted to do was this." His mouth covers mine, and a warm hand slips behind my neck, crushing my lips even harder against his. It's needy, urgent, like if he doesn't kiss me, the world will end.

The cage surges forward again, and I gasp, his tongue taking the opening. My body craves contact with him, only the bar keeps me from moving more than my arms. I clutch the back of his hair, needing more of him in whatever way I can get it. He groans into my mouth as we swing. But this time, he pulls back, and we keep going. Faster. Up and around the center arm. The cage rocks forward and back until it flips all the way over. My adrenaline spikes, and his hand glides to the side of my neck, fingers pressed to my pulse. I look out the steel-mesh front of the car. We tip all the way forward, dropping face-first to the ground. I suck in a breath, and Cass pulls my face back to his, kissing me on our way back up. His lips release mine before we spin, once, twice, and I'm dizzy, but it's from him.

The ride shudders to a stop with us swinging at the highest point. He rests his forehead on mine and watches his hand skim down to my chest. My heart hammers against his palm, and he looks into my eyes. Neither of us moves while we catch our breaths, his skin cooling slightly by the time we reach the bottom.

The ride operator wrenches the door open, and the bar releases us. Cass helps me down from the car. His hand moves to my back as we walk off the platform. It slips beneath the bottom of my sweatshirt, seeking out my skin like he can't stand not touching me right now. And really, I don't want him to stop.

At the bottom of the steps, we meet up with the others again. Jesse and Gabe are both gnawing away at massive turkey legs and holding giant glasses of beer. Terra shoves a bite of her funnel cake in my mouth, being sure to smear powdered sugar all over my face.

"Mmm, thank you."

She giggles and dusts it off for me. "So, Cass, are you ready to share yet?"

"Nope." He picks a piece off her plate and pops it into his mouth. A smirk appears, and he assaults her with a dimple as he leads me away.

I shrug back at her, and she shakes her head.

"We'll negotiate over her custody later then," she calls after us.

We walk almost to the other side of the midway before I realize where we're heading next.

"No, Cass. Any other ride." I try to stop, but his hand splays out across my back and keeps moving me forward.

"You're going on this one even if I have to carry you on."

Not doubting for a second he would, I huff and get in the back of the line for the Gravitron. Even worse, it's a long line, so I spend the next ten minutes witnessing the large disc structure spinning around on its axis and thinking about the centrifugal force that will be pinning me against the wall.

I fidget, uncomfortable with just the idea.

We're at the front of the line when Cass steps away from me. "I'll be right back."

"I'm not going on this thing alone."

"You won't," he says, jumping the metal fence keeping the line in formation.

He abandons me with the ticket taker who openly ogles me. *Great.*

I lean on the fence and pretend not to notice him. Soon the ride slows, and still, no Cass. I'm about to turn to search for him, but hands grasp me from behind. I lunge forward away from the fence and spin around.

Cass smiles, climbing back over. "Boo."

"Seriously? After all this, you still need to scare me?"

He ignores me and heads straight for the ticket taker. He grabs the man's face in his hands as the entrance to the ride slides open. I miss what he says, but the man nods slowly, eyes unfocused. Cass releases him and plucks the tickets out of my hand. The guy blinks a few times and takes them, moving the chain so we can walk through. After we pass him, he re-hooks it without letting anyone else on the ride.

"Did you just hijack a ride for us?" I ask.

He shrugs, stepping through the door into the large, open space. The only other person in there is the man in the middle who operates the ride. Cass tugs me over to the wall and pins me against it.

His hand trails up the front of my thigh. "You want me to show you a better way to get your heart rate up?"

I somehow manage to nod even though I doubt it will take much at the moment. He dips his head down, brushing his lips over mine. He keeps going to my neck, sucking and nibbling. My body responds exactly how he wants it to, and then he's gone. He reappears by the man in the center and grasps his face. After he tells him something, he's back to me in a flash.

"What did you tell him?"

He stands against the wall next to me. "I told him he won't see anything out of the ordinary happening on this ride."

I narrow my eyes at him, and the lights cut out.

We begin to spin. Smaller lights blink on and off, providing enough light to see the empty space around us. Cass's hand slides down my arm until it hits my inner wrist. My pulse throbs against his fingertips, the pace rising and rising as my body feels the invisible force holding me back. The padded boards we lean on slide up the wall until my feet no longer touch the ground.

All of a sudden, I can't feel Cass anymore. It takes an effort to turn my head to the side. He's not there. I panic, thinking he lured me onto the ride and then abandoned me. But when I look straight ahead again, I see him in front of me.

Fucking. Floating.

*Holy shit.*

A soft glow illuminates him, growing brighter and brighter. Just as the light becomes too much, they appear. The wings unfold from behind him and spread out until they span across nearly the entire enclosure. They're incredible and impossible and beautiful. The white so white that it burns to look at, turning blue around the edges. I keep my eyes open as long as I can, but eventually I have to close them. The light slowly begins to dim through my eyelids, and the air comes back, my lungs remembering how to breathe.

Cass's hand finds my wrist again. My head turns. All I see is black at first until my vision readjusts, his face slowly working its way through. He's close, only a few inches of heated air between us.

Then the spinning stops.

After we get back to the hotel, Terra insists we all have one last Farewell Florida drink at the bar. I only take a few sips of mine and slide it over for Cass to finish. He hasn't said much since the Gravitron but gives a small smile, tipping the glass back without hesitation.

Gabe flags down the bartender for another round. Cass catches my eye. He tilts his head toward the lobby, and I hop off my stool.

On my way past, I kiss Terra on the cheek. "Jesse, cut her off after one more. A hungover Terra is not someone you want in a car all day. We learned that the hard way freshman year."

He holds up his glass. "Good lookin' out, kid."

I wave goodnight to Gabe. Earlier in the day, he wanted to know why we couldn't be together, and now all I get is a nod in return.

Cass holds open the door and follows me to the elevators. An empty one waits, so we step straight in. I stand by the wall, letting him push the button for our floor. It's the first time we've been alone since the ride. Neither of us says anything. We barely even look at each other. The numbers flash one through four, and the doors open again.

It takes until I stop at my room for him to step behind me. His arm snakes around my waist and pulls me back against his chest.

"I learned something tonight," he says in my ear.

I work to keep my voice steady. "What's that?"

"You feel different." He brushes my hair back from my neck and grazes his lips over my skin, sending a shiver through me. "I can't explain it, but when I'm the reason for your heart pounding in your chest, it feels…"

The elevator dings, loud voices following right behind.

He kisses my neck and presses his cheek to my temple. "Goodnight, Hannah."

I can't feel him behind me anymore, but I feel him everywhere else.

Before anyone walks around the corner, I slide my key card. Part of me wants him to be waiting in my room. He's not, and his sweatshirt lands on the bathroom floor in a pile with the rest of my clothes. I climb into the shower to wash the carnival off me. The water's too hot, but I leave it. The burn reminds me of Cass's skin on mine, and I want to feel him.

But more than that, I want him to feel me.

# TWENTY-ONE

## CASS

You can't overdose on something that's a part of you, and that's what the light is. It's a part of me that's been taken away for so long. But tonight, I came as close as possible to the perfect high. I was me. All of me. Complete. And fuck if it's not the worst crash I've ever experienced.

I roll over to check my phone on the nightstand. It's Hannah. I shouldn't read her text. For once, I walked away without screwing everything up between us. No one argued or issued a challenge. She won't hate me in the morning. Hell, she might even still let me touch her like she did tonight. Whether I want to admit it or not, that's what I want. To touch her and kiss her and feel her and see her smile.

Fuck. I'm fucking fucked.

*You awake?*

I send back, *Depends on what you want.*

*I want you to tell me how it feels.*

I've no more than processed the words when the center of my chest heats. It spreads, slow and steady, and brings each nerve ending to life as it pushes outward. The same sensation as earlier, traveling straight to my dick. When she responded to my hands and lips on her. How she reacted to my body pressed into hers.

My breathing picks up with the high of her humming through me again.

*What are you doing, Hannah?*

*Thinking about you.*

*Just thinking?* I ask.

*No.*

I'm hard.
Instantly.
Alone in my bed without any physical contact but what I'm getting from my boxers.

She's on the other side of the wall, touching herself the way I want to, thinking about me while she does. I can tell when her pulse creeps higher, the flow of light increasing along with it. She's close. The heat intensifies in my core, my cock aches, and all I can think about is being inside of her while this feeling courses through me.

I'm at the door.

The whole don't-screw-shit-up philosophy was doomed from the moment she brought her clit into the equation. I'm an addict with no chance at recovery. I knock, and Hannah's adrenaline spikes. I'm practically panting when she answers in a robe, hair wet, cheeks flushed, biting her lip.

She backs toward the bed. My steps match hers. I pull the tie on her robe and slip my hand in the opening, running it over the smooth skin of her stomach. The fabric moves, so I can see what I've been missing, and then it falls to the floor, pooling at her feet. She's bare in front of me. Fuck, she's gorgeous. And right now, she's all mine.

I sweep my thumb over her peaked nipple, cupping her breast while we move farther into the room. She stops when she hits the bed, but I don't. I lift her, palming her ass, and our lips meet.

It's frantic, like my mouth didn't just claim hers a few hours earlier. Tongues colliding, her hands all over me, my skin burning against hers.

By the time I lower her onto the bed, I'm shoving my sweatpants and boxers down with one hand to free my erection. I run my fingers up the underside of my shaft before giving it a firm stroke. She watches, licking her lips, and I groan at the thought of them stretched around me.

I brush my hand up to her knee and press it aside, so I can see what I've only felt. Her pussy's beyond perfect, already dripping and begging to be fucked. The entire night has essentially been foreplay, leading up to this. After her little performance, we're both more than ready, but I still need time to appreciate her.

I crawl over her and swipe my fingers through her swollen lips to her clit and rub hard circles, causing her to whimper. It drives me crazy to touch her and hear her and feel her. I kiss down her neck to her breasts, and my teeth drag over one of her pebbled nipples. She arches, pushing it even farther into my mouth.

"Oh God, Cass."

I do the same on the other side, her moan sending a shock through me. As I drag my fingers to her entrance, stroking and teasing without filling her like I know she's desperate for, her hands are in my hair. She's pushing and pulling like she can't decide what direction she wants me to go. Fuck, I can't decide either. Tongue or cock, I need one in her tight cunt.

"What do you want, Hannah?"

My lips vibrate against her skin, and the sensation echoes back through me when she feels it. I lick a line from her breastbone down to her navel. Before I can go any farther, she grasps both sides of my face. She pulls me back up until I'm hovering over her. My hips are between her thighs—one thrust from being inside her.

I rub the head of my cock against her soaked pussy and brush my mouth over hers, saying, "Tell me what you want, baby."

Her fingertips trace over my jaw. "I want to feel you."

My gaze stays locked on hers as I slowly push inside her. Her eyes crush closed, and a rush of sensations floods through me. Hannah's. Mine. All of them come at me at once, overwhelming once she takes all of me. I'm desperate to move, but I wait until she looks at me.

"Like this, Hannah?" My mouth grazes hers with every word, starved for it even now. "You want to feel me bottomed out in this tight pussy?" I ease in and out a few times, letting her body adjust to me. "Feel me fuck you like I should have months ago?"

Then I thrust into her harder, and she cries out.

"Yes. Please. Fuck me, Cass."

I smile down at her. "No need to beg, baby."

I draw back and slam forward, not stopping this time. Eager hands slide down my chest and then to my back. It's all I can do to keep a steady rhythm and not lose control. Her nails dig into my skin, her hips meeting mine. Every time she moans, light ripples through me.

"Fuck," she chokes out.

My hand grasping the back of her thigh emits enough of a spark that it travels through her and back into me. As her heart rate climbs, I hook her leg over my arm, so I can sink deeper. I need more of her. Every part of her possible. My lips drop to hers, then to her cheek and neck and chest.

"Rub your clit," I tell her.

She snakes her hand between us, knuckles skimming the base of my cock where we're connected. I curse when she teases her fingers there again, my balls drawing up, and a smile plays at her kiss-swollen lips. The next time, I bite down on her shoulder. Her pussy clenches at the sting, and she gasps. I grab her wrist and press her palm to her clit.

"Fucking come for me, Hannah." I grind into the back of her hand until she whimpers at the added pressure and moves on her own. "Then I'm coming so deep in your hot cunt that you'll feel it for days." I kiss her. "Say it, baby. Tell me you want it, too."

"I want it," she rasps. "*Fuck*, I want you to come inside me."

She crushes her mouth to mine as I drive into her.

The first time I made her come, I wasn't paying attention, only interested in proving to her that I could make her fall apart. This time, I want to experience every second of it. Each erratic breath and heartbeat and wave inside her.

And I do.

Her head falls back on the pillow as she breathes out my name, eyes fluttering shut. The heat rages the hottest as she tightens around me and her body shudders. I can't even tell what's the light and what's her anymore. At this point, they're the same thing.

I quicken my pace, unable to hold back with the aftereffects of her release rocking through me. She's everywhere again, only this time I want her to drown me so I'm surrounded by everything *her*. My balls fucking throb as I pound into her harder until I bury deep and groan, spilling inside her.

I kiss her and slowly thrust even after I have nothing left, dragging in and out of her cum-soaked pussy. Hannah's not letting me go, anyway. Her chest rises against mine, and I rest my forehead on hers.

Sated green eyes stare up at me. Seeing them, and feeling her like this, I doubt I'll be looking up at the stars anymore. Not when she's right here.

Like I said … fucking fucked.

A barely-there buzzing eases me awake. Hannah's head is nuzzled against my chest, my arms around her. I kiss her hair and slip out from under her. I grab my sweatpants from the floor and pull them on, then I follow the sound back into my own room. My phone rattles on the nightstand, stopping as I reach for it.

*Jesus, fuck. Ten missed calls?*

They're all from Chaz. Before I can call him back, his name appears on the screen.

"This better be a—"

"Demon attack," he says. "Three at once. They went after my charge in the bathroom of a nightclub, not caring that humans were around."

"Fuck." I walk back to the doorway between the rooms, the anxiety of not seeing Hannah overwhelming. "All lower-level?"

"Yeah, they were sewer rats. They reeked of the worst parts of Hell. Shifty fuckers too. By the time I dropped my charge, two were gone. I lost the third after a few teleports."

I watch her while she sleeps, her breaths slow and even.

"Cass," he says, no hint of his usual *fuck it* attitude in his tone, "we might be looking at an Upper. Or at least someone who knows how to coordinate attacks. There's no way this many Lowers are working together without someone else pulling the strings."

"But why now?" I switch to the Angelic language in case she wakes up. "Nephilim have been around for thousands of years. The bloodlines have been vast, spreading across the continents. Why would an upper-level demon wait until only a handful remain?"

The line goes quiet, both of us sorting through the possibilities. It doesn't make sense. We're missing something.

"What if this is where they've been the past few centuries?" Chaz says. "Working on some demonic plan that requires us out of the way, so they can get to them. We know better than anyone the power within Nephilim blood."

"It's how we pull off most of our magic," I mutter more to myself than him.

"Whatever the hell they want, we can't wait around, trying to figure it out anymore. It's time to spell up, bro."

"Yeah." I wander back into Hannah's room. "Tell the others, and have Ros send me scrolls to read through tomorrow."

"Dude, why do I have to—"

The phone lands on the nightstand, my interest in his whining nonexistent. I crawl back in beside Hannah and move my arm underneath her to bring her to my chest. She wakes enough to sigh and cuddle against me. I hold her tighter, my eyes not falling shut again for the rest of the night. The vacation ended the second Chaz said *demon*. It's back to demons-are-trying-to-kill-my-charge reality.

Only now, it's not my eternity I care about.

It's her.

# TWENTY-TWO

## *HANNAH*

It's Cass.

Nothing is ever guaranteed with him.

I reminded myself of this when I got out of the shower last night, and when I texted him, and when I ran my hand down my body to tease my clit, and when I answered the door, and when he laid me down on the bed. But I let myself forget when he was inside me, and when he made me come apart, and when he stared down at me like I was all he could see, and when he held me close, and when I fell asleep in his arms.

Then I remember again, waking up. No Cass. The door between our rooms is shut. If not for the robe on the floor where it fell, the tender spot on one of my thighs from his hand, and a soreness between them, I might think it was a dream.

He walks in, eyes on his phone. "You going to be ready soon?"

I don't answer right away, and he looks up. It's the same look he always gives me, two seconds away from annoyed.

Pulling the sheet over my bare chest, I sit up. "Give me twenty minutes."

He looks back at his screen and disappears into his room. After months of his dismissive behavior, it shouldn't bother me anymore, but I at least thought he'd wait a little longer after screwing me to go back to it.

*It's Cass, Hannah. Nothing is ever guaranteed with him.*

No matter how much I wanted this time to be different.

By the time I've showered and finish packing my suitcase, he's waiting by the door with his. He carries both our bags down to Jesse's Jeep. Neither of us says a word. It's easy to fall back into not talking to him. I just need to pretend like the last few days never happened between us.

We all pile in the car to start the twenty-hour drive back to campus. Terra trades seats with Gabe, giving him the front. Unlike on the ride down, he's not insisting on sitting next to me. With her in the back, the drive goes fast. She creates the most ridiculous games, her favorite being Name the Driver.

It quickly develops into Name the Driver and Give Him an Entire Backstory That Always Takes a Dark Turn. Like the trucker with a gray goatee and red trucker hat. Better known as Jake from Tallahassee. He has a wife and three children and was voted Most Likely to Succeed in high school. Then, after losing his football scholarship due to a horrific car accident in which he lost seven out of ten toes, he turned long-haul trucker to support his family.

I think Jesse pulls off the highway for an early supper just so we stop ruining people's imaginary lives.

We're walking into the small mom-and-pop diner, rightly named Mom and Pop's, when Cass finally acts like I exist. He holds the door for me, a half-smile bringing out a dimple. It irritates me, mostly because my belly flips at the sight of it. I look away and slide into a booth next to Terra to avoid sitting with him. Not that he notices since his attention's already back on whatever has him so riveted on his phone.

A few hours later, he says his first words to me since we left the hotel.

I'm passing him in the aisle of a gas station, and he asks, "Do you have more than one phone charger?"

I shake my head and keep walking.

Once we get back on the road, he returns to broody Cass. Every now and then, I glance over and think I see his mouth moving. It reminds me of his lips on me, so I stop letting myself look at him.

He's made it clear that last night meant nothing to him. Whatever I thought it might have been was wrong. Cass is my Watcher. That's all he'll ever be. It's time I figure out a way to live with that.


It's late. Almost midnight.

Terra and Gabe are both asleep. Jesse's tapping away on the steering wheel, having just chugged a cup of coffee.

I'm staring out the window at shadows and brief glimpses of the world around us through headlights when Cass reaches for my hand. He pulls it onto his lap and laces his fingers through mine. Unsure what emotional whiplash awaits me, I have to force myself to look at him. He's watching me with a relaxed expression on his face. Almost peaceful, like when he stares at the sky. How he looked at me last night.

He brings his other hand to my face and leans in, sealing his lips over mine. It's unlike any other time he's kissed me. Slow and gentle, and it makes me feel everything I've been telling myself not to want from him.

His eyes stay shut for a few seconds after he pulls back. "God, I've wanted to do that all day."

"Why haven't you?"

He checks up front, but Jesse's focused on the road, drumming along to a song.

"Chaz had three demons attack last night. Ros sent pictures of a bunch of scrolls to sort through, so I could find a spell to keep you safe." His eyebrows pull tighter, his eyes dropping to my lips. "I knew the second those things were near me, I would lose all focus, and fuck if I wasn't right. Come here."

He barely finishes before his mouth is back on mine, hungry and commanding. He parts my lips with his tongue, and God, it's what I've wanted him to do all day. My free hand runs up his chest and around to the back of his neck, tugging so his tongue plunges deeper. A low sound vibrates from the back of his throat. He pushes down on my other hand, rubbing it over the hard ridge in his jeans. It's a mistake we both recognize, and he wrenches his mouth away from mine.

"Shit," he whispers, his eyes darting around. Then he calls up front, "Jesse, we good for a stop?"

I pull my hand away from his crotch. "You're not fucking me in a gas station restroom."

A sly smile forms, the shadows darkening his dimples. "Never said I was."

We only make it to the door of the men's room before he spins me around. His hands grip my ass as he backs me in. I don't even waste time pretending to be disgusted by our surroundings because, despite my claim in the car, I will let him do whatever he wants to me right now. His fingers rip open the button on my shorts, and he drops to his knees in front of me and wiggles them over my hips. I tug at his hair as he hooks his thumbs in my panties, yanking them down as well.

I gasp when he jerks me forward by the backs of my thighs and drags his nose over my bare pussy.

"All mine," he rasps.

His skin continues to warm, his breath hot and teasing against me. Then it's too bright, and heat surrounds me, the floor beneath us shifting. My eyes are still adjusting to the darkness as Cass urges me back onto a bed. He finishes taking off my shorts and underwear before nudging my thighs apart, so he can settle between them.

"Told you I wasn't going to fuck you there."

I laugh, recognizing his bedroom. It turns into a moan when he lowers his head and licks through my wet center. Growling, he drags his tongue up to my clit. He peers up at me from between my thighs and then he sucks hard enough I jerk against his mouth.

"Oh, fuck."

His arm wraps around my upper thighs to stop me from moving. I'm completely at his mercy, his tongue demanding and lips coaxing my body to give him what he wants. As long as he keeps doing this, he can never talk to me again.

A thick finger presses into me, and after a few pumps he adds a second. I claw at the sheets on each side of me while he works me over with his mouth, stubble scraping my inner thighs. He watches my face the entire time as he turns me into a whimpering mess.

It doesn't take long for me to teeter, ready to fall. But the heat of his mouth leaves me before I do. I blow out a frustrated breath as he climbs up my body, a smirk on his lips.

"Not without me," he says, shoving his jeans and boxers off.

I eat up the sight of his bare cock from the thick base up the long shaft. His mouth lands on mine, cutting off my view, but I don't care because I've already missed the way his tongue invades—tasting me, claiming me. He takes his time kissing me, his fingers keeping me torturously close. I buck against his hand and feel him smile.

*Asshole.*

"Cass," is all I can manage.

He hums, finally sinking his hips between my legs and pressing the head of his cock to my dripping entrance.

"I like you desperate for my cock, Hannah." He licks a line up my neck before bringing his lips to my ear. "But I like you coming on it more."

He drives into me all at once, and I cry out his name. He starts to fuck me, my body picking up right where I left off while he continues rubbing my clit. Only instead of the sheets, my nails dig into his blazing skin with each thrust. He bites down on my shoulder in response and pistons into me harder.

"Come, Hannah."

The command tips me over the edge, everything but Cass gone when I fall or float or maybe fly. Whichever it is, I want him with me, and I hold him tighter, arms locked around his neck, his burning forehead pressed to mine.

The pleasure's still hot in my veins when he tosses my legs over his shoulders. His breaths become shorter, ragged, and he groans, his muscles tensing as his cock pulses inside me.

He shrugs my legs off his shoulders and collapses onto his forearms braced on either side of me. Our chests rise and fall in sync, his eyes hooded as he stares down at me. Then he lazily kisses my cheeks, nose, lips.

"Think they'll notice if we just stay here?" He doesn't wait for an answer, nipping at my lower lip and pulling out. His eyes drop to my swollen pussy, still on display for him. "Don't clean up. I want my cum dripping out of you the rest of the drive."

I might argue if the possessive way he looks at me didn't make me want it too.

It only takes a minute to re-dress and return to the grimy gas station. Then we're walking back out into the cool night air, hours away from his bed. Only now his cum soaks my panties.

Tapping away on his phone, Jesse doesn't pay attention to us getting back in the Jeep.

"You want to switch?" Cass asks him.

"I have a few hours left in me." He drops his phone in the cupholder and pulls away from the gas pump.

The lights fade, and we're once again in the dark, except for the green glow of the dash. Cass's arm slides behind me, holding me close to his side. I rest my head on his shoulder, and he brings my hand back to his lap. His thumb travels back and forth. It makes the slightest hint of a spark tingle against my skin.

"What happens now?" I ask.

The dimming light appears and disappears beneath his cooling hand. "We tolerate the confines of a car for another several hours."

"I meant, after we get back." I tilt my chin to look at him.

His lips press to mine. "I do that as much as possible and spell-cast my ass off."

I cuddle into him, and he rests his cheek on top of my head.

I was wrong about nothing being guaranteed with Cass. One thing will always be true: he'll always be here. Moody and broody and pissed off at the world, but here. With me. Always.

My suitcase lands on the curb after Cass flings it out of the back end of the Jeep. He slams the rear door. "You need to bring less shit next time."

Terra's already hauling her bags inside as he nudges mine the rest of the way over with his foot. "I'm not carrying it any farther for you either. I'm done being your bellboy."

I wave at Jesse as he drives off. "You weren't that great at it anyway."

"The best one you'll ever have." He steps over it to get to me and secures his hands on my waist. "You said Terra won't stick around long?"

"She hates doing laundry here almost as much as she hates not unpacking right away."

His head lowers, lips lightly touching mine. "I'll be back the second she leaves. Until then…" He lets go of me to retrieve a keychain shaped like an alligator from his pocket. "Keep this on you."

My eyes narrow at him as he shoves it into my hand. "An alligator?"

"The hotel gift shop wasn't exactly swimming in options, Hannah."

I dangle it between us. "What is it, exactly?"

"For the next twelve or so hours, it's a solution to our demon problem. A cloaking spell slapped together with what should keep any powers or magic from affecting you. Which includes mine, so stay in your room so that if I need to find you, I can. Because the orb won't work."

Examining my new keychain, I smile. "You gave me a present."

He rolls his eyes and kisses me. "Stay in your room."

I walk into the room I've been banished to, still smiling.

Terra stops loading her laundry. "I knew it." She drops the bag and lands on my bed at the same time as I do. "I was watching out the window, you hussy. Now, this is the last time I will say this to you. Spill."

I pull my feet up on the bed between us. "What do you want to know?"

She claps her hands, wiggling around like I just promised to keep her young forever. "When did this *really* start? Because he said he'd just moved to town, but Gabe met him months ago."

"We ran into each other at the Halloween haunted house. Then a few times after that."

"But you didn't hook up until recently?"

My face scrunches up. "January."

Her mouth falls open. "When you were with Gabe?"

"No," I say fast. "Gabe and I happened after, and I didn't even see Cass again until a few weeks ago."

She nods, her eyes trailing around the room. "And now you two are together?"

"I think so."

"Think? You want to more than think with that thing walking around out there. Dude's sex on a stick."

"No, we're together."

"And do your parents like him?"

A sick feeling creeps over me. My face must show it because Terra shakes her head.

"Sorry, Han. You don't have to answer that. I know you and your parents don't—"

"My parents are dead," I blurt out. "They were killed in a plane crash five and a half years ago."

Her eyes bulge, and I cover my mouth like it will somehow take it back. But I don't want to because, as terrible as it is to say, it's not as hard anymore.

My gaze lowers to the bedspread between us. "I should have told you a long time ago, but you never asked about them, and it was just easier not to talk about it." I look up, and she's crying, and I'm a terrible person. "I'm sorry."

She shakes her head and wipes her hand across her cheek. "Don't apologize, Hannah. The reason I'm crying is really stupid."

"More stupid than not telling your best friend your parents are dead?"

Terra sniffs and nods, picking at her nails. I almost think she's going to tell me her parents are dead, too, when she takes a deep breath.

"I sent a really angry letter to your parents last year, telling them how amazing you are and how they don't deserve you. And I put a shitload of glitter in it, so it would get all over their house and their clothes and be stuck in their carpet forever." She takes another breath, and the tears are rolling down her face. "Then I snooped through your things and found an address in Colorado and sent it without a name on it or a return address. And whatever poor soul opened the letter probably still has glitter in their hair." She sobs into her hands, loud and heartbreaking.

A laugh bubbles up out of nowhere, followed by an incredibly embarrassing snort. "You glitter-bombed the Chelowskis?"

Her head pops up, eyes devastatingly sad. "Oh God, now I know their names."

Cackling even harder, I drop back on my pillow, tears spilling from the corners of my eyes. My response is ridiculous and borderline inappropriate, considering the situation. Exactly the kind of behavior that would make my parents proud.

Slowly, Terra's crying morphs into embarrassed giggling. She lies down beside me and wraps her arms around me. I try to keep my breathing even so that Cass doesn't appear in a blaze of light, ready to fight something.

"Should I write them an apology?" she asks once we calm down.

"Something tells me they don't open anything without a clear return address anymore."

She sighs. "I'm sorry about your parents, Hannah."

That's something you never learn how to respond to. *Thank you* sounds wrong. No reason why, it just does. And *it's okay* comes across as dismissive.

I roll my head toward her. "They would have loved you, by the way. And the glitter."

"What about Cass? Did they know him?"

I smile and shake my head. "No, but he remembers them."

"Would they have approved of him?"

"Probably not." Then I add, "But I really doubt he'd care."

She scoots over and rests her head on my shoulder. "Well, even if he's a dick most of the time, I like him."

"Yeah," I say, playing with the keychain in my hand. "Me too."

We stare at the ceiling until she claims she can smell her clothes. While she finishes gathering her laundry, I unpack and sneak a few things into her load before she knots the bag.

"You want to come?" She opens the door and sees Cass on the other side. "Never mind." She passes him on his way in and turns, so she can still deliver her glare. "I'm watching you, pretty boy. I have glitter, and I know how to use it."

His eyes dart to me and back, then he slams the door on her. "What the fuck is she—"

It swings back open, two of Terra's fingers pointing to her eyes and then to him. "Watching you."

This time, I shut the door on her.

Cass catches me around the middle and spins me around. "Did you stay in your room?" he asks, his mouth already on my neck.

"As commanded." I tilt my head to the side, giving him better access, and inch the hem of his shirt higher.

He reaches back between his shoulders and tugs it off. "Is that what you want?" He kisses me and jerks my hips forward.

It's exactly what I want. My fingers trail over his hard abs, heading lower and lower. I reach the button on his jeans as his teeth sink into my bottom lip. *Hard.*

"Ouch." I jerk back from him, bringing a hand to my mouth. "Cass, that hurt."

"I'm sorry, baby." He moves my hand away and rubs the pad of his thumb over where he bit. It comes back with blood. He kisses my forehead and steps back. "But it's much easier than how I usually get your blood. More fun too."

My mouth opens to ask but snaps back shut. Nope. I do not want to know the how or when or number of times.

Cass goes to the bed, focused on a small velvet pouch in his hand. "Squeeze your lip and come here. I need at least a few drops."

He sits against the headboard and pulls me between his legs, so I lean back on his chest. His arms encircle me while the tip of his finger runs over my lip. He holds it over the bag. Slowly, one drop forms and falls and then another. He tightens the string, cinching the top closed, and hands me my laptop off the nightstand.

"Find a movie."

"You want to watch a movie?" I turn my head to look at him, surprised at his choice of activity, given the empty dorm room.

"I *want* to fuck you senseless. But I *need* to chant for the next three hours to finish this spell. You can at least sit here and suffer with me." He skims his nose along my jawline until he reaches my ear. "No chick flicks. And none of the crap Fiona watched with the cheap production and everyone crying over real-issues bullshit."

I smile. She *loved* those movies. Give a woman terminal cancer and introduce her to the love of her life the next day, and my mom was a blubbering mess, watching it three times in a row. My dad actually canceled cable just so she couldn't torture herself anymore.

Cass nuzzles into my neck, his lips moving, and I hit play on a blow-it-up movie my dad liked. His hold on me tightens, and everything feels better than it has in a long time. Even if demons are trying to kill me.

With him here, everything feels right.

# Twenty-Three

## CASS

A bare foot slides over the couch cushion, up my leg, and straight into my crotch. As difficult as it is, I ignore the dick massage, not looking away from the dusty-ass book I pulled out of a bank vault a few days ago.

The keychain spell only lasted a day. A more permanent solution to hiding Hannah from demonic tracking and blocking powers exists. I know it does. Until I find it, though, anywhere she goes other than her now-protected room and my apartment, I'm with her.

Two weeks in and we're still in a sweet spot of needing sex more than air, so being on top of each other works out rather well. But one of these days, we're going to get sick of each other and need a break.

The foot starts to retreat, and I catch Hannah's ankle, stopping it. I finish my page and let the book fall to the floor, dragging her across the cushions to me. The spells have been around for millennia. They'll wait another hour.

She giggles and lands in my lap. Her mouth's all mine while she repositions, straddling me and holding my face in her hands.

And then someone knocks.

She tries to pull away, so I fist my hand in her hair to keep her in place. My tongue's in one of its favorite two places right now, and whoever the hell is out there needs to respect that.

They knock again.

*Fuck.*

"You should get that," she mumbles into my mouth.

"Not a chance." My hands grip her ass, and I shift off the couch onto my feet, bringing her with me. Her legs wrap around me as I carry her into the bedroom, slamming the door shut behind us. She lands on the bed, and I'm on top of her, pushing under her shirt and kissing my way up to her bra.

I dig my vibrating phone out of my pocket with one hand, the other cupping her breast. Unknown number. I toss it aside even though it keeps vibrating after I ignore the call.

I only take my lips off her long enough to get rid of our shirts. Hannah moans, her back arching to meet my mouth when it returns to her nipple through the lace. The feel of her is as incredible as the light pulsing through me. I make quick work of her jeans, shoving them down over her hips and off her legs.

Now they're pounding at the door, and I'm moving south. Lower. Lower.

My teeth are clenching panties when something bangs somewhere on the other side of the door.

"Tamiel!" The shrieking female voice cuts through my apartment, my old name bouncing off the walls.

Hannah sits straight up. "Who's that?"

"Someone who can't get in," I murmur. I push off the bed and lean back down, kissing the top of her head. "I'll be back." Walking away, I add, "Be naked."

I crack my neck on the way down the hall. Lydia irritates me on every visit, but interrupting me mid-Hannah destroys any chance of me having patience with her. Since the door already sits wide open, there's no need for me to answer it.

Lydia crosses her arms over her chest. Her hair's pulled back into a tight bun, and we both know the glasses are a fashion choice.

She looks me up and down, scowling. "What the fuck, Cass? A divinity blocker?"

"What can I say? You dropping in whenever you want doesn't work for me, sweetheart. Like right now, I'm kind of busy. Maybe we could schedule something a little later in the decade."

"Let me in."

I consider leaving her out there, but she looks ready to throw an arc at me, and since she can't, she might make a scene in the hall. I run a hand through the back of my hair as I walk to the kitchen, then I dig the pouch out from behind a bottle of scotch and take one of the crystals out.

She's in the living room when I come back. "Where's Samyaza?"

I shrug, positioning myself between her and the hallway to my bedroom. "Have we had this conversation before?"

"Cut the crap," she snaps. "I've given The Fallen a pretty long leash over the past few thousand years. All I ask is that you check in once a century and let me know when you relocate. Which none of you do, by the way."

"Yet, you always seem to find me. How exactly is that, Lydia?"

"Auction house receipts." She stares at her nails, as bored with me as I am of her. "I find the highest-priced item sold and check which sellers also signed new leases on apartments or bought a house around the same time." She cocks her head to the side, eyes back on me. "Mr. Asher van der Rohe."

Huh. Good to know, so I don't make that mistake again. Samy and I should probably stop cycling through the same names we've been using for the past hundred years too.

"Well," I say, "Samy's not here, and I haven't talked to him."

She straightens her shoulders, ready to lay down the law. "Well, either you track him down or I escalate the situation."

"What the fuck does that mean?" I spit back at her. "You going to banish us from Heaven and threaten us with an eternity of nothingness?"

Lydia starts with a comeback until her eyes cut to Hannah's bag on the floor. Her shoes by the couch. The almost-healed bite mark on my chest from earlier.

*Shit.*

"Is there someone here?" She takes a step toward the hallway, and I shake my head.

"Back off, Lydia."

"If it's a human, I need to make sure she didn't hear us." Again, she tries to get around me, but I don't budge. Her eyes roll. "Why are you…"

The door to my bedroom creaks open. I check over my shoulder and can't help but smile at Hannah walking down the hall in my T-shirt. She hesitates, seeing Lydia so close to me. The same harsh warmth from the night at the bar enters my chest. Before she jumps to conclusions and I have a pissed off Hannah on my hands, I pull her over and tuck her against my side.

"Lydia's looking for Samy," I tell her. "But since he's not here, she was just leaving."

But Lydia's not paying attention to me, her focus fully on Hannah. "A Nephilim." She whispers the word like she doesn't believe it.

Outside of The Fallen, very few angels have encountered one out in the wild. Mostly because very few angels ever set foot on Earth. It's kind of that part of town where no one goes unless they want crack, and even then, they don't tell anyone about it.

"Just. Leaving," I repeat.

Lydia blinks several times and clears her throat, straightening her already-straight skirt. "She knows about us?"

"Of course not."

Her eyes narrow at me. She doesn't buy it. "You know what? Whatever. It's not my job to care how you deal with your charge. Just find Samyaza, or next time, I won't be alone."

Lydia's gaze drifts back to Hannah. A look of wonderment returns to her face, and then she glares at me once more. In case I'm not lying, she marches out and slams the door behind her.

I go back to the kitchen, and I toss the crystal back in the bag and return it to its hiding spot. Next time, I'll let her throw a fit out in the hallway and cover her own tracks.

Hannah's propped against a counter.

"Why aren't you naked?"

She laughs as I throw her over my shoulder and carry her back to the bedroom. I let her down on the bed and grab my phone off the mattress. While I text Samy, I sit down. She comes up behind me, wrapping her arms around my neck.

"You think he'll answer?" she asks.

"No idea."

I send the message and twist around, pulling her face to mine. It only takes a few breathy sounds from her before I flip all the way around, crawling on top of her to resume where we left off. If I remember correctly, my tongue was about to be in its other favorite place.

My phone slips off the bed, landing on the floor, my text to Samy already forgotten.

*You have a week, brother. Then I come looking.*

A few nights later, Hannah falls asleep on my chest while I read through a collection of spells in another book. These specialize in enchanting objects to repel magic and look promising for a more long-term solution. I might spend an entire day chanting to pull it off, but if there's even a small chance it might work, I have to try.

My phone vibrates on the floor next to the couch. I rest the book on Hannah's back and reach down. I almost think I'm seeing things when I check the screen.

*Samy.*

I keep my voice low in the hopes of not waking her and answer, "What the hell, man?"

"Hey," he says just as quietly.

"That's it?" Hannah stirs, and I stroke her hair. "I've been trying to reach you for months."

"I know. I just haven't been in the best place lately."

I recognize this voice, low and somber. It's the one he uses when he's beating himself up on the inside.

"You have to stop doing this, brother. We're supposed to all be in this together, and we've really needed you lately. Have you at least been reading our messages?"

"Lydia's up your ass. Demons are attacking Nephilim."

"What about your charge?" I ask. "Any Lowers come after her?"

He doesn't answer right away. I'm about to lose my cool when he says, "Yeah, I've dealt with some. Look, I can't talk right now, but we should get together soon. You can catch me up on everything. Tell me what I can do to help."

"Your definition of soon or within the next decade? Because I have better shit to do than wait around for your ass to quit feeling sorry for yourself."

A soft chuckle comes through. "You're such a dick. I should have called Ros."

I smile, more relieved he's back than I'll ever admit. "Text me when you can meet up."

"Yeah, and Cass?" He pauses and then, "I'm sorry."

My eyes roll. "Screw you, asshole."

I end the call and drop the phone on the floor. My days of faking leader for the other two are over, and I couldn't be more fucking glad to hand over the position to its rightful owner.

"Why are we meeting him in a cemetery?"

"Because I need to rob a grave, Hannah."

She doubts me, narrowing her eyes on our way up the cracked concrete steps to the brick mausoleum. It's been at least a century since I've been here, and I don't remember which crypt I stowed my shit away in. This one or the one with the creepy headless cherub sitting outside. Or another cemetery altogether because I was drunk and hid everything away on a whim.

It's only been a few days since Samy called, so I have a hard time believing he'll show. Even if he doesn't, I needed to make this stop anyway.

I work the bolt over and grab one of the rusty metal bars of the door. The hinges creak and groan as I jerk it open.

"After you," I say.

Her chest rises, light entering my own, and she cautiously passes me. I bang the door shut behind us. She jumps at the clang it makes, and I smile.

She whips around, not nearly as entertained. "You did that on purpose."

I shrug and head to the tomb at the far back. My hand runs over the engraving, wiping away a buildup of cobwebs from the name. Hannah steps beside me, her hand on my arm for protection from nothing.

"Say hello to your great-great-something-or-other grandfather, Ivan." I shove on the heavy stone lid while I still have the strength from her. It grinds, stone on stone, and slowly shifts enough so that I can see in. "Shit."

"What?"

Hannah looks down, and fuck if I'm not ready for the rush of powers brought on by her scream. I yank the lid over and reseal what turns out to be the wrong coffin. The second I turn, she throws herself into my arms and clings to me. Her hands fist in the back of my shirt, her face burrowing into my chest.

"Calm down," I say, holding on to her. "It's just bones." The power boost starts to dip, so I pry her off. "I need to check the next one."

She reclaims her hold on my arm as I walk to the other side. Mother Mary Constance sounds familiar in a she'll-keep-my-shit-safe kind of way. Hannah doesn't need me to tell her to look away. Her eyes shut, her breathing shallow. The lid slides easily. Even in the poor lighting, I can see the chain of a long-forgotten amulet draped over the wrist bone of Mary Constance. I stop and pull out my phone. The rest of the stone coffin illuminates, and I've found my hiding spot.

A pulse of heat hits me. Hannah gets brave, opening her eyes. Staring down at the remains, she tightens her grip on me, but we do without the screaming this time. I carefully reach in, bypassing the black obsidian amulet and move a chalice, so I can get to the wand. Dark knots stand out against the white wood along with the designs etched into the surface. My fingers run over it, checking for any signs of damage, but I chose a good guardian.

I hand it to Hannah and double-check to see if anything else will be useful.

"What is it?" she asks.

"It's made of holly wood. Man thinks it has a connection to some goddess of the underworld, but that's bullshit. Really, it was the original tree of creation. It served as protection for the earliest forms of life. Which happens to be exactly what you need. Protection."

The amulet might be a useful object to bind the spell. I start to unwind the chain but stop. I have something better at my apartment I can use, so I decide to leave it with Mary Constance for safekeeping.

"Rest easy, sweetheart." I scrape the lid over, sealing her back in.

It's clouded over by the time I slide the metal bolt back in place. Hannah pulls her hands into the sleeves of the jacket and holds on to my arm, walking back to the bike. I check the time, and—surprise, surprise—Samy's late. I set Hannah on the bike seat sideways and stand in front of her while we wait. She pushes the bottom of my shirt up with the end of the wand, dragging the tip across my stomach.

"Casting a spell?" I ask.

She bites her lip. "Can you feel it?"

Her eyes lift, and I feel something, but it's not a fucking spell.

I pull my vibrating phone out of my pocket and answer with, "Let me guess. You're not coming."

"Something came up." Samy's voice sounds muffled.

Hannah's distracting me with her wand-play, so I walk back toward the crypt. "Anything serious?"

"No. Nothing like that. What if I take you out for a drink next week?"

"After blowing me off, you'd better make it a whole damn bottle if you want me to show."

"Sounds like a plan," he says. "Hey, I meant to ask the other day about your charge. She still a complete pain in the ass?"

"No, man. She's…" I stop, turning back around.

# FALLEN REBEL

Hannah's lying on the seat, back against the gas tank, staring at the clouds above. Her dark red hair hangs over the side, her fingers running over the white wood of the wand.

"Let's just say you have a lot of catching up to do."

"I'll text you the when and where."

Hannah turns her head as I approach and sits up. "So, what's the—"

My lips capture hers, my hand cupping her face. So that we don't get carried away and make another visit to MC in the mausoleum, I pull back sooner than I want.

She stares at me, her eyes sparkling. "What was that for?"

I half-smile and shrug. "It's that fucking spell."

Her nose wrinkles, and she laughs, and I feel it. Hannah Kelley and her sexy-ass light-bringing magic.

# TWENTY-FOUR

## *HANNAH*

A week after the cemetery, Cass plans to meet Samy again at a bar near campus. He drops me off at my afternoon linguistics class before he goes, and as I pull the helmet off, he dangles my alligator keychain from his finger.

"Hey," I say. "I've been looking for that."

"I know. I stole it." He tucks it in my bag and tugs me over to him, expression hard. "Stay in the lecture hall until I come back."

I blow out a breath. It's been weeks since I've gone anywhere without him other than my room and his apartment. We're ready for some space, both feeling a little suffocated.

"We're almost there, baby." His arm snakes around to my lower back. "I just need to find a way to make my powers exempt from the spell. Then we can stop pretending we aren't driving each other fucking crazy." He kisses me. "We're going to fight over all those stupid candles you have around the apartment." Another kiss. "And all the hair crap in my bathroom." One more with tongue. "Then I'm going to kick you out until you beg to come back."

I smile, backing away. "Can't wait."

He waits to drive off until I turn around at the door. A minute ago, I desperately wanted a second alone, but I immediately feel on edge without him here. I distract myself with my phone on the way down the hall, not paying attention when I walk into the lecture hall. As I descend the steps, someone runs into me.

"Shit," he says, also looking up from his phone. "Sorry. Are you okay?"

It's as much my fault as his, but I nod. We both glance down at his hand on my arm.

He snatches it back and steps aside. "Sorry. Again."

"It's fine, really." I pass him and go down a few more rows, finding an empty aisle seat.

The professor walks in shortly after. I partially listen while Cass texts me updates of his solo mission. He's in a good mood—for him anyway. The closer he comes to figuring out this spell, the more he seems to relax.

I get another message while I jot down notes about our research assignment due in two weeks. It's our final, a ten-page paper counting for a third of our grade that Dr. Stine could have given us a little longer to work on. A second and third text have come through by the time I check my phone.

*Might be a few minutes late.*

*Stay there.*

*I mean it.*

Because he usually jokes around about these things.

Everyone else files out while I wait. The room empties, except for the professor and the guy from earlier. He slows down on his way up the stairs, a hand running through his dark blond hair, and comes to a full stop in the aisle a few rows down.

"Lose the will to go on after hearing the requirements for that paper?" he asks.

I shake my head. "No, I'm waiting for someone."

He looks down at the middle-aged man with pit stains and a receding hairline at the front of the otherwise empty room, then he quirks a brow. "Hot date?"

"Ew," I say, mildly offended by his accusation. "No. He's not here yet."

He lifts his hands in mock surrender. "All right, calm down. You wouldn't be the first girl to go after a guy twice her age." He looks back at the professor again. "Or more."

I laugh, not quite sure what to make of this guy. He has one of those faces, familiar and immediately puts you at ease. Kind eyes, pouty lips.

"I'm doing this backward," he says. "I should tell the pretty girl my name's Sean before insulting her. Then maybe she'd tell me her name is…"

"Hannah."

"Hannah." He repeats my name like he's said it a million times. "And you're waiting for…"

"My boyfriend."

He gives a tight-lipped smile, nodding. "Let me guess. Tough guy. Rides a motorcycle. Would kick my ass without a second thought for hitting on you?"

"It's like you've met him."

"Nah. I saw him drop you off earlier." He climbs another step. "Tell me the truth. Can I take him?"

I laugh again, shaking my head. Despite the muscular build, Cass would destroy him with or without his powers.

"Well, good thing I never hit on you then." He winks, continuing past me. "See ya around, Hannah."

I glance back as he walks out. When I face forward, Dr. Stine's no longer at the front of the room. He must have gone out the other door. Being completely alone with only the keychain sends a chill through me. Hell, I don't even know how it works. If it works.

*Where are you?* I send to Cass.

The seconds drag out, my anxiety rising with each passing one until I can't stand it anymore. I snatch my bag and hurry up the stairs, forcing myself to look straight ahead. Almost at the top, a hand grabs my arm from behind. I gasp, spinning around.

Cass cocks his head at me. "Going somewhere?"

I clutch my chest. "Jesus, you scared me."

"*I* scared *you*?" He holds out his glowing palm and faces it toward the ceiling.

"Sorry. I worried the keychain wouldn't work if a demon attacked."

His hand flips over and settles on my arm. The light grows brighter and brighter until I have to look away. Other than his hot skin, I can't feel anything. No sparks. No tingling. Nothing.

He lets go and waits for me to look at him. "I wouldn't leave you unless I knew you were safe. You know that, right?"

I nod, embarrassed for not trusting him. It may be my life on the line, but in the grand scheme of things, Cass has more to lose. "So, how was Samy?"

Cass follows me up the steps. "No idea. He bailed."

I pause at the door. "Then why were you late?"

His shoulder shrugs. "I wanted to finish my drink with Carl before dealing with you again."

As he pushes past me, I get a grin, his arm hooking around my waist. He holds me tight against his side on our way down the hall, and I relax more than I have since he left me an hour ago. Even after he finds a permanent solution, this is the protection I'll always want. Him.

Terra and Jesse twisted my arm into staying at the house they're renting for the summer. Knowing her, she'll want to go shopping for all the knickknacks and junk we won't need ahead of moving in, which will eat up plenty of my time in the coming weeks. Between that, packing the dorm room, and studying for my other finals, I want to knock out this paper as fast as possible. So, Cass comes with me to the library, so I can get a start on it.

He settles in at the table next to me with another one of his books that historians would die to get their hands on. I dive into a stack of resources I've collected. A few hours later, I check my pile, not finding what I need. I stand up, and his hand runs up the back of my leg.

"And where the hell do you think you're going?" Cass asks, not looking away from his page.

"I thought I'd grabbed the book on dead languages, but it's not here."

His hand leaves my leg and picks the keychain off the table. "Don't die." He glances up, a dimple appearing.

God, I'll never *not* go a little weak from that. I take it and head up the stairs and to the back of the library. The shelves tower high over my head, most of the books back here infrequently used. Once I turn down the aisle, I quickly find the one I need, set on top of the others on the shelf. I must have put it down and forgotten to pick it up again.

I'm flipping through the pages, head down, and I collide with someone rounding the corner.

"Shit," he says.

And it's déjà vu, only the hand on my arm moves away faster this time.

Sean's eyebrows shoot up. "You realize running into each other is just an expression, right?"

I laugh and shrug. "I'm a literal type of person."

He tilts his head to the side, reading the spine of the book I'm holding. "Let me guess. You're getting a head start on Stine's paper too?"

"It's that or not sleep for three days, trying to finish on time."

A smile forms, his deep blue eyes softening even more. "Here I thought acting like an overachiever would save me from fighting over research materials."

He must be after the same book.

"I only need to look up a few things," I say. "Want me to find you when I'm finished with it?"

"Nah. I'll come back for it tomorrow. I have a few others I managed to beat you to." He steps aside and gestures for me to walk by. "Whenever I walk around a corner from now on, I'll call out. Just in case you're anywhere near me."

I smile on my way past him. "I'll be listening for the warning then."

A few rows from the stairs, an arm darts out at me. Cass pulls me into a dark corner and pins me between him and a bookcase. "You took too long."

"There are other people up here." My objection sounds less than convincing with his tongue trailing across my skin.

He grips my ass and grinds against me. "I don't care."

"I do." I sound more in control than I feel, but it must be enough because he groans and slows his movements.

"How much longer until we can go home?"

My belly flips at the way he says *home.* "Thirty minutes?"

He straightens, studying my face like I might change my mind. "Twenty, or I'm screwing you in the restroom."

Not doubting him, I hurry back to the table. His hand creeps higher and higher on my thigh the entire time even though his eyes are on his book. By the time he reaches the top and strokes my pussy through the fabric, I can't concentrate and finish a few minutes early. He practically carries me out the door.

We haven't made it far across the poorly lit parking lot when Cass yanks me toward him. I assume it's him not being patient enough to wait until we get back to his apartment, but his eyes sweep over the lot. His shoulders tense, and then the air shifts. An electricity surrounds us.

I look down at Cass's glowing palm, sparks crackling.

*Demon.*

The figure steps out of a shadow by a truck, slowly stalking toward us. My heart takes off as I watch the blackness from my nightmares spiral around him and disappear into his hands.

Bringing me around to his side, Cass keeps most of his body between the man and me. I look the other way, and my grip on his shirt tightens.

"Cass," I say, as another slinks out from behind a lamppost.

Cass glances over and moves me behind him, backing us closer to the building.

"Hannah." His voice is rough, commanding. "The keychain."

A third demon appears. They all move toward us, sinister smiles unfolding.

I shove a hand into my purse, digging around for the alligator keychain keeping Cass's powers from working on me. As my fingers graze over it, he jerks me to the side. A fireball narrowly misses him, hissing on its way past us. The key ring slips through my fingers. I fumble for it, losing it in the bottom of my bag.

*Fuck it.*

I throw the purse on the ground. Cass spins around, turning his back on the three fireballs flying toward us. He wraps his arms around me, but they're so close.

Heat thrashes around me, white light, and I'm not in the parking lot.

Cass isn't holding on to me anymore. The room I'm in is large and empty with plastic sheeting hanging down and broken windows along one wall. Before I figure out where he left me, searing pain rips up my arm. Burn marks streak across my right forearm, four of them less than an inch apart. The sting intensifies, almost as if whatever burned me is still being held against my skin.

The pain keeps coming. I fall to my knees and cradle the injured arm with the other. Blackness begins rising out of the wound—only this time, it's real, and I can't wake up to make it go away.

"Fuck." Cass says this from behind me but suddenly appears in front of me. His clothes are torn, more of his skin covered in burns than not, but he doesn't seem to care. He lowers onto the floor with me and grabs my arm. "Close your eyes, baby. I have no idea if this will work or not."

I do as told, only seeming to be able to breathe out and not in. The light becomes so bright through my eyelids that I lower my head to further shield my eyes. It has a sound, too, a hum that travels through my core. The burning lessens, a different type of heat replacing it, the familiar one of Cass's hands and his skin on mine. Slowly, the light fades, and all I feel is him.

Cass pulls me onto his lap and grasps the sides of my face, so I look at him. "Tell me you're okay."

I don't even check until after I've nodded. Only a slight redness appears on the flesh of my arm now, no sign of injury otherwise. But an aching sensation remains, like my mind hasn't let go of the pain yet. Or maybe it's the fear.

I throw my arms around his neck, trembling and afraid to let him go again. There's more heat and light, and then we're in his room. On the bed. In the same position we were on the floor of wherever we were.

"You're okay," Cass says, but I think it's more for him than me.

I remember his burns then. My hands frantically run down to the bottom of his singed shirt, and I yank it over his head. All the scorch marks are already gone—like they never existed. A relieved sob bursts out of me, and I press my palms against his fiery skin, his chest heaving beneath them. We stare at each other for a few ragged breaths, and then he's on me. Hands, mouth, his body crashing us back on the bed. It's frantic. Both of us tearing at our clothes, desperate to feel what only we provide for each other. His touch. My heartbeat.

We're far beyond taking what we want. This is about giving what the other needs. And above all else in Heaven or Hell or whatever else there is, I need Cass.

Maybe even more than he needs me.

# TWENTY-FIVE

## CASS

The demons aren't screwing around anymore. They shot for Hannah while I was with her and even fought me when I went back after dropping her at the warehouse. Nowhere is safe unless it's been spelled. Which means it's all I can do to stand outside Hannah's class the next day, watching her through the crystal ball. My focus stays on her and every inch of air surrounding her and on not storming in and carrying her out and locking her in my apartment until I finish figuring out this fucking spell.

I stretch my fingers, letting out a stream of light. Hannah's anxiety is running as high as mine. But I guess getting lanced with a fireball and seeing the darkness leech out of your skin has that effect on mortals. At least now I know the light can destroy it and heal any wounds it leaves her. A fact they could have included in the fucking Nephilim owner's manual rather than forcing me to use my girlfriend as a guinea pig.

She's the first one out of the room, every part of her relaxing when she sees me. I keep some kind of contact with her until her next class. I can't *not* touch her. Not after last night.

The vicious torment of waiting and watching resumes with her next class and the next. By the end of the day, we're both so stressed that she doesn't even ask to stop at the dorms before going to the apartment. The door shuts behind us, and the tension releases from my body. She's here, where nothing can hurt her. I can breathe.

It starts over again the next day, only a phone call from Chaz makes it all the worse.

Four demons cornered one of his charges while he was skydiving with the other. With the adrenaline pumping in Kai, he almost missed it, arriving as one teleported with Avery. He caught up with them before they went through the portal. Epic battle unfolded. He saved her. But barely.

Samy's next. A text two days later. Three in an elevator. We agree not to try to reschedule our little reunion until shit calms down. It sucks because, when everything goes to hell, he's the one I want with me more than anyone.

Except for Hannah.

I don't even question why Rosdan is calling two days later. The demons' pattern isn't exactly subtle.

A shrill whine comes through the speaker. I pull the phone away from my ear until it stops, and Rosdan finally says, "Demons."

Hannah's on the couch between my legs, leaning back against my chest while she works on her paper. I ease her forward and crawl out from behind her. "How many?"

"Three." He's out of breath. "We were at the fucking park, Cass. Nannies everywhere."

I switch to the Angelic language, not wanting to scare Hannah. "Everyone all right?"

"I had to wipe a few memories, and Alistair fell, skinned up his knee." He sounds more distraught with the ouchie than the rest. Chaz was right about him being a good mommy.

I already know the answer but ask anyway, "All Lowers?"

"Yeah. But there was something off about the whole thing."

"What do you mean?" I sit back down on the couch, moving my hand to Hannah's leg.

She gives me a wicked smile, light entering my chest along with it.

I almost forget I'm on the phone until Rosdan says, "I have a new theory about the reasons for the attacks." He pauses. "You're going to think I'm crazy for even suggesting it."

"Probably, but tell me anyway."

"They went straight after Alistair, bypassing the three baby Nephilim completely."

"So?" I ask.

"So, if they want to kill one of my charges, what does it matter which one? And if it turns out all of this is for some ritual and they need blood, a baby would be easier to manage than a ten-year-old. It was like they needed him specifically for some reason."

"Make your point, Armaros."

Ros takes a deep breath. "What if they want a Nephilim to read from the Book of the Speech from God?"

"No." I shake my head, refusing to even entertain the idea for a second. "Nephilim knowing the language of creation is an urban legend. Nobody's spoken it since the last reboot on Earth. Hell, we were there, Ros. We read directly from the Book of the Speech from God, and I can barely remember any of it."

"Yeah, like I said, crazy." He pauses a beat. "You any closer on enchanting that ring you were working on?"

I glance at Hannah, but even if she could hear, she wouldn't understand him. "I think if I tweak it just a little more, I'll be ready to chant."

He sighs, relieved. "Thank God, man. I already have blocking spells on the house, Mark's car, his office, and his work's gym. He doesn't go many other places, but not having to panic when he does will be nice for once."

I don't envy him or Chaz and their multiple charges. Handling the attacks on Hannah is more than enough for me.

"I'll let you know when it's done," I say.

My phone lands on the coffee table, and I crawl up Hannah, sliding her laptop to the floor. Her legs open for me, and I go straight for her chest. I push up her shirt and run my tongue over the swell of her tits. She lets out a sexy, breathy sound. "So, what's the language of creation?"

I plan on ignoring her until I fully process what she asked. Then I go cold, slowly looking up at her.

"What did you just say?"

"This language I'm supposed to know. The language of creation. What is it?"

She skims her hands under my shirt, but I pull them away. Did I accidentally switch back to English without realizing it? It's the only explanation, unless…

"You can understand me?" I ask in the Angelic language.

She nods. "Why wouldn't I?"

"Because only other angels should."

I'm on my feet, digging through her bag on the floor for a pen and paper. Rosdan can't be right. He just can't. We all thought the rumors about the Nephilim and the language of creation were as true as the "fact" that they eat humans. But if Hannah inherently knows the language of the angels, it might be real.

*Fuck.* For so many reasons, *fuck.*

I drop onto the floor between the couch and coffee table, pulling her down with me.

"Cass, what's going on?" She leans over, watching me as I draw symbols on the paper.

"The BOSG was written in the language of creation. We used it to create everything on Earth." I set the notebook on the coffee table in front of her. "Read that."

Her eyes linger on mine. A hint of light precedes them lowering to the page. And then she fucking starts reading it—a language no mortal has ever spoken. The symbols on the paper begin glowing, the ink releasing the white dust I haven't seen in over four thousand years. It lifts from the page, and Hannah gasps, clinging to my arm. The dust swirls around and dances in the air in front of us until it begins to take shape. Just the outline at first, but soon the rest weaves together, forming the intricate design of a butterfly's wing.

"Holy fuck," Hannah whispers, her nails digging into my skin, her light pulsing through me.

"Holy fuck is right." My hand waves through the dust, and it all falls back onto the table. I push off the floor, leaving her staring at what was almost a butterfly. I rub the back of my neck and pace.

If this means what I think it means, we're so far beyond fucked.

There are only two uses for the Book of the Speech from God. Hannah just demonstrated the first—creation. The other's exactly what you would expect.

The story of Noah was completely made up, his ark and animals two by two. The only things saved back then were removed and then returned to Earth later.

Because when you read from the second half of the BOSG, nothing and no one on Earth survives.

Unless you're immortal.

Hannah stands in the middle of the living room. "What does this mean?"

I stop and look at her. "It means I need to go see Ros."

I'm waiting in living room number two of Rosdan's charge's house when a small person with a brown mop on his head walks down the stairs.

"Alistair, this is my brother Cass."

The kid pauses at the end of the couch and gives me a once-over, sitting down. "You two don't look alike."

"Adopted." I toss the notebook with the symbols drawn in it on the cushions between us. "What does that say?"

He checks with Rosdan, pushing up the glasses sliding down his nose.

Rosdan nods at him. "Just try to read it."

Alistair looks at the paper, focused as his eyes examine the symbols. Then, just like Hannah, he begins flawlessly speaking the language of creation. Alistair sits back, mouth wide open while watching the divine light shine from the page, rising up and beginning the act of creating a butterfly. The anxiety seeps from Rosdan, and he steps closer, putting a protective hand on Alistair's shoulder.

"Did I do that?" the boy asks, staring up at him.

This time, I wait, desperate for the light to fizzle out or the butterfly to lose form. But soon a blue-and-black butterfly flaps its wings for the first time, coming to life. Brought into existence by a ten-year-old boy less than a minute ago.

Rosdan and I exchange a look. He kneels next to Alistair, carefully holding his face in his hands. "Ali, you won't remember reading anything or seeing the butterfly form. Okay?"

An innocent smile appears, and he nods. "Okay, Ros."

Rosdan playfully roughs up the kid's hair as he stands, but his face stays grim.

Once Alistair's eyes refocus, they go straight to the butterfly fluttering around the room. "Hey, Ros, look."

Rosdan turns, acting surprised. "How'd that guy get in here?"

Alistair's already on his feet, running toward the kitchen. "I'll get the net from the garage."

He disappears, and Rosdan collapses on the cushions where he was sitting. His head falls back, and he lets out a deep sigh. "We're so fucked, Kasdaye. The fucking BOSG?"

I check on Hannah with the crystal ball. She's at the kitchen counter, typing away on her paper. Maybe this is where her interest in linguistics stems from. Her ability to pick up languages with little effort must come from the dormant Nephilim powers.

"It's still only a theory." I drag my attention away from the globe. "We have no real reason to believe them attacking the boy instead of the babies and Nephilim being able to read from the book are connected."

"Right." Rosdan stares at the ceiling, his knee bouncing. "Even if the demons did figure this out and somehow got their hands on the book, they love Earth. What would they gain from undoing creation?"

"Nothing. At this point, all of this is more than likely a coincidence." I watch Hannah a little longer and add, "And until we have a reason to believe otherwise, we're keeping this between us."

That brings Ros's head back up, a look of concern on his face. "Cass, Chaz and Samy deserve to know. All of our eternities are on the line here. And we need to tell Lydia, so—"

"No." I shake my head, not willing to bend on this. "Remember the last time the Nephilim became a complication? They won't hesitate to finish off the entire race if they become a problem again."

It's why I never mentioned the demon attacks to Lydia in the first place—the possibility of them deeming the Nephilim a risk to God's plan and destroying them. I can't lose Hannah. No matter how selfish that makes me, I don't care. I'll sacrifice every fucking one of us if it means protecting her.

Rosdan glances over as Alistair rushes back in with a butterfly net and a giant grin on his face. He gets to his feet, heading straight to the butterfly on the wall, just out of reach of the boy's swinging net. He reaches up and gently cups it in his hands to bring it to Alistair's level. They peek at it and then go release it outside.

There's a deep understanding in Rosdan's eyes when he comes back. The connection he feels with his charges may not be the same as the one I share with Hannah, but it's real and unwavering.

He nods, watching the kid dash up the stairs. "It stays between us."


By the time I'm ready to drop back to the apartment, Hannah's finished working on her paper. She's still at the kitchen counter, laptop open while she watches a horror movie. The opening credits are still flashing on the screen when the fridge kicks on, and she jumps. I drop in behind her and startle her again, wrapping my arms around her. She sighs and sinks back into me. I press my nose to her neck. My eyes close, and I forget where I am. Surrounded by Hannah and flowers. It feels like I'm finally home.

"Stay here," I whisper against her skin.

"Tonight?" she asks.

I breathe her in and breathe out, "Forever."

The word comes out of nowhere, but I've never meant one more. I hate the thought of her not being with me, of losing this feeling when she's gone. Even for a second. Because Hannah Kelley is stubborn as hell, annoying as shit, and sexy as fuck. All at once. All the time.

She's everything.

And fuck if I'm not devastatingly in love with her.

# TWENTY-SIX

## *HANNAH*

It takes Cass over a week after his visit with Rosdan to finish the spell. He immerses himself in it. Barely sleeping or eating. At first, he takes breaks, so he can watch me during classes, but that stops after my last final. A few days later, when I wake up, he's finally figured out the missing piece that will leave him and his powers exempt. I ask what it is, and he smirks.

"You'll find out."

Those are the last words he speaks. To me anyway.

That night, I come out from my shower, and he's stretched out on the bed, arm over his face, his lips moving. He's been chanting for twelve hours straight. I crawl under the blankets and cuddle in beside him. He slips his arm around me, and with my head on his chest, I feel the words vibrating. It's relaxing at this point. His hushed voice repeating the same rhythmic syllables over and over again.

I'm almost asleep when his lips press against my temple. They go straight back to chanting, then kiss me again during the pause he takes between each incantation. He grasps my chin, tilting my face up. His lips brush mine on the break and stay there through the verse, so he can kiss me before the next one.

Mouth still on mine, Cass nudges me over onto my back. He braces himself on his forearm, one hand staying by my head, fist clenched around something he's been holding ever since he started chanting. The other slips under my tank top. His mouth moves farther down, speaking the words against my neck.

I glide my hands over the muscles of his back, his skin warming faster as he trails his fingers back and forth along the top of my panties. He rubs his erection against my hip, up and down. It sends a surge of heat through me, and I need him inside me. While I shove down his sweatpants, his voice grows huskier. He impatiently tugs at my shorts and underwear with one hand until I slide them off the rest of the way.

Cass drags his fingers through my wet center and positions himself between my legs. Before he pushes inside of me, he stops. I try to pull him the rest of the way, but he won't budge, dark eyes staring down at me and cock brushing my eager pussy. Feeling him barely touch me, I whimper—so close to what I want that it's almost painful. Each time I lift, he retreats to keep minimal contact. I'm drenched and a second away from begging when, on the offbeat of his cadence, he thrusts forward.

I gasp, my eyes rolling back in my head. His shut for a second, and then he drives into me again. He's rough, fucking me to the rhythm of his chanting. My nails scrape over the blazing skin of his biceps while he owns my body. Then he pulls out and flips me, putting me on my hands and knees.

I look over my shoulder, and he grabs his shaft. He lines up and slides back inside me, slow enough I feel every inch stretching until he fills me. Even without him moving, I'm panting, and I grind back against him.

"Fuck me, Cass." I shiver, feeling his hot palm rove over my skin, but then it disappears, his cock retreating. "Please, fuck—"

He smacks my ass, and I choke off on a moan as he thrusts. The heat intensifies while he grasps my hip and pounds into me. His words come faster and faster with every desperate sound from me.

The hand he's kept fisted hits the mattress next to mine, and his blistering skin covers my back. He keeps pumping, bringing his fingers to my clit. Heat bombards me, outside and inside, and my entire body lights up. I come so hard, my vision whites like when we drop, the pleasure splintering through me.

Cass's breath is heavy in my ear, his voice gravelly and low. I feel it in every part of me. He forces out the words through clenched teeth and ruts into me as deep as he can. His muscles jerk as he releases inside me, and then he stills.

He drops his forehead onto my shoulder but only stays for a second. I'm still coming down from an incredible high when he pulls and leaves me on the bed. He comes back with a washcloth, but then he walks away again.

I roll onto my side, my skin cooling. "Where are you going?"

Lips still moving, he gives me a satisfied grin and swipes his phone from the nightstand on his way to the bathroom. Not long after the shower turns on, I get a text.

> *I needed to infuse enough of my light with the spell to make me exempt. That should have done it.*

I sigh, reading the message. Leave it to Cass to find a way to incorporate sex into the spell.

I clean up and find my discarded clothes before I stretch back out.

Even though he's not in the room anymore, I can still hear the words. Over and over again.

The mattress dips, and my eyes flutter open. Cass sits on the edge of the bed, staring down at me like I'm the stars.

"Hi," he says.

His gaze continues tracing my face while I smile at him. "You're finished chanting?"

"I am. And if this spell didn't work, you're just going to have to die because I'm never chanting again."

"Sounds fair." I shift up on the mattress, and he leans over, propping himself on his elbow beside me. "Now can I see what's in your hand?"

One side of his mouth turns up, and there's that dimple. "I needed to enchant something you can wear all the time. Nothing gaudy or easily broken." He holds his closed fist in front of me. "I thought you might want it to be this."

After a second, his hand opens. I draw in a ragged breath at the sight of something I thought I would never see again. In the center of his palm lies my mother's wedding ring. Swallowing hard, I slowly reach for it. Afraid it will disappear if I move too fast. But then I touch it, and it's real. It's here. A white gold band with an inscription on the inside.

"Where did you find it?" My voice shakes.

"At the crash site, along with Brice's." His expression is soft, the gentleness he rarely shows peeking through. "I meant to drop them in the Colorado house for you to find. When you sold it, I tossed them in with a few other artifacts and forgot about them."

My focus returns to the ring still held between my thumb and finger. "Mom was paranoid after she watched some documentary that probably had no basis in reality. She insisted they wear them on chains around their necks whenever they traveled. Dad went along with it, claiming it was cheaper than therapy for her delusions..." I smile and look at him. "You already know all of this."

Cass nods and holds his hand out, so I give him back the ring. He picks up my hand and softly kisses the space between my knuckles. He slides the band on my finger. It stops right where his lips were, and his eyes flit to mine. When he smiles, I know I'm exactly where I'm supposed to be. Everything that's happened feels worth it for this one moment with him.

He sits up and opens the drawer on the nightstand and pulls out a silver chain. Dangling from it is my dad's ring. I don't hesitate to grab it this time. My eyes go straight for the inscription, needing proof it's really his, really the match to my mom's. And it is.

*A forever's worth of forevers.*

Cass leans over again and rests his arm on the other side of me. "I checked the chain. There's no damage, so you can wear it if you want."

He's right. The chain and the ring are perfect. Exactly as I remember them.

I lean forward and slide the chain over his head. It drops down onto his neck, the ring hanging right in front of his heart. Now, it's exactly where it should be.

He's watching me when I look up, more relaxed than I've seen him in weeks. He flips off the light and brushes his lips over mine while crawling over me. I lie back down, rolling onto my side to face him with his arm under my head.

"The inscription doesn't make sense, you know." He pushes my hair back, and my eyes adjust, so I can see him in the dark. "Forever is forever. There's only one."

"What should it say then?"

His forehead presses to mine. "You're my forever."

I stop breathing when he kisses me. His lips are gentle, sealing the words between us.

Forever's a real thing for Cass. He understands what it truly means. Forever is forever. There's only one. And I have no doubt that he is mine.

# TWENTY-SEVEN

## *CASS*

The chances of demons killing my girlfriend should be at an all-time low with the ring. Even so, I'm not too keen on testing that theory. My light still works on her, which I prove with an in-the-heat-of-the-moment hand mark on her ass. Right now, the rest is a potentially disastrous mystery, so we keep close to the apartment for a while. It works out since her summer classes won't start for another few weeks.

The night before her birthday, we're living it up on the couch. She's lying on my chest and supposed to be choosing a movie. I agreed to whatever she wants so long as it counts as her gift. But given the way her fingers inch down my torso, she's interested in another outline of my hand more than a romcom. I'm about to accommodate when my damn phone starts ringing. I pick it off the floor, seriously considering a change in number.

"What?" I bark at Rosdan.

"I need you at the house. *Now.*"

That's all he says before the line goes dead. The panic in his voice is enough to have me sitting straight up. It pushes Hannah to the other side of the couch.

"What's wrong?" she asks.

I scoop her up, and two strides have us to the sliding door of the balcony.

"Wait." She glances over my shoulder into the living room as I carry her outside. "What are you doing?"

"I'm really sorry about this, baby." Without any other warning, I thrust her out over the railing.

"Cass!" She scrambles to hold on to me, desperate not to plummet the two stories to the concrete below.

I dangle her at arm's length until the light slams into my chest, and then I reel her back in. She clings to me, and we're already dropping. Solid ground reappears beneath my feet. It's dark and quiet other than Hannah's rapid breathing. The second she touches the floor, she shoves me in the chest, trying to get away from me. I hold on to her and press my lips to hers in apology.

"I'm sorry," I whisper. "Rosdan needs me. I couldn't wait."

I kiss her once more and lead her out of Ros's room. He lives in the guesthouse a hundred feet from the main house, with an extra bedroom, living area, and kitchen all to himself. My arm stays tight around Hannah on our way across the large backyard. The kitchen lights are on, no one inside. I open the patio door, but when I try to walk in, my body refuses to move over the threshold.

I fish out my phone and call Rosdan.

"Are you there?" he asks.

"Stuck at the door," I say. "Where do you hide your blocker bag?"

Rosdan appears in the kitchen by the marble island. He reaches into the top of a cupboard and pulls down a black velvet pouch. We really are predictable. After he pulls out a crystal and disengages the spell, I step inside without issue. The bag lands on the counter as Rosdan rushes over.

"Thank fuck." He hugs me. It only takes a second for him to let go, quickly remembering which brother he called, then he drops out of the kitchen, no longer in front of me.

I bring the phone back to my ear and shut the door behind Hannah. "You there?"

"Demons attacked Mark," he says while a voice gives an announcement in the background. "When they couldn't get in the car, one landed on the hood. I got there just as he crashed into a light post. He's alive. Scarlett too. I already dropped them at the hospital, but I need to stay here at least until I can throw a spell on the emergency room."

I groan. If the dad's in the hospital along with the mom and Ros can't leave his charge unattended, there's only one reason he would have called me.

"I don't do kids, Armaros."

"Please, Cass. They're all asleep. You literally just need to listen through the baby monitor."

*Fuck.*

"You owe me," I say. "Spell the room and get back here."

"Thank you, brother."

I pocket my phone, not at all looking forward to the next few hours. "Any experience in babysitting?"

Hannah ignores me, arms crossed over her chest.

I'm plenty warm with light as I secure my arms around her. "Still mad?"

Her eyes narrow. "You dangled me off the balcony. Yeah, I'm mad."

My hands cup her ass while I kiss her. "What about now?"

She sighs and is about to forgive me until she looks behind me. "We have company."

I look back at Alistair in the doorway.

"You're Ros's brother," he says.

So much for them all being asleep. I take a step toward him, but Hannah tugs on my hand, stopping me.

"What are you going to do to him?"

I shrug. "Ritualistic sacrifice?"

She slaps me in the chest, not in the mood, and walks by me to introduce herself to the kid. He looks at me like I'm supposed to give him the go-ahead to talk to her. *Great.* He's imprinted on me like a damn baby bird.

In all the time I've spent watching Hannah, I only recall once or twice where she was around children. The one time I witnessed someone try to hand her a baby, she made a face and shook her head. She surprised me when she showed interest in having them. I assumed it was just her being stubborn.

It only takes a minute for Alistair to stop checking with me every time she says anything. Then they're raiding the freezer for ice cream, and I'm following them into the living room. Somehow, I end up on the couch between them, Hannah under my arm on one side and the kid on the other.

"We're not supposed to watch TV in here," he says, picking up the remote and turning it on. "Or eat."

A rebel. Watching TV and eating ice cream in a room meant purely for decoration and not actual living. He turns on some show about storage units. People buy them or sell them or live in them. I don't fucking know. Hannah has a spoon in and out of her mouth; I can't be expected to pay attention to shit.

The episode ends an hour later. As much as I want to send the boy to bed, Hannah's snuggled against my chest. So, when his eyes peer at me from behind his black-rimmed glasses for permission to watch another, I nod.

We're most of the way through the third one, some guy bidding because he swears he sees a Les Paul guitar hidden amid the junk of the dark storage unit, and a cry comes through the monitor on the end table.

Hannah sits up right away. "I'll check on them."

"Afraid of what I'll do to them?" I ask.

"Yes."

I look over my shoulder, watching her walk through the living room. I consider leaving the kid to fend for himself and chasing her upstairs to find one of the many empty rooms. But I never get the chance.

Light surges in my chest. On instinct, I grab on to Alistair and drop us to Hannah on the stairs. A second later, all three of us land back by the couch.

Hannah searches the room in a panic. "Demon?"

The shake in her voice adds to the power pumping through me. I nod, releasing her, and turn my attention to Alistair.

I grasp his face, and as soon as his eyes haze, I say, "You won't make a sound and won't try to run away."

I let him go and reach for Hannah, but she's not beside me anymore. She's dashing across the living room to the stairway.

"Goddamn it, Hannah!"

"The triplets," she says.

I'm about to go after her again when a portal opens between us. Three forms appear all at once, fireballs drawn. I get off an arc and catch Alistair's arm, dropping us out of the way. We land a few feet away, and the fire crashes into the television.

Hannah's almost at the top of the stairs. One of the demons starts turning toward her, so I throw another bolt to regain his attention. It strikes him, sending him flying toward the kitchen. He vanishes and reappears with the other two. With all three of them in sight, I swipe the baby monitor off the table next to me and shove it into Alistair's hand. The glow breaks through my skin, sparks spitting from my palms and ready to attack while we stand off. They want me to move first, and I will … but not yet. It takes a few seconds for the creak of the door opening in the nursery to come through the speaker next to me.

Here's hoping that ring fucking works.

The second the door upstairs shuts, I send a charge out from both palms, nailing two of the demons right in the chests and blowing them back. It's a juggling act after that. One demon pops up here while another attacks from over there. But I move milliseconds faster, always ahead. They're not smart. Patterns quickly emerge.

The one with the crooked nose that I name Hank lunges for Alistair after every third attack. Gabe Two—yes, I went there— ropes the darkness farther to the left anytime he plans to throw a fireball with his right. Bobby's eyes always land on his target before he teleports, meaning I have a bolt waiting for him every time he lands.

Alistair stays next to me for most of the fight. One time, I toss him in the air, get in a cheap shot on Gabe Two, and am back to catch him. His fingers stay tight around the baby monitor, which conveniently has a camera I can see Hannah through. She's backed against a crib, eyes on the door.

Demons are tough to kill. It can be done with enough light, but they usually give up and crawl back to the pits long before then. Not these though. They take every blast and come back for more with the dark shadows spiraling out of their wounds. I've never seen any hold out for this long, let alone a group of them.

They realize I'm anticipating their moves and switch up the attacks. It's harder and harder to predict which one will do what. But fuck if I'll let a bunch of Lowers throwing flaming balls of darkness outsmart me.

All at once, we come to a stop. Another fucking standoff, them on one side of the trashed living room and Alistair and me on the other at the base of the stairs. The only sound comes from the discharge humming out of my flaring palms. Which means the cry comes through the speaker crystal clear, followed by Hannah.

"Shh," she says. "You're okay."

The six eyes in front of me shoot to the monitor, the sound of her voice like a magnet. I can feel it shift. All their minds go to the same place at once.

*Fuck.* This fight is about to move upstairs.

Bobby's eyes dart above my head, verifying it. I grip the back of Alistair's shirt, but just before I drop, a fully glowing Rosdan appears on the other side of him.

"About fucking time," I hiss.

He winks at Alistair and hurls a lightning bolt at the demon cluster. It blasts them back into a really expensive-looking china hutch that somehow survived round one. Mine strikes Bobby after he teleports across the room. Gabe Two launches a fireball, and Rosdan and I drop simultaneously, him taking Alistair. We land side by side behind the demon and both latch on to him, drowning him in light. His head falls back, his mouth opening as darkness floods out of him, trying to escape the divinity. He goes limp, and we let him slump onto the floor.

It's as close to killing Gabe as I'll ever get, and it's beautiful.

By the time I see Bobby look at the stairs, he vanishes. I'm right behind him, landing in the nursery before he orients himself. He's right behind Hannah. She hasn't even processed me a few feet in front of her when he lunges. He nabs her around the middle. I plan to stop him from teleporting but never get the chance. The ring on her finger erupts in a golden light. It's bright and disarming, and it sends a blast of energy radiating from her. I feel it surround me, but while it throws Bobby across the room, I stay where I am, untouched. He bounces off a wall and vanishes halfway to the floor.

*Holy fuck.*

"Well, the ring works." I throw her over my shoulder, not sure how to interpret the expression on her face.

We drop back to the living room, arriving right after Bobby. Rosdan is staring down Hank when I set Hannah between us.

Without taking his eyes off the demons, he says, "Blocker bag."

He disappears, leaving me to protect his charge. I arc a bolt across the room. I'm not even sure if it reaches the demons because I involuntarily drop, cast out of the house when Ros reenacts the spell. I land in the backyard. Both of the confused demons are there with me, and then Rosdan appears beside me. We watch them try to teleport back in the house, only to be knocked right back in front of us.

"Gotta love those little spell bags," I say. "Ready to finish this?"

"Not quite, Kasdaye." The deep voice comes from behind the demons.

Rosdan shifts next to me as red eyes glow from the shadows by the swing set. The figure steps forward, the moonlight gleaming off his designer dress shoes, and *fucking great*, it's an Upper. Not just any either. No, this one has an annoying smirk, a serious ego, and once upon a time, a nice little scar on his face from one of my bolts. It's all but gone now. All wounds heal with enough time, his only visible enough to remind him who gave it to him.

"That's a cute little trick you pulled off with your charge upstairs." Abaddon steps around the Lowers, careful not to touch them and chance getting his suit jacket dirty. "We couldn't detect her in the house or teleport her. How *did* you accomplish that?"

I shrug with my face as much as my shoulders. "No idea what you're talking about, Donny."

"No worries. I'll find out soon enough on my own." The darkness cyclones around him, gaining speed as a blue flame appears in his hand.

"You sure you want to do this?" I angle my body so that Donny can't see the phone sliding out of my pocket. "Two against one?"

The smirk I loathe appears. "Not the greatest at counting, huh?"

I glance down at my screen and back at him. "Bitch minions don't count."

"Tell that to your sidekick." The words come out as a growl, and the red returns to Donny's eyes. The flame in his hand grows.

Raising his glowing palms, Rosdan lets out a sigh. "We're going to wake the neighbors."

I tuck the phone back in my pocket and bring my hands up to join the party. "Fine. We'll do it your way. Three against one."

I can see the question working its way from his brain to his mouth. "Three?"

As if choreographed, a flash of divine light illuminates the backyard. In the middle of it appears Chaz. The sparks fly off him, his eyes locking on Donny. They emit a blue glow I haven't seen since the last time the two of them crossed paths.

They have a history. It's a whole thing.

Being more than outnumbered now, the flame in Donny's hand extinguishes. He tosses a smug head nod at Chaz and vanishes along with his lackeys.

Self-preservation. No matter the demon's status.

Chaz continues to seethe at a now-empty spot of grass while Rosdan tugs at the back of his hair.

"The fucking Demon of Destruction?" Ros says. "That's who wants our charges?"

I don't answer him, already on my way back to the house. Spell or not, I need to see Hannah to believe she's safe, touch her to know she's alive. Rosdan beats me there and has the barrier down before I hit the patio. Alistair comes running into the kitchen. She's right behind him.

A new surge of light hits me as she rushes into my arms. I close them around her and reconsider the idea of hiding her away in a remote cabin for the rest of her life. When it was my eternity on the line, I could deal, but now that it's her life … *fuck*. I'm going to lose my mind by the time she hits thirty at this rate.

"Looks like it's going better," Rosdan mumbles. His hands move to the boy's face to take care of the traumatic memory of watching his fancy house be ripped apart with hellfire and divinity. Once he finishes, Alistair walks out of the kitchen in a daze, heading to bed like nothing happened, and Ros drops out of the kitchen.

I pull back from Hannah, completing my ritualistic check after a demon attack, but the ring has done its job.

Chaz struts in then, his head shaking when he sees my lips brush her forehead. "I called that."

"Triplets are already back asleep," Ros says, coming from the living room. He rights an upset barstool and nods at Chaz. "How did you get here so fast? Not that I'm complaining or anything."

"Demons attacked both charges earlier, and I decided, fuck it. It's time for lockdown." He leans back on a counter, crossing his arms over his chest. "So, all three of us were already in an apartment I'd rented out, spelled to the max, and I suggested they not leave unless I tell them to. When Cass texted, all I had to do was toss Avery in the bathroom with a snake that I'd bought for such circumstances." He stretches out his hands, both lit at full power. "I should probably go let her out. The girl's terrified of snakes."

I tighten my hold on Hannah. "Would that be better or worse than threatening to throw you off the balcony?"

She narrows her eyes at me. "Neither is acceptable."

Her glare moves to the cocky blond on the other side of the kitchen, but Chaz just grins.

"I'll go save her, beautiful." He pushes off the counter, winking at her. "Want me to come back later, so we can sort through this shit?"

As much as I want to drop Hannah and myself back to the apartment, I nod. "We'll hang around awhile."

Chaz slaps Rosdan on the back and walks over to us. His head dips down to Hannah's ear, and before I can pull her away, he says, "See you then," and disappears.

Fucking pretty boy's lucky I can't kill him.

"Sorry about him," Rosdan says, giving her a little smile. "We aren't making the best first impressions." He extends a hand to her. "I'm Rosdan, that was Chaz, and obviously, you're Hannah."

Anyone else, I might consider ripping their arm off, but I let her go when she pulls away to put her hand in his. I wander into the absolutely trashed living room to check my phone. Samy finally answered the text I'd sent both him and Chaz.

*Sorry, dealing with my own demons here. Still need me?*

Better late than never, I guess.

I send back, *No. All good. Meeting at Ros's later to make a plan.*

Even with the craziness over, I don't like not having Hannah close and go back to the kitchen. I hook my arm around her waist and check the screen for Samy's response.

*I'll be there.*

Hannah yawns, resting her head on my side.

"Since we have to wait for Chaz to come back, you mind if I take Hannah out to the guesthouse?"

"Go for it. I want to check on the kids again anyway, and then I get to play garbage man with a demon corpse." He glances into the next room and sighs. "Think I should hire someone to clean tomorrow and tell Mark and Scarlett they decided to redecorate?"

"Or buy a new house and tell them they moved."

He laughs and waves to Hannah on his way to the living room.

As we cross the backyard, Hannah's crashing hard. I don't even bother turning on the lights, heading her straight for the extra bedroom. Her adrenaline's wearing off, but I'm still warm enough to drop back to the apartment and find two of my T-shirts. One for her to sleep in and one for myself because, yet again, the one I'm wearing has fallen victim to fireballs. Fucking need a new wardrobe if this shit keeps up much longer.

# FALLEN REBEL

The moon shining in through the window gives me an incredible view of her curvy body while she pulls on the shirt. So incredible that I tug my burned one over my head and crawl into the bed with her.

"You're staying?"

I yank her over to me. "They can call whenever Chaz and Samy get here."

But once my mouth finds hers and my hands find her skin, I won't be answering my phone even if they do. The last of my three T-shirts lands on the area rug. I plan to kiss every part of her I thought about while trading arcs for fireballs, which happens to be every fucking inch. I lose focus, though, my teeth tugging her bottom lip into my mouth so I can suck on it. She sighs, and not so tired anymore, she shoves me onto my back and climbs on top of me. I groan at the feel of her lips on me, almost better than mine on her.

"God, I love you." It's the first time I've said it out loud—ever—and light shoots down my spine.

Hannah pulls back, and I sit up so we're chest-to-chest. She blinks her wide eyes at me while my skin warms hers. "You do?"

I slide my fingers down the hair falling over her bare shoulder. "Completely," I tell her.

She smiles, and even though I already know, it's not until she says, "I love you too," that I finally feel it.

Complete.

The message comes through in the middle of the night. I ease my arm out from under Hannah's head, careful not to wake her. On my way through Ros's living room, I pull on my fully intact shirt. The breeze blows warm outside, and for the first time since Florida, I steal a look at the stars. They have nothing on Hannah.

Even though he said he'd be here, I'm nearly shocked that he walks around the corner of the main house.

I'll hate myself for it later, but I throw my arms around him. "Fuck, I've missed you."

"Me too, brother," Samy says. "Now get off, or the other two might see and think you're open to hugs now."

I chuckle, taking a few steps back. He sounds more like himself than the last time I talked to him, a hint of authority back in his voice. His blond hair is the same as it's been for decades. But even in the shitty suburban moonlight, his eyes hold their usual level of guilt.

"Your charge safe?" I ask.

He nods. "Sorry I couldn't come earlier. I wouldn't have known where in Seattle to drop to anyway. I had to dig out the Christmas card Ros sent to find the address." His eyes do a sweep, checking out the place. "Is he a fucking nanny?"

I smile, shaking my head. "Are you sticking around this time? Or are you going to crawl back into your hole? Because we need you. These demons are not backing off."

"We still think it's because they want us out of the way?"

It goes against everything in me not to tell him Ros's and my theory. He's been my leader for millennia and my family since our beginning. So, I skirt around the question by redirecting. "Any better ideas?"

His eyes squint. "You look different. Less annoyed."

"Doubt it." But he's right. Partly at least—I'm just as annoyed as ever. I half-smile though. "I may have fallen in love with my charge."

Samy loses all expression. "Come again?"

"She's incredible. And frustrating. And I can't stand her. And I can't live without her. And—"

"Live?" he interrupts. "What happened to you can't be alive because you'll never die?"

I've said this to him on many occasions. Usually, I'm drunk and staring at the stars, wishing I felt like I were a part of something still. "She changed that."

His eyebrows draw in. He's concerned about my sanity, no doubt. He starts to say something but stops at the sound of footsteps.

"Well, well, well, if it isn't the son of a bitch who can't return a text in a timely fashion." Chaz shoulders past me from behind to get to Samy.

They slap each other on the backs, trading jabs.

Rosdan steps beside me. "So, he's back?"

"Looks like it." We both keep staring straight ahead, and I lower my voice enough so that the other two can't hear us. "The demon never even looked at the triplets upstairs. He went straight for Hannah."

"And with Donny the Destroyer leading the charge…"

Neither of us bothers finishing the thought. We both know. They want a Nephilim to read from the Book of the Speech from God and end the world. At least, the chances of that being the case have skyrocketed over the past few hours.

"I don't think we tell them," he says.

I look over at that, not disagreeing but surprised as hell that, of all my brothers, it's Rosdan pushing for secrecy.

He turns toward me with an unsettled expression on his face. "The motivation to keep our charges safe stays unchanged regardless of why demons are attacking. Whether they want to kill our Nephilim to get rid of us or kill our Nephilim by destroying the world, our main objective remains the same."

"Keep our charges alive."

"Exactly." He moves, so Chaz and Samy can't see him talking. "They'll fight to keep their charges alive because it's what they've always done. They don't need another reason."

My gaze drifts to the guesthouse where Hannah's sleeping. Someone so innocent to everything Heaven and Hell, and yet she poses a risk to all of mankind. If anyone in charge of carrying out the master plan finds out, they'll come for her. Alistair too. They'll sacrifice every last Nephilim to keep the design moving forward without interruption.

"He's just a kid, Kasdaye." Rosdan proves once again that we're on the same wavelength, his focus on a dark window on the second story of the house. "I can't let them hurt him. Heaven or Hell."

I check on the other two, caught up in their own conversation, and drop my voice even more. "We play dumb about the BOSG.

You three use the new protection spell on your charges. And you and I do whatever the fuck it takes to make sure no one else finds out Nephilim can read from the book."

Relieved I'm on board, Rosdan blows out a breath and nods. "It stays between us," he says, reaffirming our pact.

Before he tries to hug me or something, I pull out my cigarettes. I offer him one and toss over the lighter after I light mine. He fumbles it, nearly dropping it to the ground, and I shake my head.

"God help me when I'm keeping secrets with the Cursed One, yeah?"

Hannah stays asleep when I climb back into bed. I slide my arm under her and hold her close. Needing her against my chest so I can sleep is one of the only things that hasn't changed with her. I doubt it ever will.

My mind starts to drift until my chest warms. At first, I think she's having a nightmare, but the heat seems almost lazy as it spreads through me, not gaining or losing intensity. Only enough for my palm to emit a weak glow.

I slip my hand down the neck of Hannah's shirt. Her heart beats a slow, steady rhythm even though I can notice a difference in the temperature of our skin. My hand stays there, waiting for an increase. My eyes stay open, scanning for any potential danger. But the hours pass without anything. No rise in her pulse, no portals, and no change of the light settled inside me.

In all of my existence, I've never *not* wanted to feel the light of Heaven flowing through my veins. I've spent my time on Earth desperate for even a little bit of it to stay unwavering. But right now, I'd give anything for it to go away.

Because it can only mean one thing.

The danger to Hannah just became constant.

# TWENTY-EIGHT

## *HANNAH*

The morning after the attack, I wake up at the apartment. The other side of the bed is cold, but it doesn't bother me like it once would have. Cass left my phone on his pillow, and I check the messages.

*Helping Ros with something. Sorry about the babysitter.*

*And happy birthday, baby.*

I smile at the add-on, but it fades when something in the apartment crashes.

"Goddamn it!" The voice is husky and not one I recognize.

I pull on a pair of jeans and change out Cass's shirt for one of my own before I venture to see exactly *who* he's sorry to have left me with. When I get to the kitchen, Chaz spins around. He gives me a once-over and nods approvingly. "You look good in the morning, Kelley."

"Thanks?" I slide onto a barstool at the counter.

The microwave beeps, and he pops the door open. "Cass said to feed you. Like I cook or something." He pulls out a heated breakfast burrito and sets the plate in front of me. "Oh, hold on." After opening and closing four drawers, he drops a fork on the counter. *"Bon appétit, ma chérie."*

*"Merci, monsieur."*

He winks, tossing another burrito in to heat before he pours me a cup of coffee.

"Cass is in Seattle?" I ask.

He slides me the mug and lifts his own off the counter, leaning back beside me. "He's helping Rosdan set up everything he needs for the protection spell. Since he needs to enchant five items at once, it needs a little tweaking. Otherwise, the guy would be chanting for three days. Cass wasn't sure if you'd want to be alone after last night."

I don't. Not even with a protection spell on the apartment and the very effective ring on my finger.

"How did he get back if I was asleep?" Or get us here for that matter.

"Hold on. He left instructions on how to answer that." Chaz holds his cell phone in front of his face and clears his throat. "He said, *Shrug and tell her to eat her breakfast.*"

I roll my eyes. Dismissive and bossy, and he's not even on the same side of the country. "I assume you're torturing your charge again to be here?"

He shrugs. "Eat your breakfast."

My eyes narrow at him while I take a bite, but he just grins. I chew and study him. Between the three of them I've met, he's the odd man out. Rosdan and Cass have dark hair and dimples even though Rosdan's are less pronounced. But Chaz is blond, dimpled chin, bright blue eyes.

"Falling in love with me, beautiful?"

"No, I was just thinking how you look nothing like the other two."

He snorts. "A compliment if I've ever heard one."

"What about Samy?" I ask. "I always picture him like a less mean version of Cass."

He shakes his head. "Opposite in looks and personality. Samy looks more like me but less roguishly handsome. So, if you're thinking of trading in for a better model, I'm the one you want. Definitely not Ros."

I laugh. "I'll stick to the broody version. Thank you though."

Now he's studying me with soft eyes plenty of girls have probably become lost in.

"Falling in love?" I ask. "Because I don't think Cass is the sharing type."

"No, and you're right. He's not." His gaze brushes over my face again. "It's just … this may be the least temperamental Kasdaye has ever been. He's actually happy for once. I just can't wrap my head around the fact that it's all because of a Nephilim."

"Thanks," I say dryly.

He chuckles, his entire face lighting up with his smile. "Don't get me wrong. It's a good thing." He takes a sip of coffee but holds up a finger while he swallows to warn me of an afterthought. "Unless he does something stupid because of you. Like become mortal. God, that would be a disaster."

Now he's completely lost me. "Become mortal?"

"The only other way out of Nephilim duty." He leans back on the counter.

"I thought you only turn human if you fail."

"No, failing means you suffer through a human life and sit outside the gates forever. If we ask to be human, we have as much of a chance to go to Heaven as you. But we won't be angels anymore when we get there."

I set down my fork, even more confused. "If it means you get to go home, why haven't you all done that already?"

"Ask to be human?" He stares at me like I've offended him. "Because we're *angels*. The light of Heaven has flowed through us since we were brought into existence. Divinity is not something you willingly give up. Ever. You fight like hell for it."

"But if you fail, you lose it anyway. Then you can't get into Heaven at all."

"Trust me," he says. "It's worth the risk. Unless you've experienced it, you can't understand. It's…" He looks to the floor for a second, and his eyes come back with a Cass-level of seriousness in them. "Once you've known the divine light, never experiencing it again would be worse than ceasing to exist. Nothing can ever take away the pain brought on by its absence. The void is always there. Every. Fucking. Second." He stretches out his fingers, and a dim glow appears on his fingertips. "There are a lot of seconds in eternity, Hannah. A few thousand years is nothing if there's even a small chance to feel it again."

I'm not sure how to respond to his answer. How to even feel about it. Any time I've thought about a future with Cass, my concerns have revolved around the fact that I'll age year after year while he remains the gorgeous specimen he's always been. But maybe I should have been concerned with something else entirely.

In books and movies, the girl falls in love with an immortal and is given the choice of ending her human life to be with them. Except, in our case, I wouldn't have to die to be with Cass. He would have to live to be with me. From the sounds of it, that means sacrificing a hell of a lot more. It would require Cass to give up everything that makes him … Cass.

The microwave beeps, and Chaz slaps the button. He bites into the burrito and makes a disgusted face, chewing. "Fuck that. We're going out for breakfast." A dark blond eyebrow cocks at me. "You know where the keys for the bike are?"

I automatically look at the set on the counter. His eyes flash to them, and a mischievous smile appears. The question isn't whether I'll regret going on the bike with him, but how long it will take.

I have the answer by the time we make it out of the parking lot.


Despite all the time I've spent behind Cass, speeding through the streets, Chaz somehow makes the experience of passenger even more terrifying. Cass should be getting a power boost on every turn while my life flashes before my eyes. It makes me forget all about being another year older because, soon I'll be skidding across the concrete at a hundred miles per hour, and it won't matter.

The second he parks at a diner, I scramble off. "You realize what happens if you kill me, right?"

He chuckles and leans the bike on the kickstand. "What do you want to bet those'll be the first words out of Cass's mouth too?" His hand shoves into his pocket and comes out with his phone. He barely answers, immediately pulling it away from his face and grinning ear to ear.

*I won,* he mouths.

I laugh, heading inside with him following behind.

After watching Chaz consume half my body weight in pancakes, he terrorizes me more on the way back to the apartment. When we get upstairs, Cass is waiting for us in the living room. His glare lands on me first and then on Chaz, who stops short like he hit a wall.

"Oh, come on," Chaz says, bracing his arms on each side of the doorway. "You're divinity-blocking me?"

Cass puts his arm around me and presses his lips to my temple. "Your services are no longer needed," he says, looking back to the angel stuck in the hallway.

Chaz rolls his eyes, but he still grins and tosses the keys inside. "Whatever. Enjoy your birthday, beautiful. Don't forget to call me when his tortured-soul shit gets old."

I blink, and he's gone. I'm about to ask how he can without his charge until I notice the warmth of Cass's skin.

"You have your powers?"

He lets go of me and swipes his keys off the floor. "Enough to travel if we concentrate hard enough at least."

"What does that mean?"

"That the demons aren't giving up yet. But we already knew that." He shuts the door and comes back to me. "You let him drive my bike?"

"You can't be mad at me." I drape my arms over his shoulders. "It's my birthday."

His eyes are harsh, but his voice doesn't match as he holds me tighter. "You're right. But tomorrow? We're fighting about it." He kisses me quickly and digs something out of his back pocket. "As for your birthday, we have a busy day."

I take the paper from his hand, narrowing my eyes while I unfold it. "What's this?" When I look down, my heart skips. My eyes fly back to him. "Are you serious?"

"What else would we do on your birthday?"

He shows a dimple, and I fall even more in love.

The list started on my seventh birthday with a new item added every year. You can tell the years my parents were lazy or unprepared. Although those often turned out to be the best ones. We completed everything on the list each birthday without fail until they died, but I haven't done a single item on there since.

Cass stares down at me where I sit cross-legged on the linoleum floor. "You ready?"

I nod, grinning so big that my cheeks hurt. Hands down, the first one's my favorite.

He shakes his head on his way to the door and pulls it open. A dozen puppies come dashing out. All colors. All sizes. All barking. Their paws slide across the floor as they scramble around, and then I'm covered in them. One bigger one bounds into me. I fall back and laugh and bask in the joy of being attacked by fluff balls.

After a while, Cass lifts me off the floor and out of the chaos. He brushes his thumb over my cheek, and I turn into the touch. The temperature difference in our skin is more soothing than ever.

We stay with the puppies until a worker from the dog rescue comes in to wrangle them. Cass picks up the smallest one from the corner to help. A mix between different breeds with long reddish fur. It stares at him with sad eyes until he scratches it behind the ear. He hands it off to the employee and scrunches up the puppy's face one more time. He turns back around, and I smile.

He rolls his eyes. "Shut up. I have a thing for half-breeds."

"And I have a thing for angels who have a thing for half-breeds."

He pushes his forehead against mine. "It had better be a thing for *one* angel."

One fallen rebel angel. Heaven help me.

His fingers intertwine with mine, and he leads me back to my car. Next on the list: cakes. Plural.

# FALLEN REBEL

We park in front of a small bakery with *Life's Better with Sprinkles* painted in the window display. My parents couldn't agree on flavors, which meant in order to avoid bloodshed, we bought two cakes for every occasion.

So, when the man returns with an extra box, I squint at Cass. "Let me guess. We need three cakes because you don't like strawberry or chocolate."

"No," he says, opening his wallet. "*You* don't like strawberry or chocolate. If I'm buying you birthday cakes, I'm at least getting one of them in a flavor that you do." He hands cash to the guy behind the counter and flips the lid to one of the boxes. "Vanilla without frosting."

I laugh at the bare dessert. "All this time, I thought having three cakes would be over the top."

"It is. I have no idea why the fuck I'm encouraging it." Cass closes the box. Then he leaves me to carry out my three different cakes, swearing under his breath about my family's ridiculous traditions.

Fifteen minutes later, we're back at the apartment. Cass takes the cake boxes to the kitchen. He comes into the living room with a large paper bag and sits down on the couch, setting it on the cushion next to him.

"You actually made the grab bag?" I ask.

This one originated on my fourteenth birthday. Each of my parents thought the other was taking care of the birthday idea, which led to neither of them doing it. They rummaged around the house and threw random stuff in a grocery bag, so I could reach in and choose one surprise "present." Over the three years they put together the grab bag, I chose a coupon to an auto parts store, a pair of my mom's earrings she would steal back a few days later, and a fifty-dollar bill.

Cass pulls me onto his lap, so I'm straddling him. While his interest in the bag was never there to begin with, mine vanishes the second his hands slide up my back, bringing me forward until my lips meet his. The kiss deepens, and soon enough, I'm grinding shamelessly against him, his hips flexing to meet mine.

*Happy birthday, Hannah.*

His phone vibrates in his pocket. I expect him to ignore it, which he does until it goes off again. The hand on my back disappears, and he shifts around beneath me. He growls, breaking his mouth away from me, irritated eyes on the screen. "How long will you be mad if I make Terra forget she knows you?"

"Right now, I don't care."

I lower my lips back to his, and he drops the phone. He grabs my hips, pulling them down so he can thrust up against me. But just as we regain our rhythm, he pulls away again.

"Fuck," he says, panting. "She's downstairs, waiting for me to let her in the building."

"Why?" I ask, equally out of breath.

He moves me onto the cushions and disappears down the hall, abandoning me on the couch.

*Unhappy birthday Hannah.*

Coming back from our room, he carries a pair of purple-and-black Rollerblades in his hand. "Because you two are going to skate around our apartment like lunatics."

"You're joking," I say, rushing over to him. "Carpet-roller-skate tag?"

Skating and tag started out as two separate activities until the year it snowed a foot. Both were moved inside and ended up combined into one. The results were just disastrous enough for it to become permanent.

"It's on the list, Hannah." As soon as Cass says my name, he mutters, "Goddamn it," and reaches for his wallet.

Another forgotten year. They paid me anytime they said my name.

I smile as he hands me the skates along with a ten-dollar bill.

"Midnight can't come fast enough," he says, going to let in Terra.

She skates in, fully decked out in elbow and knee pads and a helmet. Give the girl a mouth guard, and she's ready for a roller derby. After clearing out any potential hazards, including the coffee table, Cass disappears to avoid the madness. We half-skate and half-run around the living room, slapping each other whenever close enough. It's exhausting, and as excited as twelve-year-old Hannah was about this, the twenty-two-year-old version calls it quits after ten minutes.

Terra collapses beside me. She stretches out her legs, and her skates *thud* on the floor. "We should do this every week. Then I won't need to go to the gym anymore." She rolls her head toward me. "Happy birthday, Hannah."

I let her off the hook for saying my name, too tired to collect. "Thank you."

"So," she says, sitting up, "any big plans for tonight?"

She's fishing to see if I know about the surprise party she has planned for later. I figured it out a few weeks ago after she asked for Cass's number in case she ever needed to track me down. Within a few hours, he was glaring at his phone and muttering vague threats all aimed at her.

"You'll have to ask Cass," I tell her.

"Well, whatever you end up doing, I hope you have fun!" Her voice shoots up an octave at the end. She pushes off the floor and offers me a hand, but I wave her off, comfortable where I am. "Tell Cass bye for me?"

I nod. "See you later."

Her eyes bulge a little, but she recovers quickly. "Yeah, maybe we can get lunch tomorrow or something."

Before she blurts out every last detail I know she's dying to tell me, she skates out the door. I force myself up and take off the Rollerblades. I set them by the couch and go in search of Cass. We have one item left to complete, but I want a quick shower.

He's on the bed, reading. I peel my shirt off on the way through and toss it at him. Without glancing up, he places the bookmark and follows me into the bathroom. And there goes any chance of my shower being quick.

But it's totally worth it.

Cass sets the motorcycle helmet on my head, my hair still wet underneath.

"Where are we going?" I ask.

He kisses the tip of my nose and gives the perfect answer: "Nowhere."

The last year my parents and I spent together, we finished everything on the list and then got in the car and drove. For miles and hours. Through towns and countryside. Someone would call out a direction, and we'd turn, or the flip of a coin would decide our fate at an intersection, but a true destination never existed. We were driving to nowhere. It's the last favorite memory I'll ever have of them.

Cass takes us out on the highway, but his speed stays relatively slow. For him anyway. We're still passing every car in sight. I wonder if it's because the light already flows through him, so there's no need to terrify me. Or maybe he wants me to enjoy the ride for once. Either way, I tighten my hold on him and do just that.

As he drives, he drags his fingertips across my skin, sending a tingle up my arm. He hates the fact that I'm in danger, but having his powers all the time must be incredible for him and the others. To feel the light consistently again after all this time, it's what Cass has been wanting since having them taken away. Surely, that's why he never brought up the possibility of becoming human. He'd never consider it as an option—and neither would I.

Our ride ends at the bar for the party. Aware of the reaction Terra will have to the helmet hair, I run my fingers through it, doing what I can. I bend down to check the side mirror, and Cass steps behind me, his hands planting on my hips.

"Tell me you want me to make everyone inside forget why they're here."

I spin around, and he leans me back on the seat. "You could have made Terra forget she wanted to throw me a party in the first place, you know?"

"Where was that advice two weeks ago?" He kisses me and backs away. "Let's get this over with before I change my mind."

I receive one last eye roll on our way inside as a group yells, "Surprise!"

Terra barrels into a girl, trying to get to me first. She throws her arms around me and bounces, and she really is amazing to care so much. "Were you surprised?"

I nod, but the uncomfortably large smile spread across my face gives me away. She gives an exasperated sigh and hauls me across to the bartender for a drink. As we mingle, I pretend to know more than a few in attendance. Most are friends of Terra's that I've met a few times at parties or the other mandated social outings. If it wasn't for her, it would be a handful of people. Maybe the drunk guy Cass knows, who just so happens to be passed out at the end of the bar, which is exactly where Cass stays, drinking for both of them.

Close to midnight, an arm slinks around me while I'm talking to Terra and Gabe. Cass pulls me away from them in the middle of our conversation, not acknowledging Terra's objections. We head to the hall on the far end of the bar, and I slow down as we approach the men's room.

"What is it with you and public restrooms?"

He turns around and walks backward, tugging me forward. "I'll take you wherever I can get you."

But we pass them, and he backs out the exit at the end of the hallway. I glance over my shoulder as the door closes, leaving us alone in the gravel parking area behind the bar.

"We can't leave without saying goodbye to everyone."

He traps me in his arms, smirking. "We can't?"

The blinding light surprises me along with the heat. Once both fade away, my feet aren't on rock anymore but sand. It's not entirely dark either. A small sliver of the horizon above the ocean is still on fire from where the sun recently set. The waves roll onto the shore only a few feet away.

I recognize the rock formation down the beach, my breaths coming harder. "Cass, what are we doing here?"

"We're adding something new," he says.

He unfolds the completed list, and it's already written in at the bottom: *Visit Brice and Fiona.*

My thumb rubs over the band on my finger as I remember the night I left them here. Where she always found peace and he made a lifetime worth of promises he would never be able to keep.

These are the memories that always send me running. The absence of them so overwhelming that I need to get away from everything reminding me of them so that I can breathe. Only this time, instead of crashing over me all at once, the loss and heartache creep up like the water on the sand and retreat before drowning me. Tears fall on the paper, and I miss them so bad that it hurts, but I want to stay. Be close to them in whatever way I can.

Cass lowers onto the sand, pulling me down with him. I sit back between his legs, and he rests his cheek against the side of my head. Night falls, everything around us quiet, except for the waves. I can't imagine a better ending to the day he's given me than watching the water with his arms around me.

"Can we do this every year?"

He kisses just below my ear. "We can do this whenever you want. Just say the word, and we're here."

I fall further into him, not sure I ever want to move and risk losing how I feel at this exact moment. Where nothing can reach me because I'm safe with him.

We stay a while longer, listening to the waves crash before Cass drags me to my feet. He kisses me as the world goes white. For an instant, we're all that exists other than the light and its warmth. Then we're back in the real world, our feet on gravel in the parking lot. Everyone's gone home, the bar closed hours ago, and my birthday's over.

After we get back to the apartment, Cass walks into the bedroom with the long-forgotten grab bag. "You never chose anything." He sets the sack in the middle of the mattress and slides onto the bed next to me. "I may have cheated though."

I sit on my knees. "Cass Daye, not playing by the rules? I refuse to believe it."

He half-smiles as I reach in. There's only one item at the bottom.

I suspiciously eye him and pull out the box, dark blue and velvet. "You got me a present?"

"You really thought I wouldn't?"

He slides the box out of my hands and tips open the lid. On the velvet lies a white gold necklace with a star pendant. Cass and his stars. My finger runs over the diamond embedded in the center.

"It's perfect." I look up and caress his cheek. "Thank you."

He pulls me onto his lap, so I'm straddling him. As he dangles the chain around my neck, an engraving on the back of the star catches my eye. I move my hair, so he can hook the clasp. Once he's done, I flip over the pendant to see the inscription he chose.

*You're my forever.*

"I mean it, Hannah." He cups the side of my face, tilting my chin up. He stares into my eyes like I'm his sky, and I stop breathing. "I love you. You're my one. There's nothing else for me. There will never be anything but you."

Cass kisses me slow and deep, reinforcing every word. I feel everything he feels for me and want nothing more than to disappear into it. Let him make me forget everything but him. Only this time, I can't. His words are a promise of us always being together. The way he's touching me and kissing me leaves no doubt that he'll sacrifice the eternity he's been waiting on, his immortality, to be with me.

Except I won't let him. I refuse to be the reason he loses everything.

Cass said it himself. I'm his last Nephilim. After me, he finally goes home.

He'll return to Heaven when I die, and I'll do whatever it takes to ensure he has his light when he does. Even if it means giving up a life with him, I'll make sure it happens..

Forever in love with him or not.

# TWENTY-NINE

## CASS

The ring allows me to return to pre-demon Watcher duties once Hannah starts summer classes. Determined to graduate by December, she's signed up for more than she planned. A full course load means the crystal ball and I need to become reacquainted with each other. It's quite an adjustment from being at her side every second to hovering around the edge in case she needs protection.

For the record, watching your girlfriend feels a hell of a lot more controlling than when it's just your charge. And a hell of a lot more irritating in a number of situations.

Like on Friday, some tool slides into the seat next to her at the beginning of her philosophy lecture. He leans over to chat her up. I crack my neck and take a long-ass drag off my cigarette, running through all the ways I'll destroy him if he touches her. She hands the dude a pen, and his eyes wander all over her bare legs, lingering on the hint of cleavage her tank top shows. I wave my hand over the orb to clear the image before I drop in and fucking level him.

The longer my powers hum through me on the low setting, the easier I can differentiate between the constant danger brought on from Donny's plan and light from any added threats or spikes in adrenaline. So, as much as seeing her safe eases my mind, I limit my use of the ball for the next hour to keep from losing it over whatever else Pen Guy might pull. But the second she emerges from the building with him following like a puppy, I'm jogging across the street. I don't stop until my mouth is on hers. It's possessive as shit, but Hannah doesn't seem to care. The strap of her bag falls off her shoulder, and she lets me gratuitously and unapologetically claim her until her shadow disappears.

My hands on her ass and lips still on hers, I let out a frustrated sigh. "Tell me you're done for the day."

The second she starts to nod, I throw her over my shoulder. She squeals out my name while I carry her and her bag to my bike. The rest of the world had her all week. From now until Monday morning, she's mine. I'll fight anyone who tries to tell me otherwise.

Including her.

On Saturday afternoon, lightning flashes, and thunder roars off and on in the background. The wind blows rain against the windows. Gray and gloom cast a depression over everything outside while Hannah and I lie on the living room floor. My aim was the bedroom, but I got distracted.

She lies on her back, watching me trail my hand over her stomach. My palm and fingertips glow. I let them spark against her skin. Her chest rises faster in response, and I nudge her shirt higher to move farther up her rib cage.

I've become more in tune with the *mood* of the light she gives me. Edgy when she's angry. Demanding if she's scared. Liquid gold in my veins anytime she's turned on. And every once in a while, she'll look at me, and I can't describe it any other way than to say, it's … Heaven.

As if she's in my mind with me, she asks, "What does it feel like?"

I watch the brief flash between our skin, the power leaving me, only to come right back when her pulse picks up. "Absolutely intoxicating." My eyes meet hers, and I add, "There's only one thing in existence better than divine light."

"What's that?"

One side of my mouth turns up. "You."

Her heart rate speeds as I lower my lips to her body. The skin's still warm from my touch, her fingers tugging at my hair. Fuck the light pumping through me. It's her I want to feel. I glide my hand down to the button of her jeans.

"What happens when I get older?"

"A lot of things," I say dryly, tugging down the zipper. "You want the list?"

"I mean, with us."

The light alters enough that I stop and look at her, not recognizing this one. Not scared, but something else. Heavy. Looming.

She undoes the progress I've made on her pants and sits up. "It's delusional to think you'll still want to be with me when I'm locking in low rates on a burial plot and you still look, according to your driver's license, twenty-five."

I sigh, sitting up next to her, and sweep her hair away from her overly concerned face. "You really don't need to worry about that."

I lean in to kiss her, but she presses her hand to my chest. "Why not?"

"Because I told you, you're my forever."

Again, I attempt to bring my lips to hers. She stops me. I lower my head and take a deep breath. She's not going to let this go until we have, what I consider to be, a pointless conversation. My fate was sealed the second I realized I never wanted to exist without her. There's only one way for that to happen.

Once I clear my mind of everything I want to be doing to her right now, I look up. "You don't need to worry because I'll be old with you."

Hannah's expression stays the same even though an intense weight settles into my core. "How?"

"The Fallen have the choice of becoming mortal," I tell her. "We can live a life, die, and face judgment alongside the rest of humanity."

I never expected to even consider the option. It sounded like a ticket straight into a devastating nothingness. Until her. Now, a chance to live and die with her—to give her everything she deserves and then spend the entirety of the beyond with her—it's the best gift I've ever been given.

"But then you won't be an angel when you go to Heaven."

"No." The sensation inside intensifies with a dash of panic added to the mix. I reach out and skim my finger across her cheek. "And I don't want to be. If I am, we'll never see each other again."

"Never?" she asks, her voice unsteady.

I shake my head. "Not if I'm immortal. It's hard to explain, but me being human when you die is the only way we can be together. Since I promised you an eternity…"

The light shifts—demanding—as she scrambles to her feet. She secures plenty of space between us, and then she stops and holds a hand to her forehead. "I don't think I can do this, Cass."

"What the fuck does that mean?" I ask, shoving off the floor.

"It's too much."

She looks at the ceiling, the walls, everything in the fucking room, except for me. It's irritating as hell, so I close the distance and make her look at me, tipping her face to mine.

"Tell me what you mean." The command is harsh, but between the way she's acting and the feeling I don't recognize that continues to spread through my chest, I can't help it.

Her eyes settle on mine, her heart pounding and the light surging. "What if I change my mind?" She pauses and then clarifies, "What if I change my mind *about us*?"

At first, I feel nothing. Not her. Not me. Fucking shell-shocked. Then it all slams into me at once. My hands drop to my sides, and I back across the room. I can't trust myself near her right now. Not when all I want to do is make her forget what she just said. Remove the possibility of this ending in a way other than with her in my arms.

"I'm only twenty-two," she says fast. "I have no idea what I'll want in ten years or twenty. But if you become human for me, I won't feel like I have any choice other than to be with you. It's not fair to expect me to decide what I want for the rest of my life before I even know what's out there. I've only been here a few decades, but you've been alive since—"

"Existed," I say flatly.

She locks eyes with me. "What?"

"I've *existed*, Hannah. I wasn't alive until the first time you said my name."

Looking back now, I know that's when it started. A trickle that turned into a goddamn waterfall.

The way Hannah looks at me changes the heat coursing through me into something perfect and pure. How it's supposed to be, with her and me and nothing in the way. I try to hold on to it, but she averts her gaze, and it slips away. We're back to the heaviness, stronger than ever.

"I need time, Cass," she says to the floor.

"Great. You'll have plenty of it," I bite at her. "I'm not asking to become human tomorrow. Or anytime soon for that matter. It's years away and not even an option until the demons stop attacking."

"It's not just that."

I let out an exasperated groan. "Of course it's not."

She keeps her eyes cast down. "I'm finally getting to a point where I'm not lost in grief. I owe myself a chance to see what that life is like without—"

"Me." My jaw tenses as I realize what she's saying. "You want to know what it's like without me."

She nods, gutting me with every up-down.

I shake my head in disbelief. How the hell did we go from about to fuck on the living room floor to a fight about my mortality to… "Where exactly are you heading with this, Hannah?"

My chest burns hotter.

She fidgets, taking her sweet time with a response. "I think it's better for both of us if we go back to being Watcher and Nephilim. Nothing more."

*Jesus Christ.*

My hand scrubs over my face as I laugh at that gem. "How the *fuck* am I supposed to do that?"

She blinks away tears and wipes the one escaping down her cheek. She still refuses to look at me. I start toward her but stop a few feet in front of her. Any closer, and I'll erase everything since the last time she said she loves me. And she does love me. I feel it in my *soul* when she looks at me and would feel it with or without the connection to her heartbeat.

"This isn't what you want, Hannah. I know it's not."

"It is," she whispers. "I'm sorry."

Another two words powerful enough that they rip through me. Only this time, they shred me the fuck apart on their way in. I stand there and watch her chest rise and fall slower. Each deep breath she forces, the less I feel her. The less I feel at all. Before I lose all the light from her, I have to walk away. If I stay, I'll find a way to make this shitshow even worse.

"You want us back to the way we were?" I snag my keys off the counter. "You got it, sweetheart."

As much as I would love for that to be my parting line, this isn't one of the times where I walk out, cool down, and then we fight again until we're ripping each other's clothes off. When I slam the door behind me, it will mean more than the end of the conversation. Apparently, it'll mean the end of us.

I pause in the doorway, not letting myself turn around. *God, do I want to turn around.*

"However long it takes." My voice sounds cold, but I can't manage anything else. "Ten years. Twenty. Hell, make it fifty or a hundred. I'll wait forever because, now that I know what a life with you is like, I can't go back to an existence without you."

A long time ago, I reached a point where it was nearly impossible to alter even the most minor aspect of who I was. Falling in love with Hannah ... that's changed me in ways that can never be undone. It's there now. Ingrained in me. Always. Whether she spends eternity loving me back or not.

My hand still grips the side of the door, ready to slam it shut when I drop to my bike instead. I rev the engine and focus on anything but the heaviness returning to my body. Part of it me, part of it Hannah. Heartache weighs the same on the soul regardless of whether it's pouring out of you or the heart of someone you love. For a long time, it rolls over me in waves. Then the sensation from her stops, and I'm alone in the pain. It's just the divine light inside of me, devoid of anything Hannah.

I've never experienced a loss like it.

I already know what waits for me back at the apartment. A half-empty closet, not a candle in sight, and a key on the counter connected to a fucking alligator-shaped keychain. I throw it with enough power to send the lamp it hits crashing to the floor. The tiny release breaks way to an unleashing of pent-up emotions. Anything that reminds me of Hannah is fair game. Which just so happens to be whatever I come across. Books, cushions, shelves, everything on a flat surface. I tear the place apart.

The entire world lurches to a stop the second I feel her again. A burn fills my chest, so I'm no longer empty inside.

She's thinking of me.

I frantically search the ransacked living room for the crystal ball. I find it on the floor under the notebook with the symbols from the language of creation drawn on the pages. It's only been a few hours, but I ache to see her, hold her, love her.

Hannah's image appears in the globe. The room is dark, but moonlight shines through a window, reflecting off her face. Her eyes are closed, face relaxed while she sleeps.

*A dream.*

It's a fucking dream.

The ball leaves a hole where it hits the wall. It bounces off the couch and onto the floor where it stays. I swipe a bottle of whiskey out of the tossed kitchen and head to my mess of a bedroom. A few long pulls in, I set the bottle down. I light a cigarette and drop back on the mattress. I stare at the ceiling, a hand behind my head.

For all the time I spent worrying about what it would feel like to lose everything, I never once thought it would play out like this. A slow unraveling of what I want and need until the only reason I've ever craved a life decides she wants to live hers without me. The real kicker is what happens next. I'll watch. Witness it all.

*Every.*

*Fucking.*

*Second.*

Screw ever going back to Heaven. I need to fight my way out of what has somehow become my own personal Hell.

# THIRTY

## CASS

The first day without Hannah, I only leave my bedroom to retrieve the crystal ball and alcohol. I spend the next twenty-four hours drinking with the orb on my chest, watching her.

Fake smiles.

Fake laughs.

Fake nods at whatever advice Terra and Jesse give her to heal a broken heart.

Most of the time, she looks completely unaffected by what's destroying me. It wrecks me to see, but I keep watching, waiting for when no one else is looking. That's when she closes her eyes, sucking in short, shallow breaths. The light flooding through me turns heavy, and she lets herself feel the hurt. In these moments, I'm not alone in my grief. Because that's what I'm doing. For the first time in my existence, I'm grieving. And it's over the loss of us.

The next two days, I shadow at a distance while she attends classes. Anytime she's about to walk out of a building, her adrenaline tips me off, a nervousness to the light. She keeps her head down, staring at her feet. With so few students on campus, all it would take is one glance, and she'd see me standing across the street. But the look never comes.

On day four, I ignore a call from Chaz. I've been curbside at Terra and Jesse's house for the past four hours. The first three, I spent chanting, using one of the extra vials of Hannah's blood I stored away in case of emergencies to make a blocker bag. I texted her that I left it in the mailbox and parked my ass on my bike. Over an hour has ticked by since then. No word. No light from her other than when she read the message. I'm waiting for her to step outside, and she's waiting for me to leave.

It's a battle I intend to win. Until a deluge of texts comes through. I sift through the creative insults to get to the reason Chaz insists on river dancing on my nerves. He snagged a Lower out of a gutter and is holding an impromptu interrogation. A chance to crack open Donny's plan trumps another hour of loitering.

I'm less than a block away when I feel her—the light on edge.

By the time I show up at the warehouse in Colorado, Chaz and Rosdan are already mid-torture session. From the looks of the demon—face swollen, broken extremities, and burn marks from bolts marring most of its flesh—they've been at it awhile.

Chaz looks back as I step out of the shadows. "Where the fuck have you been?" Then he gets a better look, and the discharge vanishes from his palm. "Never mind that. What the fuck happened while you were there?"

I assume he's referring to the four days' worth of stubble and the fact that I look ready to commit murder. And I am. Not that killing a demon is anything but a service. God knows what this one would do with enough time on Earth.

Rosdan straightens up from next to the demon, deep lines between his eyebrows at the sight of me. He opens his mouth to say something, but I don't give him the chance.

"You get anything out of him?"

"No," he answers, smart enough not to push it. "If he knew anything about Donny, he would have talked by now."

Without any warning, I hurl a bolt. Low charge, but my powers are stronger than yesterday. Chaz barely drops out of the way in time, and the light strikes the demon dead center in the chest.

"What the fuck?" Chaz shouts from somewhere behind me.

I ignore him on my way to finish off the demon. I grip his jaw and tip his head back. The black of his pupils swim outward through his irises and the whites of his eyes until only darkness remains. It seeks an escape since the physical body has nowhere to go with spelled ropes keeping it from teleporting.

My other hand covers his mouth and nose, blocking the potential exits. "What was he doing when you found him?"

Shadows seep out of his wounds and snake down to the floor, keeping as far away from our light as possible. Chaz steps beside me and covers the largest gash. The dark retreats from the glow in his palms.

"He was lurking outside an elementary school," he says.

Rosdan places his hands over the demon's ears. "Do we know what he planned to do?" I quirk a brow, inquiring if he really wants to know, and he quickly shakes his head. "Forget I asked."

Light leaks out from under his hands where they connect with the demon's skin. The muffled grunts of panic under my palm go ignored while we smother the darkness. Anything he'd tell us at this point would be complete bullshit. As soon as he goes limp, we all release our hold. The blackness screeches as it's finally freed, shooting into the rafters and through a hole in the roof.

"A little dramatic," Chaz deadpans.

Cleanup includes a trip to the Andes. Mountain ranges are an easy place to dump evidence of the eternal pissing match between light and dark. And that's what it is since neither side can ever win. Both are required to keep the wheel turning. If the balance ever tipped too far in one's favor, it would wipe out far more than Earth. The entire cosmos would revert to chaos.

Always late to the party, Samy calls right after we leave the warehouse. Rather than pinpoint where the hell we are, Chaz tells him to go to Ros's guesthouse. After we finish, we're supposed to drop there, but the side of a mountain, miles away from any other soul, is far more desirable.

I stare over the face of a cliff, standing at the edge with the world spread out below me. I reach for my chest, for the ring resting under my shirt. Right over my heart. I've been rubbing my fingers over the band lately, thinking about the inscription that matches the one on Hannah's finger. Brice promised Fiona a forever's worth of forevers. I can't even convince Hannah to be with me for one.

"Kasdaye," Rosdan shouts over the wind whipping around us. "You coming?"

He steps beside me, and my ledge becomes crowded. His concerned gaze plasters to the side of my face while I hold the ring, not acknowledging him.

After a while, I drop my arm to my side. "I told Hannah I want to be mortal."

His head jerks toward me. "You what?"

"Don't worry," I shout back. "The idea of eternity with me sent her running."

"Shit." He goes quiet for a minute before he says, "So, what are you going to do now?"

I look over at him and shrug. Then I take the step forward I've been wanting to. I close my eyes and fall. Nothing but the wind howling, ripping at my clothes until just before I hit the ground and I drop. My feet land in Ros's kitchen, the others already there. Bottle of whiskey open.


A hand slaps on my back as I nurse my tumbler. Rosdan sits back down next to me at the table. The pity in his eyes matches what I'm getting from Chaz across from me. The only one not looking at me like I might burst into hysterics is Samy, leaning against the counter.

My swan dive only afforded Rosdan a minimal head start. All he managed to tell them was that Hannah left. The three of them have been feeding me drinks for the past hour, no one saying a word. But given the way Chaz fidgets, he's about two seconds away from—

"You plan on telling us what happened this millennium or…"

Right on time.

"Jesus, Chaz." Rosdan kicks him under the table.

"What? If we wait for him to open up, we'll be here at least that long. I'm trying to save us some time."

"There's nothing to tell," I say, slumping back in my chair. "Classic angel falls for mortal girl, and she freaks when he decides to become human to be with her."

With me voted Least Likely to Walk Away from Immortality, the admission shocks the room into silence. I look up at Samy, his eyes an odd storm—disappointment for not telling him about planning to give up the light maybe.

I don't talk about my feelings and shit, but since they're already staring at me like I sprouted a second set of wings, why the hell not? "The fucked up part is, I never considered she wouldn't want me to be human and experience all that life shit with her. I thought once she found out I could, she'd annoy me over it until it happened, but she acted like being mortal would be the worst thing I could do." I finish my drink and reach for the bottle. "Maybe I shouldn't have told her becoming human was an option until after everything calmed down."

"Shit, Cass," Chaz says. "Hannah's known about the mortal escape clause for a while now."

I stop mid-pour, my gaze lifting to him. "What?"

He winces and leans back in his chair like he wants to get away from me. "I might have mentioned something over a frozen burrito on her birthday. But to be fair, it wasn't in the list of banned topics you gave me when you asked me to Nephilim-sit."

Rosdan slides the bottle from my still-suspended hand and sets it between us. "Cass, maybe you should—"

"What did you say?" I ask, my voice calm despite the rage building beneath the surface.

Chaz's head droops, avoiding eye contact. "I'm sorry. I never thought it would—"

"What the fuck did you say?" I growl across the table.

I knew something was wrong. She went from zero to *piss off* way too fast, and whatever he'd planted in that thick skull of hers is the reason.

He lifts his head, the guilt seeping out of his pores. "That becoming human for her would be the biggest mistake you'd ever make."

The chair crashes back as I dive at him. I knock over the bottle, the table, fucking everything to get to him. With our powers, we're an equal match. Without, too, but I have fucking rage on my side. Each punch only fuels me and my desire to destroy his pretty face. Rosdan tries to pull me off Chaz as I beat the shit out of him. It does little to slow me down, so Samy steps in. He hooks Chaz's arm, hauling him off the ground.

"Tamiel," he shouts, placing himself between us, "enough!"

He barks the command, and like a good little soldier, I obey. I shove Rosdan away and drop back to my apartment. I'm only there a few seconds when someone pounds on the door.

"Let me in, man," Rosdan says from the hall. "You don't want to be alone right now."

"The fuck I don't." But I go to the kitchen and pull a crystal from the blocker bag anyway.

I pass by him on my way to the couch, full whiskey bottle in hand. With the light burning off the alcohol, it takes a distillery to hit numb, and that's what I'm aiming for.

He glances around at the post-Hannah destruction. "You're just all about redecorating places lately."

"If I can't fix what he destroyed, I'll scour the Abyss for the Dimming Blade and end him."

Ignoring the idle death threat, Rosdan makes himself comfortable on the other end of the couch, legs crossed and sipping from the glass he brought with him. "'The most devastating thing that could ever happen to one of us is to live and die as a human.'" He pauses for effect or some shit and then says, "Those are your words, Cass. You've been saying it since we were cast out of Heaven."

I wipe a hand over my face and sit forward, resting my forearms on my thighs.

"I was wrong," I tell him, the heaviness inside all mine. "It's immeasurably more shattering to love and lose one."

# THIRTY-ONE

## *HANNAH*

It's just breathing.

I've done it every second of my life. In, out, repeat until you die. But for the past four days, it's been anything but simple. Each inhale needs to be measured with the exhale even. Otherwise, it will all come crashing in, and he'll feel it. He'll feel me and know the truth.

When I decided this was the only way to keep Cass from giving up being an angel for me, I thought the hardest part would be lying to him—making him believe any part of me doubts I will belong to him forever. Turns out, words are easy. It's living with how much mine hurt him that threatens to destroy me.

After an hour of Terra begging me to go to a movie, Jesse scoops her off the couch. He gives me a wink as he carries her out, and I mouth, *Thank you.*

She's been extra attentive since I showed up a crying mess on the doorstep. I told her Cass and I broke up because I couldn't see it going anywhere. Considering I sobbed my way through the bullshit explanation, it would shock me if she bought it.

As soon as the door latches, the house falls quiet. Too quiet.

With nothing to distract me, I go upstairs to what would be my room if I unpacked. Right now, it's a guest room with Jesse's weight-lifting shit in one corner and my boxes in another. And that probably won't change tonight.

When I turn on the light, I flinch and grab my chest. "Jesus, Cass."

He lifts his head from where he's sitting on my bed, arms braced on his thighs. My heart thrums in my chest but not from the scare. It's from seeing him—what I've been dying for and avoiding all week. For someone who only needs a few hours of sleep a night, he looks exhausted. Knowing I'm the reason twists at my insides. I have to fight the urge to run to him.

"What are you doing in here?" I ask, shutting the door.

He stares at me for a few seconds. Then he's up, his long strides closing the distance between us fast. He doesn't stop until my back's against the door and my chest is against his. "You lied."

I swallow, once again focused on breathing evenly. "No, I—"

"Breakfast burrito," he says. His hand sweeps over my fingers, and he traces the band of the ring he put there. "You. Chaz. A conversation about my mortality. Ring any bells, Hannah?"

All the bells.

But I shrug, trying to play it off. "So I knew you could ask to be human. It doesn't mean I want to be with you."

He studies me, my face and then my lips. "Your mouth keeps saying that, but the rest of you…" His hand slides to the hollow of my neck. My pulse throbs beneath his fingertips, betraying me and giving him exactly what he wants.

"This always tells me the truth. And it says your mouth is a fucking liar."

I slap his hand away, but he's unfazed and brings the other to my cheek.

"Chaz is a tool. He has no idea what he's talking about. I love you, and the mistake would be letting you do something stupid like throw all this away over some savior complex."

"That's not what this is."

"Are you sure about that?" he asks, leaning in.

The scent of him fills the air between us, smoke and leather and something distinctly Cass. I've missed it, and I need distance or else I won't stand a chance. I start to sidestep, but he puts his arm up, blocking me. I'm boxed in. The door, my dresser, his hard body inching closer. It's the moment I've been dreading over the past few days. Face-to-face with him and nowhere to go.

"Cass…"

He looks up at his name, but his gaze goes straight back to my lips as he licks his. "What do you want, Hannah?"

It's the question he always asks, and I've practiced what to say a thousand times, so my voice won't tremble and give me away, but when I open my mouth, he moves his finger to my lips and shakes his head.

"Not with this. I need an answer from something I trust." He lowers his feverish palm and presses it flat to my chest. "Tell me what you *really* want."

More than ever, I regulate my response to him—air in, air out. But then he releases a small charge over my skin that radiates through me. It breaks the carefully calculated rhythm of my breathing, and the rest dominoes. My heartbeat speeding, my breaths shallow. As soon as my control slips, his eyes dart back up. He can feel how much I want him. How much I've always wanted him.

In the next second, his soft lips are on mine. He presses me into the door and slides his hands up to my face. I thought breathing was difficult without him here, but it's damn near torturous with him invading all my senses. I should stop him, but I can't. I've longed for this. Dreamed of it. Feared it. I close my eyes, feeling the warmth of his lips brushing over mine and fighting the desire to respond.

"Kiss me," he pleads against my mouth. "I know what you're doing, and you don't need to. Please, baby."

Weakness is foreign to Cass, but right now, he sounds broken, and it kills me to be what's hurting him. I don't know how I'll survive doing it the rest of my life. As the agony in his voice cuts through me, he growls, low and deep, enduring my pain as much as his own.

"Fucking. Kiss. Me." He reissues the command with his lips, kissing me harder.

It takes every ounce of willpower I possess not to submit to them. To not be selfish and let him sacrifice everything, so I can keep him forever. But I love him too much. I can't stand the thought of him suffering all of eternity without his light because of me. Tears spill down my cheeks until they pool against his hands.

I shake my head as much as I can against his hold. "Stop!"

His mouth instantly leaves mine. The torn expression I haven't seen since before we went to Florida returns to his face, and then he dips his head and locks me in his gaze.

"I could make you forget," he whispers. The heat from his hands creeps into my cheeks, his voice turning velvety and enveloping me in calm. "Tell you that you're as desperate for me to be mortal as I am to live a human life with you."

His touch soothes me from the inside out, like my mind's sinking into a hot bath. I can't remember why I was crying anymore. Why I would ever need to cry again. I relax against his chest, lost in his eyes, never wanting him to let me go.

"I could erase your doubt about how perfect that life sounds to me because I promise you, nothing in existence feels as right as being with you." He takes a deep breath. "But I won't. No matter how much it destroys me or how miserable you make me, I won't take this away from you." He pushes his forehead against mine, my face still secured by his now-glowing hands. "I've never needed anything as much as I do you, Hannah," he says, the light humming, "but it has to be all of you. Every fucking stubborn piece—"

It's like someone hit the off button, sound and video gone. I blink my eyes open and jerk upright in my bed. I frantically look around. The room's dark, no sign of Cass.

It was just another dream. I've had them every night I've spent away from him. Instead of shadows attacking me, they're of being with him, and rather than feeling relief when I wake up, I wish I had stayed a little longer. This one felt different though. More heartbreaking.

As my head struggles to regain a foothold in reality, I check the clock to see how long I slept. Except I only came upstairs a few minutes ago. Confused, I try to remember what happened after I walked in, but all I have is the dream.

# FALLEN REBEL

I throw off the blanket and rush across the room to the window I've stayed away from until now. It overlooks the front of the house. Down onto the street. Onto him.

When I see Cass next to his bike, I freeze. He's staring at the window like he's been waiting for me. I feel my cheeks with the back of my hand, and the same tormented look from my dream darkens his face. Only I'm not so sure it wasn't real anymore, not with my skin still hot where he was touching me.

# THIRTY-TWO

## *HANNAH*

"He's still out there?" Terra peeks out my bedroom window.

I rip the curtain back, exposing both of us. She ducks like Cass hasn't caught her spying on him half a dozen other times this past week. Ever since my dream or not-dream or whatever it was, I've focused on returning to life before Cass. Or life before I *knew* about him. But the more I pretend he doesn't exist, the less discreet he becomes with his Watcher duties.

"At what point does it become weird?" she asks, crouched beside me.

"I'll go talk to him."

She tugs at my hand to keep me from walking away. "Take Jesse in case he tries something. He'll go all hulked-out football player and scare him off."

"It's Cass, Terra. He'd never hurt me."

"Han, the guy's practically stalking you. Everywhere we go, I see him hovering around. It's only a matter of time before it escalates into a serious problem."

Her concern is genuine, even if misplaced. To her—and everyone else in my life who's met him—Cass is behaving like a possessive and controlling ex. His following me will send up red flags until it either stops or she doesn't remember him. And only one of those can happen.

"Don't worry," I tell her, knowing what I need to do. "I'll be fine."

But I'm far from it once I step outside. Like any other time I see him in front of me, I want to run to him. Jump into his arms. Tell him I'm sorry and I need him and I'll never spend another second without him. Then I remember it's his eternity at stake and coolly walk down the sidewalk.

"You ready to act like I exist?" he asks, flicking his cigarette into the street.

He pushes off his bike, and I stop five feet in front of him, not trusting either of us enough to go closer.

"If you insist on being out in the open, we're going to—"

"*We?*" His voice is harsh, the irritation loud and clear. "According to you, there isn't a *we* anymore. There's you and your life. Then there's me and my job."

As his glare settles on me, I try to remember how I used to deal with all this. When we went around and around on the merry-go-round without any reprieve. Only it feels so far away and distant that I can't.

I cross my arms and try again. "Terra and Jesse think you're stalking me because we broke up. You need to make them forget you."

"You want me to erase myself from their memories?"

"Yes."

He rubs a hand through the back of his hair, jaw clenching. "Is that what you really want?"

I nod and turn for the house, hoping to get inside without any part of me going rogue. If my dream wasn't a dream, then I already know how that would play out.

"No," he says, his gruff voice stopping me on the step.

I spin around. "What?"

"No," he repeats. "I won't do it."

Muscle memory must kick in because I storm toward him, a surge of annoyance steeling me for battle. "Are you joking? You can't keep popping up all over the place and expect them *not* to think something's wrong. They'll never understand why my ex refuses to accept that we're over."

He relaxes back on the seat, clearly pleased with my reaction. "That's the thing though. We're not over, Hannah. You can pretend all you want, but we both know how this ends. You and me. Together."

"You don't get to decide how I live my life, Cass."

"What about how I spend my eternity? The forever I want with you? You have no problem making that choice for me."

As I bite back a groan, a smug smile tugs at his lips, and I realize he's trying to bait me. Heated fights always lead to the same place with us.

I close my eyes long enough to regain my center. "I'm not doing this with you anymore. I'm sorry that I hurt you. And I'm sorry we have to go through this instead of having a clean break like other people, but our connection doesn't change anything. It's over."

"Look me in the eye and say it then." He straightens and marches toward me.

At first, I step back but then decide to stand my ground. Cass walks straight into me, his arm behind me by the time I change my mind and try to move away. He holds me there with his breath on my face.

"You don't love me. You're happier without me. You've moved on. Make me believe even one of those things," he says, "and I'll fade into the background like I never existed."

I open my mouth but can't force the lies out. Even if I could, it wouldn't matter since as soon as he mentioned never seeing him again, my chest tightened, the thought smothering me.

The look in his dark eyes that cuts through me loses intensity, the gentle one he only gives me emerging from the storm.

"That's what I thought." He releases me and backs to his bike. "I'll hang back more. Not let them see me. But I'm not taking away their memories of us."

The engine snarls as he speeds away. I stay there until long after he's out of sight. As hard as it's been to not be with him, I have a feeling it's only going to get worse.

Cass keeps his word. I don't see him parked at the curb or outside my classes or at the frozen yogurt shop Terra and I frequent with Gabe. But the real test of his restraint comes only a few days later.

Terra insists I continue with her mandatory social outings over the summer. I don't even fight her on it. Honestly, anything that keeps me from dwelling on what Cass said earns my stamp of approval. At least, that's what I think until Thursday when she pops into my room in spandex workout gear, spouting off nonsense about the gym.

"Endorphins are good for you," she says, throwing her hair up in a high bun. "Plus, when you exercise, your body burns off all this adrenaline, so afterward, you feel calm and relaxed. And if anyone needs to relax, it's you." She gives a smart-ass grin and jogs out. "Be ready in ten!"

I shut the door, so I can change and text Cass, certain he'll be as unenthused about the evening's activities as I am. I toss my phone on the bed and peel off my shirt.

"Hannah."

I start at his voice behind me, which conveniently covers up the rush of emotion at hearing it. I stay facing away from him, unsure of what to expect from his little drop-in. "How do you want to handle this?"

"Warn me before anything high intensity." His shirt brushes across my back as he reaches around me. He hands me my top off the bed. "And keep your ring on the entire time."

"You know I'd never take it off."

No matter what happens, that's one thing that will never change.

I turn around after pulling on the tank top, and he looks down at my bare midriff. The mood shifts, his features darkening. I can almost see big, bad, broody Cass resurfacing.

"So," he says, eyes returning to my face, "you move on yet?"

In the time it takes me to blink, he's gone. I hate it when he does that.

I give myself a minute to re-center before I finish changing. Terra's jogging in place as I lug my rarely used gym bag downstairs. She's "pumped," and she keeps throwing out motivational sayings on the drive. With all the added enthusiasm, she must be worried about me—that, or she's afraid the cloud of gloom surrounding me will challenge her position as BFF.

After an hour-long spin class, I sneak away from her to track down something with sugar in it. I luck out and find a random candy bar in the bottom of my bag. Leave it to me to bring a stash with me to the gym. With a mouth full of chocolate, I round the corner from the locker rooms and run straight into a chest I've bashed into on more than one occasion.

"We have *got* to stop meeting like this."

I look up into Sean's melty blue eyes, and he grabs on to the ends of the towel slung around his neck.

"This time is clearly your fault," I say. "We had a warning system worked out."

He looks at the half-eaten candy bar I'm gripping, a grin following right after. "Speaking of workout…"

"You're just jealous because you didn't think to bring snacks."

His head tilts, eyes on my other hand. "Did you run off and marry the bad-ass biker dude without inviting me?"

I run my thumb over the band on my finger. "That would be the left hand."

Sean raises his left hand and twists a little, double-checking which hand the ring's on. "Thank God," he says, his arm falling to his side. "If he would kick my ass for hitting on his girlfriend, I'd be terrified to talk to his wife."

I force a smile and shrug. "We're not even together anymore."

"Shit. I'm sorry, Hannah. Are you okay?"

"Yeah, I'm fine."

Or I will be. Eventually. *I hope.*

He arches an eyebrow. "You sure? Because I happen to be an amazing rebound. I can get you references."

I laugh and glance away, twisting the ring around my finger.

"Seriously though," he says, more sincere, "if you ever need a sort-of acquaintance to listen, let me know." He steps around the corner, out of sight. "I'll be here."

I smile again as he reappears. "Good to know."

"Bye, Hannah." He spins on his way past me, walking backward down the hall and watching me a little longer.

As he turns around, I remember Cass's comment about moving on, the acidity in his voice. It reminded me of how he used to act with Gabe. I've been failing miserably at convincing Cass I don't want to be with him. Maybe it would be more believable if he thought I wanted to be with someone else.

I take a few steps down the hall, not letting myself overthink. "Hey, Sean?"

He whirls around, a wide grin on his face. "Run into you at the corner in fifteen minutes?"

Ignoring the unease settling into my gut, I nod. What's a few more lies at this point? Hell, Heaven—neither one will have Cass.

Before I shower and change, I check in with Terra to tell her I'm bailing. She tries to talk me into staying with promises of a smoothie. It might have stood a chance if we shared the same definition of smoothie, but she thinks green and veggies, and I think neither of those things.

On my way out of the locker room, I dig through my gym bag for my phone. I might not mention the why or with who, but I at least need to text Cass that I'm leaving early. I stop searching as I cautiously approach the corner.

"Sean?"

"See, and this time, I was ready for you." He pops his head around, and I can't help but smile.

He really is a nice guy. Funny, compassionate, and I'm a terrible person for using him like I'm about to. Especially if this backfires and Cass ends up dropping him in the middle of a jungle or something.

We walk toward the lobby, and Sean slides the strap off my shoulder.

"Here," he says, taking my bag, "I'm sure all those snacks are heavy. I'd hate for you to leave the gym, having actually exercised."

"Careful. You're starting to sound like you might be a dick."

"No, that would be my brother."

He holds the door open and tips his head toward the parking lot to the side of the building. Through the windows, I see Terra running on a treadmill with her earbuds in. Sweaty and happy and full of nutrients.

"Just the one sibling?" I ask, determined to make a genuine effort to get to know him.

"Three. I'm parked over here," he says.

He puts his hand on my back to guide me around the corner of the building. The second he touches me, my mind goes straight to Cass.

*Shit.* I never texted him I was finished.

We pass the only working light post and all the other vehicles. I'm about to check if he's sure he parked over here until I notice a sports car in the very back corner, blending into the shadows. With my knowledge of cars as sharp as ever, I quickly identify it as black and ridiculously expensive. No wonder he parked so far away from potential door dings.

The car beeps, and the trunk pops open. Before I can say anything, he tosses my bag in.

"Hold on. I need my phone." I step forward, but Sean grabs my wrist, stopping me. When I turn back to see why, his kind blue eyes are ice cold, matching his hard expression. "Sean…"

He tightens his grip when I try to pull away and jerks me toward him. His arm wraps around me from behind, pinning me to him while I struggle to stop him from sliding the ring off my finger. It clinks, bouncing off the ground, and he clamps his hand over my mouth, muting my cry for help.

I'm unprotected. Isolated.

I breathe in short spurts, my heart pounding like during cardio, but if I panic enough, Cass will know the difference. He'll sense something's wrong and come for me. But the fear fades fast as Sean murmurs the same words in my ear, over and over— chanting. Everything slows inside and around me until I can't stand anymore, and I go slack in his arms.

"I'm sorry it has to be you, Hannah," he whispers as my eyes fall shut. "I just need all this to end."

# THIRTY-THREE

## CASS

"Just take it."

I shove the crystal ball into the crook of Carl's arm on the bar and walk away. It's the only thing that will keep me from watching Hannah. After almost wiping her memory last week and then losing my temper the other day, I'm trying to give her the space she claims to want. Not so easily done with the steady stream of light constantly reminding me of how she feels—how *I* feel when I'm with her. It makes the moments I'm not all the more torturous and the ache of being near her unbearable.

Right now, my entire world is burning to the fucking ground, and the only thing that can extinguish the flames is what set the damn fire.

*Fuck.* I'm going to lose my damn mind before this is over.

Carl shifts on his stool, and I dash back and catch the globe that's rolling out onto the bar. I'm about to break down and call up her image, but my phone vibrates.

*Ros.* He probably wants me and Chaz to sit down for a fucking couple's therapy session. But it will take a lot more than a polite request for me to forgive. And I'll never forget the role he played in this entire mess.

"What?" I answer.

"Do you feel it?"

"I feel a lot of things, bro. Annoyed, heartbroken, drunk."

"Kasdaye," he says. "Do. You. Feel it?"

"Armaros, what the fu—"

The entirety of my powers drives into me so hard that I stumble back onto the barstool. The phone falls to the floor while I fight to control the cyclone inside me. I manage to maintain a solid grip on the crystal ball. Not even needing to think about it, I summon Hannah's image. All I see is black. My hand moves over it, trying to pull further back. Nothing. I mutter the incantation for sound and pick up my phone. As I call her, the faint buzz of hers comes through along with another noise. Constant and muffled.

Without any idea where I'm going, I focus on her—her touch and light—but instead of dropping to wherever she is, like I should, I'm still next to a semi-conscious Carl. Someone's using magic to block me, and they know what the hell they're doing, not leaving me a single opening.

"Shit," I yell, then I drop from the middle of the bar.

I land in an empty hallway at the gym. It only takes me a few seconds to find Terra, running on a treadmill. I rip her earbud out. "Where's Hannah?"

She pulls out the other and straddles the belt. "She left already."

I only need one hand on her cheek for the light to affect her. "You won't remember seeing me."

Another drop, and I'm in the mausoleum at Mary Constance's tomb. While sliding the lid, I call Rosdan back and tuck the phone between my shoulder and ear.

"Power surge?"

"Full strength in a millisecond," he says.

I carefully unwind the amulet from MC's wrist bone, glad it's not around Hannah's neck right now. "You have all your charges accounted for?"

"All of them."

"Samy and Chaz?" I reach into the chalice and pull out the brown paper package wrapped in string. Damn, am I glad I stocked up on her blood when I did.

"No answer from either one. What about Hannah?"

I move the lid back and drop to my bedroom. In the closet, I open the box where I hid all the random shit Hannah left, so I'd stop trashing the apartment whenever I spotted a reminder. I find her sweater and drop to the kitchen for the map shoved in the back of a drawer.

"Cass." He's panicked. "Where's Hannah?"

"I'm working on it."

Spread out, the map of the city covers most of the counter. I rip open the package and break one of the vials over the sweater. I wrap the fabric around my hand and hold the amulet over the map. Old-school dowsing for something lost with a divine power boost—courtesy of Nephilim blood. Drawing on her essence from the sweater, the amulet begins to swing. When the gem tugs downward, I let the chain slip through my fingers, and it hits the map. She's local, so maybe the return of our powers isn't directly related to her missing. She might have just left early. I check where the amulet's sending me.

*That can't be right.*

I attempt to pull the gem off to try again, but it won't budge. Like it's fucking magnetized to the spot.

"Rosdan." My voice is gravelly, so I clear my throat. "Call Chaz again."

"What about Samy?" he asks.

Sparks fly from my palm, igniting the map. The flames burn around the amulet but leave it untouched along with the paper underneath.

"There's no point in calling him."

No point because he already knows.

Chaz is pacing. So is Rosdan. I'm not. I'm just standing in the middle of his charge's kitchen.

*Fucking seething.*

"I need you to go over it again," Chaz says.

"Me too." Rosdan tugs at his hair. "You named yourself after streets?"

"Kind of." I rub the back of my neck and try to calm down, but it's useless. I won't be anything but ready to rip someone's head off until Hannah's in my arms. "Over a century ago, we decided to start using fake names Lydia couldn't track. I was too drunk to be very creative, so most of mine ended up being random street signs we passed. Walter, Douglas, Norris, Park—"

"Asher," Chaz reads off the shred of unburned map I brought, part of it being Asher Park. "It can't be a coincidence?"

Not one to throw around accusations of ultimate betrayal lightly, I've already been down this path of doubt. I toss him my phone with the name of the new owner of the collapsing church across the street—where the amulet landed.

"Walter Norris. Fuck!" He flings it across the room and drops to catch it before it shatters against a wall.

The magic, the names, the church—with all those breadcrumbs, Samy has left me no room to doubt he has her. I just can't figure out *why* he'd lead me straight to them. It's the only reason I haven't descended in a fiery ball of light, palms blazing. Every instinct I have tells me that's exactly how he expects me to play it, and his plan shifts into neutral until then.

"Samy took Hannah," Rosdan whispers to himself before he turns to me. "Which means…"

"He wants to undo creation."

My eyes dart to Chaz. "What did you just say?"

"What?" he says. "You think you two are fucking clever? All of a sudden, we have our powers. Demons are attacking. Ros has a notebook in his kitchen with a symbol from the language of creation scribbled in *your* writing." He cannons my phone across the room, and I stick out a hand to catch it.

"I get it, okay? I'd choose protecting my Nephilim over each one of you too. But when it comes to something this existence-altering, you'd better believe I'd tell you assholes, so you were with me when shit went down."

"Because who else would you want there?" I mutter.

Chaz rants his way into the reason Samy Hansel-and-Gretel'd me. Even if he's using the only thing I've ever loved to trigger the end of the world, he wants me with him when it happens, just like I would him.

"Hey, Cass." Tantrum over, Chaz scratches his jaw, focused on the empty space between us. "If you needed a Nephilim to destroy the world, which one would you pick?"

I'd choose Hannah, but the way he looks up, eyebrow cocked, he already knew that.

"And I'd want Avery," he says. "So, why the fuck isn't Samy using Chloe?"

*Holy shit.* I've been so blinded with everything Hannah that I never considered what's now the most glaring hole in the scenario Samy's crafted. He has a charge—a sexy-ass doctor, saving the world one underprivileged child at a time.

"Because she's dead." Rosdan looks up from his phone, his face paling. "A year ago. Random stabbing in South America."

A cold shock rocks through my core, numbing me as it goes.

"No." Chaz shakes his head, almost amused, and steals the phone. "That's … no. That would mean…" He trails off, his expression sobering while he reads the screen. "Samy's human."

No one moves or breathes, like the words deliver a death sentence. They do. Except what's supposed to come after never will. Nothingness for eternity.

"Maybe it's not true." Rosdan finds the piece of hair he's always yanking on. "Chaz makes jokes about taking his charges underground all the time. Samy might have—"

"When's the last time he said her name?" I ask, cutting him off.

"I don't know," he says. "Why?"

"You two have always used a Nephilim's name when talking about them. Chaz and I are the dicks who usually call them charges."

It's something I should have noticed when he popped up again. I would have if I hadn't been so wrapped up in Hannah.

"But how'd he get from Colorado to Seattle without any powers?" Chaz sighs and answers himself, "He's working with demons. They teleported him wherever he needed to go." He slumps back against the fridge. "I thought he felt a little weak when he was dragging me off the floor."

The quiet resumes, but it's different. Rosdan and Chaz are looking at me, waiting for me to tell them what they already know. Samyaza's mortal, and with enough knowledge and magic to bring about the apocalypse, it appears he wants a little company on the wrong side of the heavenly gates. Only one thing will guarantee he's not successful.

I dismiss the friends-forever highlight reel playing in my head and clear my throat. "I need to go to the church and save Hannah. Then, after she's safe, I'll…" I can't finish. What I need to do is an acid eating away at my entire being.

Chaz blows out a breath and straightens. "Not just you. We're all going to get your girl, man."

"And then," Rosdan says, letting his hand fall to his side, "we'll kill Samy before he fucks us all."

# THIRTY-FOUR

## *HANNAH*

At first, it feels like I'm underwater. Their words slosh around me, lapping at my subconscious. Then, slowly, my head begins to clear, and I recognize the smooth voice closest to me. The last thing I remember is hearing it utter an apology. The other voice also belongs to a man—gravelly and cold with an unmistakable boredom to the tone. It moves closer until it sounds almost on top of me, every syllable perfectly clear.

"Time to wake up, princess."

The touch on my temple is so icy that I can't help but open my eyes. I was right about the voice being on top of me. I just never thought that would mean the speaker was as well. He's crouching over me in a black-on-black suit with a foot on either side of my hips and a dark smirk lifting one side of his mouth.

"Bummer," he says, dragging his frigid fingers over my skin. "I thought I'd get to tell Kasdaye I played prince and kissed you awake."

Before I decide whether to scream or punch him in the crotch, he vanishes. I sit up from the hard bench and glance at the crumbling insides of a long-forgotten church. Plaster hangs from the ceiling, obscuring parts of a faded mural. A massive hole in the roof leaves the bare floors to rot, and only a small pane of stained glass remains. The rest of the large windows bordering the candle-lit chapel are boarded up.

"St. Olga's."

I still at Sean's voice, any ease it once brought replaced with foreboding. The wooden pew behind mine creaks. He steps into my row from the aisle and slides in beside me, but I stay facing forward.

"Interesting enough," he continues, "before she found *the light*, an assassin murdered Olga's husband. She exacted her revenge by massacring his entire village. And yet, here we are, sitting in an abandoned house of worship named after her. Someone once stood right up there"—he points to what remains of the altar and pulpit at the front—"preaching about loving one another and cardinal sins and all that other bullshit."

I've heard half a dozen other rants end the same way. Any question of who he is vanishes. Blond hair and blue eyes like Chaz, the opinions of Cass.

"You're wrong," I tell him.

"About Olga?" he asks.

I shake my head, still not looking at him. "About your brother being the dick and not you. I've met them all, and you are by far the worst."

"Right." Samy chuckles and stretches his arm across the pew back behind me. "All it took for me to out-asshole Cass was dragging you along for the ride to help destroy all of creation."

I look over then, sure I misheard him. "You … I'm…"

The words stick in my throat, and I try to swallow them back down along with the alarm creeping up from my chest.

His eyebrows draw in, the humor gone as he leans closer. "Nephilim are the only ones left who can read from the Book of the Speech from God. And while only the words of the book possess the power to create, it's only with the words of the book that all that's been done can be undone."

The pieces Cass refused to tell me fill in seamlessly.

All the demon attacks, the panic over the butterfly, and how they have their powers again after all this time.

Samy plans to end the world.

And he's going to use me to do it.

Feeling sick, I bend forward and cover my face with my hands. I squeeze my eyes shut, ready to wake up but this time in my bed. Far away from broken churches and plots of mass destruction and rogue Guardian Angels.

"You okay?" There's sincerity in his tone. Surprising, considering he plans to force me to kill myself along with everything else in the world. He rubs my back when I don't answer. His fingers graze over the bare skin at the base of my neck. They feel almost cool against the balmy air. Except they shouldn't.

I sit straight up. "We're the same temperature?"

A rigidness returns to his expression as well as the rest of him.

The other times his skin touched mine—in class, at the library—it wasn't warm then either. Not even earlier at the gym. Maybe it's because Cass talks about him all the time and has never uttered a negative word, other than bitching about him being flaky, that I bring my hand to his forehead without thinking. He sets his jaw as I run it down to his cheek and then his neck, searching for the missing heat.

"I don't understand. You should be burning up."

Cass has been since the attack in Seattle when his powers kicked on full-time. The heat comes from the powers and the powers from the Nephilim. I check around the church again for any sign of someone else like me, but every grimy body posted by the exits looks like it crawled straight out of Hell.

"Samy…" I look back at him, almost more worried for him than myself. "Where's your—"

"Wanna feel me up too, princess?" The demon reappears out of thin air in the pew in front of ours, turned around to face us.

I jump, jerking back from both of them.

The demon shakes his head, entertained by my reaction, and drags back the sleeve of his suit coat to check his designer watch. "Am I going to need to dangle her off the roof for Kasdaye to show up? I mean, this plan isn't exactly going to go over well with Heaven *or* Hell, so tick-tick, Samyaza."

"Back off, Donny," Samy says, "or I'll summon every bit of divinity I can into this place." He reaches for a chain around his neck, and the clear stone hanging from it glows white.

Out of the angels I've met, none have needed anything other than their powers for light, but the way he clutches the stone, it's clear he does. No heat, no powers, no Nephilim.

Samy's not an angel anymore.

"See, this is the problem with these guys." Donny rests his chin on his arms, folded over the back of the pew. "They're all threats and no fun." He smiles, and the curve of his lip on the right side highlights a faint scar almost invisible in the limited light. "Did he tell you the best part of all this yet?"

The way he asks turns my stomach, and I spit back, "Unless it involves Cass harpooning your ass with a lightning bolt, I doubt I'll care."

I've no more than finished when a flash of lightning illuminates the sky through the gaping hole above us. Then another and another.

Donny's eyes narrow, the centers emitting a red glow. He scans the church, his expression hardened by the time it returns to Samy. "They're here," he snarls. "You hesitate, I kill you."

With one last crack of lightning, three blinding shapes drop through the opening and land in the middle of the sanctuary. As their wings fold in behind them, the brightness dims enough that I can tell them apart. Rosdan and Chaz on each side with Cass in the center—fully lit and fully pissed. He immediately locks his gaze on me with a *goddamn it, Hannah* look in his furious eyes. And I've never been more relieved to see it. After a second, his attention shifts to the demon in front of me.

"Abaddon and I have been there, done that with the lightning bolt." He taps his cheek where I noticed the scar on Donny, and the disdain in his tone morphs to mocking when he adds, "You show her your little reminder of me, buddy?"

In a blink, Donny's in the aisle with a flame in his hand and unkempt demons on all sides of him. "You think it's smart to taunt me when I have your Nephilim, Kasdaye?"

Chaz snorts. "What are you gonna do, Baddo, kill her and go fishing for another one?"

"No," Rosdan says, "he'll do his little swirly thing with the darkness, trying to scare us, and then run off to the pit, crying about how the big kids were mean to him on the playground."

The flame grows in Donny's palm the more they badger him.

Samy sighs. "This will go on for a decade," he says, grabbing my arm.

Cass's focus snaps back to us as I'm hauled out of my seat. He is rarely a fan of anyone touching me, and right now, he looks like he might start his own apocalypse. His nostrils flare, and sparks fly from his hands. "Let her go."

Once in the aisle, I tug my arm away from Samy with surprising success. I race past Donny and his lackeys, and as soon as I'm out of the way, Rosdan and Chaz both unleash arcs of lightning. I don't look to see who they aim at, only caring about getting into Cass's arms. He flashes to meet me, but then I hit a wall—an invisible one that he reappears on the other side of.

"Cass?" It comes out as a panicked sob. I pound on the empty air in front of me, so close to him that it aches not to touch him.

"Hold on, baby." He presses his palms against the barrier and circles me, running his hands along it in search of any opening. "Fuck you, Samy. I already planned on killing you, but now I'm going to make sure it fucking hurts."

The other two stop their attack, so I glance behind me. The demons, protecting Donny and his flaming hand, all appear singed and at the ready with fireballs as an unharmed Samy walks toward us.

"You know, you should at least hear me out before hurling light and making death threats." He effortlessly crosses whatever blocks Cass and stands next to me. "You're going home, brother. All three of you. I'm finally setting everything right."

Cass nods once, detached when he looks at him. "Yeah, Samyaza. You're going to kill all our Nephilim, so we rot outside the gates with you. Not exactly the homecoming we were working toward."

The confirmation that Samy's charge is dead and he's human sinks like a stone in my belly. Then it gains several friends when I think about the rest of the charges and Watchers suffering the same fates.

"You misunderstand," he says. "The words from the BOSG come from God, Cass. Anytime they're spoken, it's an act of God! Don't you see?" He holds his hands out and smiles. "You'll return to the light of Heaven like none of this ever happened."

Cass's expression remains unchanged, if not a little more irritated. "So, should I drop to my knees and thank you for devising a plan in which you use my girlfriend to wipe out all of humanity?"

Samy drops his arms back to his sides and sighs. "*Ex*-girlfriend. And I believe she was about to go out on a date with me, so—"

Cass lunges at the barrier, flattening his palms against it and letting off a massive charge. Samy tenses, the shock appearing to go straight into him as he struggles to grab the stone hidden under his shirt.

The next thing I know, everything goes black. Coldness stabs at my skin, and then I'm on a deteriorating balcony that overlooks Cass and the sanctuary. Samy is propped against a pillar beside me, catching his breath, and Donny's arm is snaked around my waist from behind. I shove him off, my body rewarming once he stops touching me.

He steps to my other side and smirks down at Cass. "While I love listening to the four of you squawk at each other, it's time we get this show on the road, huh?"

"You expect us to believe you have the BOSG?" Chaz asks. Both him and Rosdan still hold sparks in their hands, monitoring the demons quietly spreading around them. "A book that no one has laid eyes on since the angels stashed it after the last reboot?"

"I'm the Demon of Destruction, Chazaqiel. You really think I haven't had my finger on its whereabouts since last creation? I mean, I never expected to use it, but deals were struck, and here we are."

"What deal?" Rosdan asks. "What are you possibly getting out of this?"

He smiles, wide and sinister. "The exact location of the Dimming Blade in the Abyss, which only opens when the book is read."

Cass paces back and forth like a keyed-up lion in his cage, close to losing it. Rosdan takes a few hesitant steps toward him, reluctant to go much closer with him ready to snap.

"It's not enough you're fucking working with him, Samyaza?" Cass asks. "You gave up the only weapon he could use to kill us? What the *actual fuck*?"

Samy doesn't answer, still seeming to be recovering from Cass's attack with the stone clutched to his chest.

"Angels can die?" I whisper.

Donny leans to the side and whispers back, "He's being dramatic. They don't *die*. They're simply drained of their light so they can either be turned or wiped from existence." He straightens up and, with a clap, rubs his palms together. "So, let's put our little Nephilim to work reading, shall we?"

With the snap of his fingers, a shadowy object appears on one of the few intact sections of banister in front of me. It doesn't even look real. It's transparent but with solid and defined edges.

"Sure," Cass says, barely holding it together. "And when she tells you to fuck off because she's not sacrificing every living thing for funsies, try tacking on a *please*."

"Oh, she'll read the book." Samy pushes off the pillar and comes closer. He's tucked the stone back in his shirt, only the chain still visible.

I want to rip it off his neck and see what happens without his magic to protect him.

"In fact, Cass, you're going to tell her to. Otherwise…" He trails off, tilting his head toward Donny.

The muscles in Cass's neck strain, his fists tightening. "You wouldn't dare."

"You wouldn't dare to what?" My head jerks toward Samy and then to Donny on the other side. "What are you going to do to me?"

Donny shrugs and says, "The best part. Turn you into a demon."

A cold shock slams into me, starting at the nape of my neck and tearing down my spine. I cry out, my knees folding underneath me. Donny catches me before I hit the floor, his hand still latched on to the back of my neck.

A guttural roar rips through the church. "Fucking *fuck*, Samyaza!"

I try to hold on to Cass's voice, to block out the ice searing off my nerve endings, but all I can think about is the pain and how I'll do anything to make it stop.

Then it does.

Someone says, "Enough," and Donny lowers me to the floor.

I can barely breathe, the thought of it coming back cutting off my airway. Even when the crashes start down below, I hug my knees tight to my chest, afraid to move and feel it again. Death would be a gift.

Donny kneels beside me and lifts my head into his lap. "All right, princess, as much fun as you'd be, I need to fix you before Kasdaye brings the whole house down."

He cradles my face in his hands. I try to push him away until I realize the memories of the pain feel further away. He strokes his thumbs over my cheeks, and they become more bearable with every pass, no longer choking me. Air returns to my starved lungs. I suck in breath after breath, and when Donny releases me, I scramble across the plaster-covered floor, away from him.

With most of the banister missing, I can see Cass in the middle of the chaos on the ground—Chaz and Ros doing all they can to restrain him, the rest of the church torn apart and covered in limp demon bodies. The torment on his face is worse than the darkness. It's soul-crushing.

Before I can cry out for him, Donny hooks me under my arms from behind and drags me to my feet. "She's good as new," he calls down.

All at once, Cass stops fighting against their hold and looks up. His shoulders heave when he finds me, as if a weight leaves them. It takes some away from me too. And if, by some miracle, I survive this, I'm never leaving his side again. Not in our human lives or the forever that comes after.

Donny dusts off his pants and retrieves his suit jacket from where he draped it over the banister. "Now, if she doesn't do as she's told, she'll have to go through that all over again. The beginning of the transition really is the worst part with the darkness ramping up to snuff out your soul. I do not envy her experiencing it more than once."

He winks, adjusting his collar. I'm about to mouth off, doubting I have much to lose at this point, but Samy steps beside me.

"Game time's over," he says. He grasps my shoulders and moves me to the book.

The composure he's shown since the moment I met him as Sean has worn away. He's on edge, and I can't help but think it has more than a little to do with Cass not even hesitating at the first chance to kill him.

"You're really going through with it?" Rosdan asks. "After everything we've been through?"

Samy clenches his jaw and reaches for the shadow. It fills in where he touches it to form a black cover with a ridged design twisting across it. He slides his thumb between the pages and lifts, opening the book to the middle. I jump as a shadow shoots from the pages. His grip on me tightens to keep me in front of the inky-black swirls that I've never seen before and yet somehow understand.

*This can't be real.* I even start to consider the possibility of still being in a coma from hitting my head months ago.

"Come on. Think about it." Chaz readjusts his hold on Cass, still straining to contain him. "It's all of humanity, Sam."

"We disobeyed God to save them," Rosdan adds.

They're trying to get to him like they did Donny. Pushing and pushing for a reaction. And it's working. Samy's fingers dig in, the more they talk. His exhales sharper.

"You can't eradicate mankind," Chaz shouts. "You fucking love mankind!"

"And where has it gotten me?" Samy yells back. He rushes to the edge of the balcony, hand wrapped tightly around the glowing stone. "We gave mortals knowledge to survive, and they used it to senselessly kill. Murderers, rapists—we've been charged with truly cruel beings who deserved every death we'd prevented a thousand times over. Humans are hateful and unforgiving, malicious and overconfident. Profiting from others' pain and taking advantage of those most in need. I don't love humanity. I've lost everything because of them. My light, my existence, *her.*"

His charge. It has to be.

"Do you know how it happened?" Samy shakes his head, his tone heavy when he continues, "Someone started stabbing people in a crowd—no reason. Women, kids, anyone they could get to. And Chloe…" He stumbles over her name, his face crumpling. "There was a little girl screaming in the middle of the chaos. Just before we dropped, Chloe jerked away from me to try to help her. I caught her within seconds, but there was another guy that I'd missed. She was beyond saving by the time I dropped. Our bond broke, and I was cold. So cold and empty. Without her for eternity."

Samy stops and looks around at the ruined church, appearing just as broken. It's the first glimpse I've seen of what I imagine is the real him. Or was before he lost his light. The brother Cass wanted me to meet. The one he respected more than anyone.

"Hannah."

Cass's voice is calm, carrying through the silence Samy's left us in. He's no longer restrained by Rosdan and Chaz but standing in the middle of the sanctuary with them behind him, faces solemn. He stares up at me like he has so many other times, eyes soft just for me.

Then he says the last thing I expect—"Read the book."

"What?" I wait for one of the other two to jump in to tell him he's out of his mind, but they don't react in the slightest. "Cass, no. I can't. I won't—"

"Hannah," he says again, not a hint of suggestion in his tone. "Read the fucking book."

# THIRTY-FIVE

## CASS

The second Samy said her name, I knew. The sadness that edged its way into his eyes, I recognized it all too well. Not only did I see it from afar in Hannah every day for five years, but I've been up close and personal with it in the mirror every damn day I've spent without her.

Samy loved Chloe. He loved her, and he's lost her forever. And I've never understood him more.

Hannah's staring at me like I've lost my mind—so are Samyaza and Abaddon. The only ones who know better are behind me. Our plan was to find a way to put a crack in Samy's plan, no matter the cost, and now I know how I can split the fucker wide open.

He said it earlier, *"I'm finally setting everything right."*

He couldn't save Chloe, and he can't save himself; the only ones left to save are us. The brothers he blames himself for being cast into the darkness. He wants to spend his eternity of punishment knowing we have our light.

At least, that had fucking better be what this is about, or what I'm about to do will suck so much worse than just letting Samy trigger the apocalypse.

"Plan?" Chaz whispers in the Angelic language.

Being mortal now, Samy lost the perk, so even if he's using magic to listen, he won't understand.

"He wants us all to live happily ever after in Heaven, so I'll give him an ending he doesn't see coming and make him choose."

"You think he'll choose you?" Rosdan asks.

I shrug with one shoulder and look over the other. "If not, I'll be with Hannah."

Donny smirks when I bring my head around. "Well, you heard him."

Samy watches me, trying to figure out my play, but he'll have to wait a little longer. Right now, I need to focus on convincing my girlfriend to trust I'm not insane. I reach in my shirt and pull out Brice's wedding band. The light she gives off changes when she sees it, the one that feels like Heaven. Home.

I force a small smile to further reassure her before I step forward. "Not so fast, Abaddon. I want to make a deal."

"What are you doing, Kasdaye?" Samy says, but I ignore him.

Abaddon quirks a brow. "I'm listening."

"You turn her into a demon after she reads."

Even though Hannah's light flips to terrified, she keeps a poker face. Samy, not so much. But Donny … he doesn't even think about it.

"Done." He shakes his head and slaps a hand on her shoulder. "I get the Dimming Blade, so I can hunt down Chazaqiel at my leisure and a new pet? Best apocalypse ever."

He positions Hannah, her panic growing, and I have to bite the inside of my cheek, not daring to utter another word until she's opened her mouth. The second she does, I hold up my hands.

"Wait. There's one more condition."

"He's playing you, Abaddon." Samy shifts around beside Hannah and clings to his stupid fucking amulet. "There's nothing he could possi—"

"After you get the Dimming Blade, you turn me too."

Hannah gasps before she catches herself. She presses her lips together to regain control of her outward reaction.

"No," Samy commands. "You're going home, Tamiel."

"She's my home. If I can't be with her in Heaven and I can't be with her here, then we'll make fucking adorable Nephilim-demon babies in the pits."

He glances between the three of us on the ground, his disbelief on full display. "You two are just going to stand there? He won't be in darkness … he'll *be* the darkness."

I don't need to check; both Rosdan and Chaz are staring at him, expressionless. We're in the highest-stakes game of chicken in the history of everything, and not one of us can chance swerving. The muscles of Samy's jaw work beneath the skin, his knuckles losing color the tighter he clutches the clear quartz. He's hauled it around since creation. By now, the power of it is enough to rival an Upper on their best day.

"I'll do it," Donny says.

"What?" Samy turns back to him. "That's not part of our deal."

"It's not against it either. Light or dark, we're all big fans of the free will. Now"—he snaps his fingers, and a dozen Lowers teleport in around us—"every being in this room has trampled over my patience, and if the Nephilim isn't reading in the next thirty seconds, I'm killing anything mortal."

His hand bears down on Hannah's shoulder, making her cry out. I have to fight every urge inside me to drop up there and rip him to shreds.

"Careful, Donny," I call through clenched teeth. "She'll be one of you soon."

He squints for a moment but then relaxes, and his obnoxious smirk is back in business. "You know, it's always been between you and Armaros that I would spare. I'm glad it's you."

I monitor every movement Samy makes next to Hannah while Donny fiddles with the book. I see my twist ending working its way through him—the doubt sinking in, the worry over my soul. I don't care how lost he is; compassion is a part of him. His default setting.

Donny turns a page, and a familiar shadow rises from the book.

"How much can she read before we're fuck-fucked?" Chaz asks.

"To the end of the first line," Rosdan answers. "That's when the Abyss will be fully opened. And once it is…"

"There's no resealing it," I finish.

*No going back.*

I tuck the ring in my T-shirt before all Hell literally breaks loose. "Well, boys, it's been real."

Hannah looks down at the words and then peeks up at me, waiting for confirmation. I give it to her, and Samy curses my old name. She hesitates, the light thrashing through me, fierce and pounding as fast as her heart, and then her eyes fall back to the page in front of her.

It's not a slow-growing tremor like they would portray in a movie. You don't need to build suspense at the actual end of the fucking world. So, with the first syllable out of her perfect mouth, the ground erupts in a violent earthquake. The walls shake, and a giant fissure cracks through the floor in front of me. After all the structural damage I caused, the church will be nothing but a pile of holy debris by the time the real action starts.

Darkness floods from the book, encircling Hannah and Donny. I hate to do it, but I shift my eyes from her to Samy. I need to know if I've sentenced her to an immortal existence of damnation. He grips his crystal, staring down at me. I stare right back, refusing to blink first.

"Come on," Chaz grinds out behind me.

"She's almost there," Rosdan says. There's not the slightest emotion to his voice. Just a fact.

They're probably thinking the same thing at this point; that if Hannah hits the end of the line, they have to get to the dagger in the Abyss before Donny. Then, I have to do everything in my power to get it back from them. Because I wasn't lying. If Hannah's a demon, I'm a demon. Even if it means I have to kill them to make it happen.

The crack in the floor busts wide open to make room for whatever the book will release once the Abyss fully unseals. That's the fun thing about the BOSG. You never know what annihilation it will unleash.

Even as the ground erupts in front of me, I don't take my eyes off Samy. But I do take a casual step back to get out of the way, and because no matter what I am—angel, human, demon—I'll forever be a defiant asshole, I arch my eyebrow in a final challenge.

And that's when he blinks.

His eyes dart to the side, and a flare from his amulet knocks Donny away from Hannah, her lips forming around a word she never finishes. I get about two solid seconds of sparkling relief before the Lowers attack from all sides. I dodge a few poorly aimed fireballs and drop to the balcony. Samy's magic bounces me right back, almost landing my ass in the gaping hole that leads straight into the pits.

I shoot off an arc at a brave demon and look for another point of entry. Donny's regained his bearings, the darkness churning around him. It'll be a race to the book—and Hannah. She glances between him and Samy on either side of her in a standoff. The blue flame overtakes Donny's palm, and Samy holds out his amulet.

A bolt cracks a support beam overhead, and a rogue fireball slams into it right after, crashing it to the ground. It inspires me, and I drop. I hit Samy's barrier, as expected, but this time, I barely feel the ground beneath me before I drop to bash into it again. I go a few more times, only pausing long enough to see his brow pull in. His attention is split, not sure which direction he needs to focus his power—Donny's cyclone of shadows or my attacks.

The plan to break through with brute force works, getting me farther with each drop. Until Donny catches on. He times a step with each of my strikes. Samy matches every one. And now every time I get closer to Hannah, so do they. They're closing in on her. The flame grows, and the light brightens. I can't even tell her to run because of the invisible cage she's stuck in.

Two arcs collide with the barrier at the same time as my next attempt. Rosdan and Chaz provide some much-needed backup and return to the Lowers still pouring in.

The unexpected voltage causes Samy to fumble with his amulet. As soon as it's not pointed at him, Donny lunges for Hannah and the book. He lands a hand on her wrist, but before he can teleport, Samy floods the balcony with light. It throws Donny against the wall on one side, and in the same breath, Samy turns the magic on me.

When he brings me down, I narrowly miss the rift and slide across the floor. A busted pew stops me, and I push up, ready to go right back. Except I can't. I can't drop. Not even my wings can unfold.

"Samy," I shout up at him. "Let me go!"

I strain against the invisible weight bearing down on me, struggling until I reach my hands and knees and can see him on the balcony. He has the book cradled in one arm and the other wrapped around my world. Tears stream down her face as she twists at her finger where her ring should be. The first thing I'm doing when I get us out of here is tracking down where Samy stashed it.

I reach for my own ring beneath my shirt. Hannah sucks in a breath when I do, the sharp rise of her shoulders visible. The light shifts all over the place. I can't tell what she feels. She closes her eyes, and when she opens them, she grabs Samy's amulet, breaking the chain as she rips it from his neck.

Without direct contact, the effects of his magic begin to fade. I fight my way forward, crawling through the middle of a war zone. Fireballs fly, and bolts retaliate while Hannah struggles against Samy for the crystal. She manages to throw it away from them. He pushes past her for it as Donny gets up. His flame is as furious as his darkness, igniting whatever he touches.

I'm clawing at the boards, drawing on the light to break the hold that's lessening by the second.

But I'm out of time.

Even with all the threats around her—an Upper ready to fire, an inferno engulfing the church, a raging Hell pit below—I zero in on a random fireball. A misfire that ricochets off the last standing column and soars straight toward the balcony.

"Hannah!"

She turns, and everything slows as I watch, battling against the magic binding me and helpless to stop the fireball from barreling toward her. It's worse than any ending I could have imagined. Being right here. Witnessing Hannah die in front of me. On my hands and knees in a church when I lose everything. When I lose her forever.

It's simultaneous. The magic releases me as Samy collides with her. The impact knocks her off the balcony, and I drop with my wings spread behind me. I catch her midair directly over the mouth of Hell and land on the other side with her in my arms. Where she's staying until they pry my cold, dead human hands off her in fifty to seventy years. Then I'm starting all fucking over for forever.

Hannah's taking short, shallow breaths, her eyes clamped shut. She realizes she's not falling anymore, and she peeks to see who's holding her. Fuck if I haven't missed the rush I get when she sees it's me.

But no amount of light has anything on how she feels, scrambling around and wrapping her arms and legs around me. "I'm sorry. I'm so, so sorry." She smashes her lips into mine. "I love you. I want you."

The woman chooses a hell of a time to make up, and while I'd give up existence to do it a little longer, I pry my mouth off hers. "We'll fight about it later."

She huffs out a breath, relieved or looking forward to it.

With the fallout of a near-apocalypse left to handle, I set her down.

Her feet have barely touched the ground when Chaz shouts, "The book!"

I look up just before Donny teleports across the balcony. Chaz beats him there and strikes him with a bolt when he reappears. Not sure where Samy went, I tuck Hannah against my side and drop to give backup. We land beside the book as Chaz dodges the blue flame streaking toward him. The second Donny's outnumbered, he stops his advance.

His gaze falls on each of us and then to the floor behind us. "So," he says, his mouth hooking up, "think I can get to the Dimming Blade?"

Chaz growls and hurls a bolt, only to hit empty air. "Fuck." He looks at me, more than a little panicked. "Does it work like that? Can he squeeze through the cracks or something?"

I shake my head, not having any idea. The Abyss has never been partially opened. It's usually an all-or-nothing sort of thing.

But if he does get to the blade, there is no question he'll come after Chaz first.

With Donny gone, all falls quiet, except for the crackle of the rapidly spreading fire. I'm unsurprised his posse bails as soon as he does, but there's still no sign of Samy and his amulet. I expected a final showdown, one last stand.

"Guys," Rosdan says behind us.

We turn, and Hannah clamps down on my bicep. She brings a hand to her mouth while Chaz, Rosdan, and I stare at Samy on the floor. Darkness escapes the massive wound to his chest that rises in quick, ragged breaths.

"The fireball." Hannah looks up at me. "It must have hit him when he shoved me out of the way."

Chaz kneels next to him. "His crystal should have protected him."

"He never made it to the crystal," I say.

My eyes land on the amulet, still on the floor where Hannah threw it. Where he was heading when I yelled her name.

Samy turned back for her without it. He saved her when I couldn't.

"What do we do?" Rosdan asks with the same emotionless tone from earlier. Distant. Which is what all three of us need to be right now.

I rub a hand over my face and give one last glance at the church, somehow still standing despite our best efforts. "We need to go."

I lower next to my dying brother and drop him and Hannah to the park. Rosdan and Chaz are right behind us with the book and amulet. Across the street, the flames flicker through the hole in the roof with smoke billowing out.

Samy's breathing has slowed, his skin graying. Fireballs take very little time on humans.

Holding on to my anger toward him should be easy. An hour ago, I was in Ros's kitchen, planning to kill him myself. But seeing him weak and broken, all I can think about is what made him this way. How easily our roles could have been reversed if I wasn't as lucky as I've been with Hannah.

I hold out my palm over the wound and emit enough light that the shadows disperse, so he's not suffering. His eyes open once the pain eases. They hold the guilt they always have. His cold hand grips my forearm. I know he's about to try and choke out a deathbed apology, and I shake my head.

"Don't. The moment you saved her, you set everything right between us."

His gaze travels to the other two behind me and then lands on Hannah, offering each the same silent apology before he closes his eyes again. The crease in his forehead smooths when his chest stills. I move his hand to the grass. It's the most peaceful I've seen him since our beginning.

As I get up, Rosdan steeples his fingers, pressing them to his chin, and Chaz hangs his head. Samy's the first of us to fail, and we'll all mourn him in our own way. I'll down a bottle of whiskey and prattle on about the universe, Rosdan will pore over the scrolls and spells Samy left behind, and Chaz will find a cliff to dive off with his charge.

"We're not leaving him on a mountain," Rosdan says.

Chaz nods. "He deserves better than that."

"Find out where Chloe's buried," I tell them.

I don't know if it's what he would have wanted, but it sounds like him.

Hearing the first sign of sirens, I haul Hannah to her feet. She sees the still-very-much-on-fire church and takes a few steps toward it, which is all the farther I'm letting her go.

"How long do we have?" I ask no one in particular. "A few minutes?"

Chaz snorts. "Sounds like plenty of time to close a massive gateway to Hell." He dangles the amulet between the three of us. "Anyone know how to work this thing?"

"In theory," Ros says. "It will drain all of its power, though, and even then, it might not be enough to completely close it."

And then we'll have a swarm of mortals buzzing around and have to suggest they all forget they've seen into the depths of Hell. The three of us go quiet, trying to think of a backup plan in case it doesn't work. Or at least a Band-Aid to slap over this until we find one.

The sirens grow closer, and I check on Hannah.

She's not where I left her. I suffer a flashback to the nursery debacle and am about to panic when I notice her off to the side of us. She's sitting cross-legged in the grass with the BOSG in her lap. Her lips are moving and then—

"Whoa." Chaz throws his arms out to catch his balance. "What the fuck?"

Rosdan stretches out his fingers. "Powering down."

I feel it, too. Not a complete loss, but very little light other than what I'm getting from Hannah's lingering adrenaline.

She stops reading and looks up. "Did it work? Is it closed?"

Chaz drops and is back in a few seconds. "Nothing but a big-ass crater in there, Kelley."

Proud of herself for bailing our asses out, she stands up with the book already fading back to shadows. I tip my head to Ros when Hannah holds it out, and he reluctantly takes it.

"What am I supposed to do with it?" he asks.

I shrug. "I don't know."

"Should one of us check up on Donny to see if he got the blade?" Chaz asks.

"Go for it." I tug Hannah toward me and ask, "You ready to go home?"

A smile answers me, and she relaxes against my side.

I plan to lock her away and not share her with anyone as long as she'll let me. Longer if I can't find her ring.

"Wait a minute." Chaz holds up his hands, shaking his head. "You and your Nephilim can't just make a mess and leave us with the cleanup. Back me up here, Ros."

Rosdan wipes a hand over his mouth, hiding a smile and not offering any reinforcements.

"Oh, come on," Chaz says. "This is bullshit."

I secure my arm around Hannah while he continues complaining, and because I've never given a shit about his whining, we drop.

# THIRTY-SIX

## CASS

It takes three days for Hannah to convince me to leave the apartment. Honestly, if it wasn't for my bike still being at the bar where I left it to go save her ass, it would probably take longer. I put her off until late afternoon before she sets her jaw and slips on her shoes.

Since my powers have returned to only when needed, I drag her onto my lap, ready to get her heart pumping the best way I know how. We're really getting somewhere until someone knocks.

She tries to get up, and I say, "Leave it."

"Cass, you need to—"

The rest cuts off when I kiss her. I can already sense my least favorite unsolicited visitor on the other side of the door. Sure enough, after a second round of knocking—"Tamiel, answer the damn door."

A familiar light enters my chest at Lydia's voice. The one brought on by anything female sniffing around me.

I smirk against Hannah's lips. "Still want me to get it?"

Instead of answering, she shimmies her way off me and onto the floor. She hits her knees, already jerking open the button on my jeans. Her fingers dip into the waistband, and I lift my hips, so she can tug them down.

Once she frees my dick, I arch an eyebrow at her in challenge. Another demand from the hall, and Hannah grabs my shaft, her eyes flicking up to mine as she sinks her puffy lips over the head. I groan, fisting my hand in her hair as the heat of her mouth envelops me, her hand working the rest of me. "Just like that, baby."

When I gently guide her head, she moans around me. So, I thrust up, hitting the back of her throat, and the light spikes through my veins.

"That's right, Hannah." I press her head all the way down, holding her on my cock. "Choke on it while she's on the other side of the door."

She whimpers and rubs her thighs together, loving every second. Once she gags, I let her up, and her watery eyes lock onto mine. They stay there while I fuck her mouth, heat coursing through me, and every time Lydia makes noise, I hold her down.

It doesn't take long before I'm thrusting faster. "Fuck. *Fuck.*"

Hannah moans, vibrations and light and her, and I groan, pushing deep and keeping her there. She swallows around my cock while I spill down her throat, taking every drop.

The light turns to a satisfied hum, and my hand slides down to her jaw. She sits back, lips swollen, cheeks pink, and her claim made on me.

"Fucking gorgeous." I lean forward and kiss her before I stand up, pulling her to her feet. She smiles as I tuck my dick away.

Then I cross the living room and swing the door open, so Lydia can scowl at me from the hallway.

"Sorry, we were just on our way out." I sling my arm over Hannah's shoulders when she steps beside me.

Lydia crosses her arms and tips her head to the side. "So, you don't want to know what happened to Samyaza?"

"What about him?" I ask, feigning a vague disinterest, as always.

Lydia looks between us, still unsure how much Hannah knows.

Hannah puts her out of her eye-bouncing misery. "I'll let you two talk."

She disappears into the hall, where she'll listen to everything.

I prop my shoulder against the doorframe, and Lydia waits for the decoy click of the bedroom latch before she straightens her jacket.

"I'll assume you already know that Samyaza lost his final charge and has been mortal for over a year," she says, tugging at the hem.

It's not a question, so I don't answer, but she takes my silence as one.

"Look"—she brings out her disappointed-soccer-mom tone—"I'm not here to reprimand you. I wanted you to know he's returned to Heaven."

"A rather misleading statement," I say, not hiding my irritation as well as I'd like. "Why don't you call it like it is and say he started his sentence outside the gates?"

"Because he's not. He passed judgment and entered as a mortal soul." The *what the fuck* must flash in neon on my face because her expression softens enough to count as friendly. "I don't know how, but there must have been a loophole. Something he did while mortal that was so worthy of redemption—"

"Self-sacrifice."

The ultimate act of love.

Samy gave up his life to save Hannah. To save me from losing her like he had Chloe.

Lydia perks up at my comment, so I clear my throat and straighten.

"I mean, if I had to guess," I say dismissively.

"Right…" And with that, she slides into suspicious and accusatory. "You wouldn't happen to know anything about the rumors going around about the Book of—"

"Really, Lydia, it's been great catching up. Let's do it again in seventy years."

The door shuts before she can even spit out one shrill Tamiel.

I smile on my way to the hallway, and around the corner, a grinning Hannah jumps into my arms.

"You'd make a terrible spy," I tell her.

She beams even bigger. "Samy's in Heaven with Chloe."

I nod. "And the first thing I'm doing when I see him again is kicking his ass for hitting on you."

She laughs, but it's true, and I'd bet my existence Samy knows it's coming.


In case Lydia plans the same pop-by for the other two, I give them a heads-up, and then I drop us to the bar restroom. I raise an eyebrow at Hannah when we land, and she rolls her eyes, reaching for the door handle.

"You and public restrooms."

The place is empty, except for the bartender playing with his phone at a booth. He doesn't notice us slip out the front even though we never walked in.

I hook my arm around Hannah as we walk down the sidewalk to my bike. She doesn't know it yet, but we have a stop to make before we go home. I stole a page out of Lydia's book and tracked down a storage locker Samy was renting in the city. I have a hunch about something that might be in there. Something I want ahead of her returning to the classes that I doubt she'll agree to skip much longer.

A man bumps into her shoulder and turns back. "Sorry," he mumbles. When his gaze lands on me, he stops. "D-do I know you?"

I study him hard, not sure why the grimy man looks familiar. Then I imagine him under shitty lighting with his cheek flat against a bar top, softly snoring.

"Carl?"

"Oh my God," he whispers. He brings his hands to my cheeks, poking and prodding with stubby fingers. "It's you." As soon as he says it, he pales, his eyes growing wide. "You're the angel banished from Heaven. And time's not real and you…" He glances at the bar door we came out of, then he's back to me. "You vanished into thin air. I tried to tell them you were in front of me, and then, *poof!*"

*Shit.* Maybe he wasn't as unconscious as I thought he was all those times.

Before he screams any more about angels in the middle of the goddamn street, I lunge at Hannah.

Of course, she flinches. "Really, Cass?"

Carl tries to back away, but I catch his face, and a dreamy look replaces the fear in his eyes.

"I'm not real," I tell him, my voice calm. "You drink too much and imagined me. Stop hanging out in bars all day. Go to a meeting. Find a job that makes you happy."

He nods, and I start to release him but pause. I've always been curious about something, and if I don't ask, it will drive me mad.

"What's your name?"

"Jeremiah," he says.

I make a face and let him go. He blinks a few times, coming out of the daze, and heads the way he came from, away from the bar and off to start a better life.

When I turn around, Hannah's leaning against my bike, shaking her head.

"What?"

"Nothing," she says. "That was just sweet of you."

I look down the sidewalk after him and sigh. "Yeah, but I should have suggested he change his name to Carl."

After bidding farewell to the best bar buddy I've ever had, I inform Hannah about our pit stop. The drive doesn't take long, and within a few minutes, I find what I'm looking for in the storage unit. The rest of the stuff is mostly scrolls and various magical elements I leave behind for Rosdan to deal with.

I slide the door down and turn around to Hannah and her narrowed eyes. She's annoyed I wouldn't tell her why I dragged her here.

"Calm down," I tell her, backing her to the bike. "It was worth the trip."

Once she cools it with the glare, I hold out my hand and open my fist.

"My ring," she says, lighting up.

Our fallen brother liked to magically store things away. A quick spell and an item popped into his stash. He might have stowed the ring in case shit went sideways, but I think it's so I could find it if he failed. Samy's heart couldn't completely turn black even after he lost everything.

Hannah picks the silver band from my palm and twists it to check the inscription. Once she's verified it's hers and not some knockoff I found and spelled, I take it back from her. She gives me her hand so that I can put it on for her, but I shake my head.

"I want the other hand."

Her eyes flick up to mine. "What?"

"I said, I want this one." I lift her left hand as the light floods in. "And I want your tomorrow and all the days after. I want every laugh and birthday and Christmas." I kiss between her knuckles where I'm going to put this ring, and it's never coming off. "I want you, Hannah Kelley. What do you want?"

She bites her lip and smiles. "I want big, bad, broody Cass to ask me to marry him."

I arch an eyebrow and slide the ring down her finger. "Marry me."

The light answers faster than she can, so she barely nods before I kiss her.

"Close enough," she mumbles against my mouth.

She sighs and pulls me closer, and I should have waited to do this because I'm about to drop her ass back to the apartment to finish what she's starting. To keep from abandoning my bike again, I force myself away from her.

"I get it now," I say, pushing her hair back.

She tugs at the hem of my shirt, not making this any easier. "Get what?"

"The inscription. I understand why Brice promised Fiona a forever's worth of forevers."

"Why?" she asks.

I lower my forehead to hers and smile. "Because even forever with you won't be enough for me."

Her nose wrinkles, and she laughs as I kiss her once more and set her up on the seat.

I'm more than ready to take her home, and the way she runs her hands over me when I start the bike, so is she. But as I pull out of the parking lot, the sun is beginning to set.

I turn the opposite direction, heading away from it.

Hannah starts tugging on my shirt, probably wondering why, but I ignore her. I just asked the love of my existence to marry me and waxed poetic about wanting a forever of forevers. The last thing I'm about to do now is drive us off into the fucking sunset.

# EPILOGUE

## *CHAZ*

The gig of immortal being is supposed to be badass. Powers. Near impossible to kill. Savage good looks from here to eternity. The last one's not a guarantee, but the point remains the same. Immortal equals badass.

So, why the fuck am I standing on a roof in Colorado, mid-July, with a handful of burned-out twinkly lights?

Hannah. Kelley.

She's not even my charge. Yet here I am, stooped down to hook cords around nails put up by another mortal—also not my charge—all because my brother fell in love with a Nephilim who has a fetish with Christmas.

"You plan on finishing anytime soon?" Cass asks from the ground. "Or should we just skip Christmas in July and see if you're done by December?" He cocks an eyebrow, not even trying to hide his smirk.

I twist in a new bulb, and the entire string illuminates.

"Hallelujah," I deadpan.

Cass steps back when I jump down, and we both check out my handiwork. The multicolored lights crowded onto the roof of Hannah's parents' old house spell out, *Ain't no Christmas like a Kelley Christmas 'cause a Kelley Christmas don't stop*. It's impossible to read and most likely a significant fire hazard.

"You sure you want to encourage this?" I ask.

He shrugs, walking toward the house. "If it means she doesn't give a shit about any other holidays, I'll deal with this one twice a year."

I follow him inside the poor two-story house with more decorations on the outside than siding. Hannah has crammed more ornaments on the entryway tree, which sags at the top from the weight. Rosdan ended up anchoring the one in the kitchen to a cupboard, so it wouldn't fall over.

When I step into the living room behind Cass, Hannah brings me a giant glass of eggnog.

"You realize it's ninety degrees outside."

"It's almost all whiskey," she says, shoving it at me.

She goes to the couch, and Cass pulls her down onto his lap. It's the first time they've been back since he suggested the previous occupants sell her parents' house back to her, but they look at home. Which says something when talking about Cass. As much shit as I give him over falling for a mortal, Hannah's good for him. He went from pissed off all the time to only mildly irritated most of the time.

Rosdan walks in with another box of decorations and a pair of antlers on his head. He settles in next to them, and he and Hannah start picking through it. Cass looks over and rolls his eyes.

Spending my day in a Christmas jumper might not be my cup of tea, but it would be nice if he and Hannah moved back after she finished school. With Ros in Washington, we'd all be on the same side of the continent again. A plus since I still have no idea if Abaddon weaseled his way into the Abyss and found the Dimming Blade before Hannah closed it.

"Chaz, you should bring your charges to dinner."

"Yeah," Cass says dryly.

"Sure, Kelley." I sink into an oversize easy chair across the room from them. "I'll drop them in and suggest they drove here to spend the evening with a bunch of strangers."

She squints at me, and I grin, winking at her.

Her mention of my charges reminds me to text Kai about rafting in the morning. Kasdaye and I have always existed by the motto of the less interaction with our Nephilim, the better, but we've both relaxed that recently.

A few years ago, my charge, Kai, discovered he was an adrenaline junkie. The constant surges of light—while fucking awesome—drove me nuts. I never knew if he was in actual danger when they hit. Then, I realized if I bro'd out and went with him when he threw himself out of planes, I could enjoy the rush and not chance him dying and ruining the rest of my eternity.

Because when you're only two Nephilim away from finally going home, shit gets serious.

*K-bro, we hitting the rapids in the morning?*

It doesn't take him long to shoot back a response.

*Before the sun? Make it interesting?*

Junkie, through and through. Hell, I might have to worry about landing myself in a Cassannah situation if he were a woman. Or if his sister were anything like him, but Avery is quiet and shy. The most exhilarating thing she's done in the past ten years was give a valedictorian speech at their high school graduation a few years ago.

*Ten-four*, I send.

*New bar on Koenig Ave. We can go out tonight and 4G it.*

I'm about to ask what the fuck he's talking about when the answers vibrate in my palm.

*Get drunk.*

*Get laid.*

*Get showered.*

*Go to the river.*

I snort and look at Cass, Hannah, and Rosdan on the couch. Other than the redhead in the middle, I've spent most of my existence around them. What's the harm in bailing on one family dinner in favor of a night of booze and a hot hook-up I never need to see again? I mean, one of us has already fallen in love with a mortal and almost started an apocalypse. It's not like that's going to happen again.

# ACKNOWLEDGMENTS

Joe, you truly deserve the first shout out this time. Thank you for the crazy idea that I should write a book about fallen angels. And thank you for then spending the next five hours plotting not only one book, but an entire series. I really do like you. Swear!

My beta readers. Sara, Callie, Dmitri, Amanda, Joe, and Lauren, your feedback was priceless and your encouragement irreplaceable. Thanks for tolerating my neurotic-ass.

Emmily, I'm glad Brad found you and brought you to me. You read all my words—ones from five minutes ago and ones you've memorized because it's taken that long for me to get them *just* right. Cass loves you. (hey B-rad!)

To Madison and Jovana, my incredible editors. You help sculpt the details and push me to be a better writer. I learn from each book, and much of the credit goes to you ladies. And to Christina, but not Hannah's mom, Fiona.

Murphy Rae, you killed it as always. Thanks for turning my vision into art and saving us from those pants.

To the LitChicks and my author friends. You are rock stars. Straight up. The indie author community is amazing and uplifting, and a place where even this socially awkward chick can feel like she belongs.

LB—Bruh. Thanks for the memes. And the voice messages when you're at Walmart. And all the shit-talk. You've reached the top-ten. But it's whatever. No feelings or anything.

A page worth of thanks belongs to my early readers and bloggers. I can't tell you how much I appreciate every second you spend reading my words, reviewing, sharing, and just being your awesome selves.

Finally, to my readers—the ones who've been spinning on the merry-go-round with me and those just grabbing on for the ride. You've all taken a chance on me at one time or another, and that's cool as shit. Thank you will never be enough.

CG

# About The Author

CG Blaine writes unapologetically messy and emotional romance novels. She loves her characters complicated, the connections intense, and rip-your-heart-out feels.

She is obsessed with her vicious cat and aggressively cute bunny. Her favorite stories hit with the hurt and then apologize oh-so well.

Never miss a thing!
Join my reader group: CG's Cool Kids
Instagram: @cgblaine
Facebook Author Page: @cgblaineauthor
Website: cgblaine.com

Be sure to stay in the loop and sign up for CG's newsletter. You'll also snag a **FREE** short story.

Sign up at https://www.cgblaine.com

www.ingramcontent.com/pod-product-compliance
Lightning Source LLC
Chambersburg PA
CBHW061658190726
48289CB00006B/1924